Praise for Juliet Blackwell's
Secondhand Spirits

"Solid plotting and realistic but odd characters bring a cozy tone to this wonderful debut . . . looking forward to the second."
　　　　　　　　　　　　　　　—Mystery Scene

"Juliet Blackwell provides a terrific urban fantasy with the opening of the Witchcraft Mystery series."
　　　　　　　　　　　　　　—Genre Go Round Reviews

"An excellent blend of mystery, paranormal, and light humor, creating a cozy that is a must-read for anyone with an interest in literature with paranormal elements."
　　　　　　　　　　　　—The Romance Readers Connection

"The story combines fun and seriousness for an entertaining read."　　　　　　　　　　　*—Romantic Times*

"It's a fun story, with romance possibilities with a couple hunky men, terrific vintage clothing, and the enchanting Oscar. But, there is so much more to this book. It has serious depth."　　　　　　　　*—The Herald News* (MA)

IF WALLS COULD TALK

A HAUNTED HOME RENOVATION MYSTERY

Juliet Blackwell

AN OBSIDIAN MYSTERY

OBSIDIAN

Published by New American Library, a division of
Penguin Group (USA) Inc., 375 Hudson Street,
New York, New York 10014, USA
Penguin Group (Canada), 90 Eglinton Avenue East, Suite 700, Toronto,
Ontario M4P 2Y3, Canada (a division of Pearson Penguin Canada Inc.)
Penguin Books Ltd., 80 Strand, London WC2R 0RL, England
Penguin Ireland, 25 St. Stephen's Green, Dublin 2,
Ireland (a division of Penguin Books Ltd.)
Penguin Group (Australia), 250 Camberwell Road, Camberwell, Victoria 3124,
Australia (a division of Pearson Australia Group Pty. Ltd.)
Penguin Books India Pvt. Ltd., 11 Community Centre, Panchsheel Park,
New Delhi - 110 017, India
Penguin Group (NZ), 67 Apollo Drive, Rosedale, North Shore 0632,
New Zealand (a division of Pearson New Zealand Ltd.)
Penguin Books (South Africa) (Pty.) Ltd., 24 Sturdee Avenue,
Rosebank, Johannesburg 2196, South Africa

Penguin Books Ltd., Registered Offices:
80 Strand, London WC2R 0RL, England

First published by Obsidian, an imprint of New American Library,
a division of Penguin Group (USA) Inc.

First Printing, December 2010
10 9 8 7 6 5 4 3 2 1

To Carolyn J. Lawes
For your unconditional support, wicked wit, and
Superwoman smarts
Thanks for being my sister

Acknowledgments

I would like to especially acknowledge John Sperling, a true patron of the arts, and the first client to suggest I "just take care of" his massive historic home renovation . . . and then the one after that. And thanks to Nic Ehr and his entire construction crew, and to landscape architect Vera Gates at Arterra, and mosaic artist Karen Thompson of Archetile. Thanks also to Peter Simoni, Bruce Nicolai, Gomez Gomez, and the many Bay Area builders and architects I've worked with over the years, for answering my incessant questions and helping me learn the ins and outs of historic renovation.

To all my writer friends . . . you are too many to enumerate, but I appreciate you all every single day—especially my grog mates, conference pals, and all the Sisters and Misters in Crime. Remember: What happens at (fill in the blank) stays at (fill in the blank).

Special thanks are due to Steven Strouhal, Bee Enos, Pamela Groves, Jan Strout, Anna Cabrera, Mary Grae, Claudia Escobar, Shay Demetrius, Suzanne Chan, Susan

Baker, Kendall Moalem, Chris Logan, Brian Casey, Beth Bruggeman, and Kim Sullivan Green, and all the members of the (extended) Mira Vista Social Club for sticking with me despite my crazy schedule and writing obsessions.

As always, thanks to my wonderful editor, Kerry Donovan, and my great agent, Kristin Lindstrom. Your support means more than I can say.

And finally, thanks to Bob Lawes for inspiring Mel's dad, to Susan for passing on the dadisms, to Carolyn for her manuscript tweaking, to Jane for being such a loving mom, and to Jace and Sergio for the daily laughter. And to Oscar for being Oscar.

Chapter One

This was one pitiful-looking mansion.

As I pushed open the heavy front door, an empty beer can rolled across the dusty oak floor, its metallic rattle echoing off bashed-in walls and broken bookcases. More cans, wine bottles, and an impressive assortment of power tools lay strewn about the floor. Half-filled cups spoiled the once-shiny black lacquer of the grand piano and littered the graceful sweep of the circular stairs leading off the octagonal foyer. A damp, salty bay breeze blew in through a broken casement window. I tried clicking on the overhead chandelier to shed some light on the dim interior, but either the fuse had blown or the electricity had been cut.

My former client lay sprawled on a worn black leather couch, a gash between his eyebrows still oozing blood.

I had warned him.

Long, freckled fingers gripped a half-empty bottle of a local favorite: passion fruit–infused Hangar One vodka, brewed in an abandoned navy airplane hangar just on the other side of the San Francisco Bay. At least the fool had taste, if not sense.

I pried the bottle from his hand.

With a snort, Matt Addax opened red-rimmed bright blue eyes.

"Wha . . . Mel? What're you doin' here?" he asked in a British-accented slur.

"Your son called me," I said. "He was afraid that last night's 'Do-It-Yourself' remodeling party might have gotten out of hand."

"The lad's wise beyond his years."

"Mmm." I kicked at a stray piece of old molding, lying rusty-nail-side up, with the steel toe of my work boot. "What happened to your face?"

He sat up and raised a hand to probe the cut between his eyes. "Ah, *bloody hell*, I've got a photo shoot tomorrow. A piece of wood snapped off—the stuff that they used to put old plaster onto. What's that called?"

"Lath?"

"Yeah. I was prying off some lath and it snapped and beaned me. I loathe lath." He smiled. "Try saying that five times fast."

"You promised me you'd wear safety glasses."

He shrugged, looked me up and down, and lifted his eyebrows. "You always look like you're on the way to a fancy-dress party. Don't the boys tease you?"

"Not if they want their paychecks signed, they don't."

Provided I wore the proper footwear—my ever-present work boots—and knew my single-bevel miter saws from my random orbital sanders, the construction workers in my employ didn't much care how I dressed. Today I was wearing a multicolored spangled shift dress under a leather bomber jacket I had borrowed from my dad's closet as a concession to modesty and the weather. The carnival nature of the dress was a little over-the-top for a woman just a couple years shy of forty, and strangers on the street frequently mistook me for a Madonna groupie, but after years of wearing the "proper" faculty-wife wardrobe, I had sworn never to hold myself back. Besides, even in progressive California, people were so surprised to see a woman running a construction company, I figured the clothes gave us all something tangible to fixate on.

I sank onto the sofa next to Matt, held my hand out for the vodka, and took a little swig. It was barely noon, but the havoc that forty or so drunken amateurs had managed to wreak on this formerly gorgeous, if down-at-the-heels, Pacific Heights mansion was motivation enough for a quick drink an hour or three before happy hour.

Matt leaned his elbows on his knees and cradled his head in his broad musician's hands, his thinning sandy hair sprouting between his fingers. Looking over at him—and at the once-elegant mansion falling apart around us—I could feel my resolve melting away.

I had sworn I wouldn't get involved with Matt's scheme to flip upscale houses, trading on his celebrity and social connections to market to an exclusive clientele. But I liked Matt, and it wouldn't take that much for me to help him out. After all, remodeling historic homes is my business.

Still, my relationship to the former rock star was tenuous at best. My stepson, Caleb—*ex*-stepson, actually—went to school with Matt's son. Matt and I had met a couple of years before over cupcakes at a Parents' Association meeting, and then last year Matt hired me to remodel his kitchen in Sausalito. A couple of months ago, as a special favor, I had done a thorough inspection of this house before Matt bought it.

As far as I was concerned, that was the extent of our relationship. But a lot of rich and famous people wind up growing abnormally close to their contractors. We camp out in their homes for weeks, sometimes months, at a time. We have no particular stake in their wealth or celebrity—though our rates might spike when we enter the poshest neighborhoods. But aside from obvious budget considerations, ripping the toilet out of a crumbling Victorian in humble West Oakland is essentially the same as ripping one out of the fanciest Pacific Heights Beaux-Arts mansion.

The very banality of this interaction can transform a good general contractor into a client's trusted confidante. There's nothing quite like a protracted remodel project to devastate a marriage or threaten family harmony, and since taking over my dad's construction business two years ago I've mediated more than my fair share of domestic disputes. I respond to panicky calls about leaky faucets in the middle of the night and find myself hearing much more than I want to know about unfaithful spouses, shady corporate deals, and murky political alliances. I'm like a confessor to some of these people.

Matt Addax, whose long-haired, blue-jean-jacketed, guitar-playing image had adorned my bedroom wall in my teenage years, was one of those people.

"Anybody else get hurt?" I asked.

"I don't remember much past the . . ." He held his hand up toward the jagged shards of glass remaining in the smashed window frame and trailed off with a defeated shake of his head. "It seemed like a good idea at the time. Ya know that remodel show on cable, where they do their own demo?" Matt asked, his voice recovering its familiar upbeat tone. "Like Kenneth said, it always seems like a blast. He arranged to have a photog here from the *Chronicle* to document the whole thing. He thought it'd make a brilliant human interest story."

"Why am I not surprised that Kenneth was involved?"

"He means well."

I found that hard to believe. But as my mother used to say, if you can't say something nice, change the subject.

"I'm pretty sure that on TV they don't encourage participants to drink while using power tools," I pointed out, passing the bottle back to Max. "They also have professionals running things."

"You're right. I'm an idiot. I should have hired you to supervise."

"You called and asked me to, remember? I refused, because I'm smart."

"Right. Now I remember."

"Besides, Kenneth doesn't like me."

"He just doesn't like your rates."

"Believe me, he doesn't like *me*."

And the feeling was mutual. Kenneth had acted as project manager on Matt's kitchen renovation in Sausalito, but he kept insisting on cutting corners and fudging on little things like code requirements. I had finally walked off the job after an incident involving threatening words concerning the creative use of a jackhammer.

"I give up on this place," Matt said with a defeated sigh. "Will you fix it?"

"Which part?"

"All of it. I'm tired of it. I don't care what Kenneth

says. Just take over the remodel. If you cut me a break on your fees up front, I can offer you a share of the sale price. We should still be able to make some good money."

"You're one week into a remodel and you're already tired of it? You might want to reconsider this house-flipping venture."

"We made a killing on the last place."

"One lucky sale is no foundation for such a risky line of business."

"Kenneth got this place cheap, though. Because of the haunting deal."

I was afraid to ask. But I couldn't stop myself.

"*Haunting* deal?"

"You don't know about that? People say this place is haunted. So we got it cheap."

"Seriously?"

"Previous owner had to disclose it in the sale."

"Let me get this straight: The owners have to tell you if they think their house is haunted?"

He nodded. "Real estate law. It's part of full disclosure and all that." His red-rimmed eyes scanned the disaster area surrounding us. "Maybe it really *is* haunted. Maybe *that's* what happened last night."

I held up the bottle of vodka. "*This* is what happened last night. These are all the spirits you need to screw up a construction project."

"At least I followed your advice on one thing: I packed up all the glass lampshades, a lot of the door and window hardware, and anything else that looked valuable or historical."

"You forgot the chandelier." I gestured toward the obviously homemade monstrosity hanging in the entryway. Colored rocks and murky crystals had been wrapped in copper wire and hung limply amongst amber, flame-shaped electric bulbs. I sort of admired the concept, but the execution left a lot to be desired.

"With good reason." Matt snorted. "The former owner considered himself an artist, it seems. There are a number of his creations, here and there."

"I take it the mosaic in the bathroom is his handiwork? And the homemade fireplace in the den?" I asked, recalling the ugly rock-and-shell-studded surround.

"Yup. And the funky garden walks and the homemade pond. Seems he owned his own cement mixer." Matt dug into the pocket of his faded jeans and brought out a chain with two keys, one small and one large. "The crate's in the garage. Could you arrange for storage? It's padlocked—here's the key."

"What's the other key for?"

"The front door. Say you'll save me."

"It'll be a huge job if we do it right."

"I know that."

"Pricey." Just wanted to be clear.

"I'll make the money back in the long run. This is Pacific Heights, after all. The sky's the limit. . . . Listen, Mel, I can't afford to look like an idiot with this one. I'm too high profile. I need to flip it—fast."

He looked grim. Matt Addax may have started his professional life as a teenage rock god, but as is the case with so many of us, advancing age brought with it certain unavoidable insights. His big blue eyes and adorable British accent took him only so far. For the past several decades his music career had been in free fall, but during a stint in the exclusive New Leaf rehab center up on the Mendocino coast he had befriended an elite array of socialites—the same place he met the well-connected Kenneth Kostow.

Soon Matt became an all-around San Francisco celebrity, one of those people who didn't actually have to *do* anything—at least anymore—to be famous. Since he wasn't a skinny young female who could achieve notoriety by forgetting her underwear, he had to use other methods to distinguish himself. House flipping gave him a semiartistic, cutting-edge career; as he explained to me once, *everyone* loves home design. And I had to hand it to Kostow—he and Matt had done surprisingly well so far.

I looked at the living room, the entry, and the dining room beyond. Yes, there was trash everywhere, holes in the walls, cracked and peeling paint and varnish, and signs of dry rot along some of the windows. But I knew from my previous inspection that the all-important foundation was solid and the main wood supports were intact. And, like most historical structures, Matt's house had been built with more care, better skills, and finer materials that one would find in any modern home.

Indeed, the bones of the place reflected the grace and refinement of an era long past. Ceilings were high, with peaked arches leading from one room to the next. Wide-plank oak floors were dressed up with an inlaid Greek key border design. The crown moldings were intact, boasting intricate fleur-de-lis and acanthus leaves. The living room fireplace mantel, crowded at the moment with plastic cups and beer cans, was elaborately carved limestone complete with spiral columns and frolicking putti.

I could practically feel the people who had once come to this parlor for a cup of tea, hear the rattle of a newspaper, smell the aroma of pipe smoke, and sense the tinkle of laughter through the years.

Who was I kidding? I had fallen under the house's spell the first moment I walked in to do the inspection two months ago. The signs of its long neglect and recent abuse hurt my heart. I was already itching to get at it.

"All things considered, the damage looks pretty superficial," I said, patting Matt on the knee and giving in to my inevitable impulse to save the place. "Nothing a big fat check won't fix. As long as no one broke a water pipe or compromised a load-bearing wall, you'll be okay."

Matt's bloodshot eyes fixed on me. "You're a peach, Mel. I mean that."

"Let's go survey the damage, shall we?"

First things first. Matt showed me the loaded crate in the ground-floor garage and I made a quick call to my transport and demo guy, Nico, asking him to rescue the grand piano while he was at it. Half Italian and half Samoan, Nico had a big strong truck and an endless supply of similarly sturdy nephews. I felt confident that together they could lift the entire house, much less a piano.

As Matt and I mounted the steps to the second floor, I bit my tongue, trying to keep from commenting on the vodka. It really wasn't any of my business.

I made it almost halfway up the flight of stairs.

"I thought you quit drinking."

"I'm in a new program. Booze isn't strictly forbidden as long as it's taken in moderation. Besides, my new neighbor brought over a bottle of eighteen-year-old scotch. Old enough to vote. What's a man to do?"

Sounded more like rationalization than science to me, but who was I to say?

I had to smile as we stepped into the master bedroom. A sheet of wallboard had been hung both crooked *and* backward. There were several nails placed, seemingly at random, in one multipaned window frame. And the pièce de résistance: a lacy red bra hung over a closet door.

If this was Matt's definition of moderation, I'd hate to witness his version of overindulgence.

As I stepped over an empty champagne bottle, my boot kicked something that clinked and skittered across the floor. I squatted and picked up a few of the small brass objects.

"Are those shells?" Matt asked. *"Bloody hell."*

"No, they're bullets. Thirty-eight caliber."

"What's the difference?"

"Shells are cartridge casings that are expelled upon firing."

Matt looked bewildered.

"The shells hold the gunpowder," I explained. "They separate from the slug when the gun is fired. The slug's the part that kills you. These bullets haven't been fired."

"You Americans and your guns. What's the deal?"

My father was an ex-marine who had grown up hunting in the Adirondacks. His dismay at having sired a pack of three girls was alleviated by taking us all to the firing range when my mother wasn't looking. My sisters soon bowed out, but I had tried my best to be my father's son and went as far as to take a hunters' safety training course before I realized there was no way I'd ever be able to shoot Bambi, or any of his relations or other furry woodland friends.

Assessing the cold weight of the metal cartridges in

the palm of my hand, I felt a tingle at the base of my neck.

"What exactly went down here last night, Max?"

"I'm telling you, I don't remember. My ex walked in with her new boy toy, and I started downing that great scotch. I'll admit, I lost it."

"Who was invited to this shindig?"

"Everybody. The A-list. Rory Abrams—the guy with that hot new restaurant in North Beach?—took care of the catering. Everyone thought the whole do-it-yourself demo idea was a scream."

"Oh, sure," I said, "brandishing Sawzalls and pneumatic drills and *handguns* while downing tequila shooters is a real hoot."

"It wasn't that bad. The photographer gave me the name of a guy to handle security at the front door, and he brought along a couple of friends to make sure things didn't get out of hand."

"Sounds positively sedate. You guys trashed the place, cut the lights, and someone had a gun?" My eyes scanned the floor for more cartridges. "Tell me, Matt— what would 'getting out of hand' look like?"

"Be kind to the man with a beastly hangover. Besides, those bullets could have been here for years for all we know. Maybe they were behind something, just got knocked about in the hubbub."

"Was there anyone at the party that I'd know? Who was the photographer?"

"A kid—Zachary something. He's new. Cute. Looks like a young Antonio Banderas, except, ya know, not Spanish."

I crossed over to the crooked wallboard and peered

into the deep recess beyond. Because of the line of the eaves, there was more than the standard six inches of space behind the wall. A dark niche extended back several feet. The perfect hiding place.

"Hey, Matt, I think I see something back in here."

Matt wrinkled his nose. "I hate that—when they open up the walls. It smells funky."

"Are you serious? That's the fun part."

"It's the anthropologist in you coming out. The love of digging up old bones. I'm telling you, it's bad juju."

"I was a *cultural* anthropologist, not an archaeologist. I dealt with live people. And anyway, I relinquished my badge when I became a contractor, remember?"

"Once an anthropologist, always an anthropologist. You guys are like musicians. You can't shake it."

He was more right than he knew.

To me, old houses might as well be ancient pyramids. They hold secrets and messages from the past; I feel them whispering to me as I walk the hallways. Walls, attics, basements . . . over the past five years I had found newspapers from the thirties, liquor bottles, old coins, address books, even the occasional stash of money or stocks. I once unearthed a button-up baby's shoe and a dress pattern book from 1916. I even liked the smell: the distinctive, musty aroma of history, reminding me of used bookstores . . . promising the serendipitous discovery of the perfect novel or family relic or beloved treasure.

I dug through my satchel for my key ring, on which hung a miniflashlight. Holding the light with my teeth, I crouched, grabbed onto a stud with one hand for balance, leaned in through the hole in the wall, and reached.

It was frustratingly close, but my arm wasn't quite

long enough. I stretched just a little more, managing to knock at the item with my fingertips. Unfortunately that just pushed it farther until it fell into a well between the floor joists. I couldn't see anything anymore, even with the flashlight.

"Darn it!" I swore under my breath. "I almost had it...."

Behind me, Matt screamed.

Chapter Two

"*Kenneth!*"

I swung around to see Matt's business partner lurching through the bedroom doorway, his chest, stomach, and arm soaked with blood.

Kenneth held a bright green pneumatic nail gun in one hand. The other arm was wrapped tight around his abdomen. His normally sleek blond hair was sticking out every which way, and bits of sawdust and white powder clung to one side of his body. But scariest of all were his eyes—they were wild and unfocused.

Kenneth lifted the nail gun and pointed it toward us.

I grabbed Matt from behind and shoved him to the side just as Kenneth managed to squeeze off a single nail. It sailed halfway across the room before lodging its tip in the window frame. Our would-be nailer then fell over onto the floor, moaning, rolling in the dust and debris.

I scrambled over to him, wrenched the nail gun from his flailing hand, and passed it to Matt. Stripping off my jacket, I balled it up and put it under his head.

"Matt, call nine-one-one," I commanded in a calm but urgent whisper. His eyes looked dull when they met mine, but after a beat he pulled out a cell phone and dialed.

I turned back to the injured man.

"Kenneth, talk to me," I said in a loud, authoritative voice, holding his face, trying to get him to meet my eyes. Shock takes away reason and focus. "Where are you hurt?"

He mumbled, but the words were nearly unintelligible and mostly consisted of "Damn, Matt . . ." Kenneth's wild eyes held mine for a moment, telegraphing his terror. I tried to lift his arm off his body, but he held it pressed to his side with surprising strength. There was too much blood to see the extent of his injuries, so I started feeling, gingerly, around his abdomen. Was there a bullet wound? Then I felt something small, flat, and hard. Lifting his soaked shirt and gently wiping away the blood, I peered at it.

It was the head of a nail. I searched further. Kenneth had been shot with the nail gun. . . . repeatedly.

Continuing with my tactile exploration, I came to a terrible realization: Kenneth still held his arm to his abdomen, but that was all there was—an arm. At the wrist was a tightly drawn leather belt serving as a tourniquet.

There was no hand.

I swallowed, hard, took a deep breath, and listened to Matt giving our address to the 911 operator. When he finished, I told him, "Run and get the cooler from downstairs, and then go find Kenneth's severed hand."

"Severed *hand*?" he whispered weakly.

"Just do it. Don't think about it." I remembered seeing an object that looked like an inflated latex glove lying in the hall near the door of the den, at the other end of the hall. I now suspected it might not be a glove. "Look in the hallway, or wherever he might have come from—the den, maybe?"

Construction was among the most dangerous jobs in the world. My father was nearly fanatical about job site safety, and he had enrolled me and my sisters in annual emergency first-aid courses starting at the age of twelve. But all the care in the world couldn't stave off the occasional sliced fingertip or tumble off a ladder. Fatigue, stress, shortcuts, alcohol . . . any of these, combined with the tools of the trade, could lead to tragic mistakes in the blink of an eye. One of my dad's best friends, after twenty years on the job without incident, had gotten sloppy one day and slid off a roof, fracturing two vertebrae. He had never walked again.

Matt seemed frozen, swaying slightly on his feet, his skin an unnatural shade of green associated with the bottoms of birdcages.

"*Matt*, listen to what I'm saying. We might not have much time. You need to move, *now*. There'll be plenty of time to be sick later. Is there a first-aid kit anywhere?"

Matt shook his head, and I felt a surge of rage. What had been absurd, even laughable, before—a drunken celebrity do-it-yourself demo party—now seemed criminal. What business did these dilettantes have playing around with deadly tools?

"Go, *now*!"

Matt finally shifted into gear and loped out of the room. I wrapped Kenneth's stump as best I could, then just held his head in my lap and murmured to him. He had a small birthmark on his neck, a Port-colored splotch that moved slightly with his pulse. I watched it, synchronizing my breathing to his, willing him to continue as I did. There was no love lost between Kenneth and me; but now, in my arms, he was just a man, terrifyingly vulnerable. Like the rest of us, nothing but soft, yielding flesh and blood: human. Fallible and prone to injury. He was someone's son, maybe someone's brother, or uncle. I had never thought to ask.

A lifetime passed before I finally heard the shrill, escalating whine of emergency vehicles heralding the arrival of the paramedics.

"It was a do-it-yourself demo party." I yelled to be heard over the sound of the retreating siren.

Sunlight glinted off the chrome of the ambulance as it disappeared down the street. Matt was accompanying Kenneth and the paramedics to the California Pacific Medical Center; I stayed behind to close the place up.

"A *what*?" asked the cop. He was a middle-aged, jowly man whose paunch strained at the buttons of his SFPD uniform. His watery blue eyes kept wandering from the notepad in his hands to my overexposed chest. It had become a warm, sunny February day, so my sleeveless dress was equal to the weather, but perhaps not to the company.

After the paramedics swooped in and took over with Kenneth, I had washed up in the powder room sink as best I could, scrubbing my hands and arms raw, trying to pull myself together. I smoothed my dark curly hair and did my best to ignore the wan, hollow look in my eyes. Amazingly my dress had emerged from the ordeal dusty but unbloodied, but my father's jacket wasn't so lucky—I would have to take it in for professional cleaning before he discovered it was gone. At the moment it hung, grimy and stained with blood, over my arm. Without the jacket on, I really did look like the last gal left after a wild party.

"The idea is to do part of the demolition and beginning remodel with the help of a lot of friends." I straightened my spine, tried to rally my spirits, and continued. "Unfortunately, there was alcohol involved. But that was last night—those injuries must have been recent. Kenneth couldn't have survived—"

"You're saying it was a construction accident," the officer said with finality, as though he were filling out a form with only a certain number of choices.

"A single nail might have been an accident," I protested. "Maybe two. But he's been shot repeatedly."

"According to the victim himself, it was an accident. First with the . . . uh . . . table saw and then with the nail gun."

"Kenneth's able to talk?" I asked.

"Like I said, he told me it was an accident."

"But that doesn't make any sense—"

"Listen, sweetheart, you'd be surprised what these power tools can do, all right? I once saw a guy got shot in the head with a nail gun and he was standing clear across the room. And this other time . . . Well, look, I don't want to upset you, okay? But it's like they say— accidents are stranger than fiction."

"I'm in the construction business myself, *sweetheart*. And I'm telling you: This doesn't seem like an accident." I reached into my jacket pocket for my business card and realized I still had the bullets. "Oh, I found these in the master bedroom. Sorry I touched them. I guess they could be evidence."

He held out his hand, and I relinquished the cartridges. A flicker of interest sparked in those bland eyes.

"Was the victim shot? I mean, with a gun?" the cop asked me, as though I would know.

"As far as I could see, only with the nail gun, but it was pretty hard to tell. I'm sure the hospital will discover more."

I handed him my business card:

Mel Turner, General Contractor
Turner Construction
Remodeling—Renovation—Repair
Historic Home Specialists

The officer looked down at it, then back up at me with a doubtful don't-that-beat-all look on his broad face.

"This your job site, then?" he asked.

"No, I wasn't involved in the project. I just dropped by to check up on Matt. As a friend."

"Okay, look, what we need here is for you to tell me what you saw. Period. You arrived a little before noon and found the first gentleman downstairs, asleep, and the second individual upstairs missing a hand and shot with nails. Okay? Is that about it?"

I nodded.

A large, rattling truck pulled up to the curb, air brakes wheezing. Three smiling men the size of Wisconsin were squeezed into the cab. Nico and his nephews.

"Matt Addax asked me to move a couple of things out of the garage and then to close up," I told the police officer. "Is that a problem?"

"Nah, seems okay. That your dog?"

I turned around to see a medium-sized, long-haired brown dog with a red bandanna around its neck sniffing at the garbage. I shook my head.

"Off leash, no collar." The police officer shook his head. "There's an infraction right there."

I studied him. He seemed as concerned about a dog without tags as he did about Kenneth's grave injuries.

"Look, you might want to call a cleanup outfit; you got a real mess in there. Somethin' like this happens out on the street, we could call the fire department to hose things down. But seein' as how it's on private property, you're responsible for doin' it yourself." He scratched his head, consulted his notepad, and nodded with finality. "Anyways, we'll take another look around, and then you can lock up. Cal-OSHA usually sends out an accident investigator to file a report in construction accidents such as this, but since it's a private homeowner deal, I'm not sure if they'll get involved. Depends on permits. We'll call you if we need anything else."

With that, the cop hustled back into the house.

Nico jumped down from the cab of the truck, a huge smile splitting his pleasant, smooth face. He gave me a bear hug and lifted me clear off the ground.

"Mel! You look gorgeous. How come you not remarried yet?"

"I learned my lesson the first time, remember?"

This exchange had become our ritual when we saw each other after a long separation, and despite Nico's propensity for dousing himself with cheap aftershave I felt a surge of gratitude for the safe, familiar feel of his muscled arms.

I gave him and his nephews the short version of

what had happened. After clucking their sympathy, they tromped up the stone stairs, tape measures in hand, to assess whether the piano would make it out the front door. If not, it would have to be maneuvered through the expansive living room window. Many of these old houses still have anchored hooks under the roofline that were used to winch large pieces of furniture up the three or four floors that make up the typical ritzy townhome.

The sight of a piano being hoisted two stories above the sidewalk always made me think of hapless cartoon characters getting squashed flat by falling pianos before reinflating like blow-up dolls.

If only real humans recovered so easily.

I lingered on the sidewalk, not yet willing to force myself back into Matt's house of horrors. The views from the peak of Pacific Heights were unparalleled, and today the Tuscan red Golden Gate Bridge and the emerald green Marin headlands beyond were crystal clear, as were the vistas of Alcatraz, Angel Island, Sausalito, and Tiburon. Sailboats crowded the smooth, blue-green bay waters, vying with a handful of China-based container ships lumbering to and from the Port of Oakland.

Somewhere nearby a dog barked, a motor revved, neighbors chatted.

I felt removed from it all, altered by recent events. My mind cast back to the morning my mother died, when I couldn't believe that the world refused to stop, even for a moment, to acknowledge its loss. I remembered watching people rush about in their everyday routines; I had despised them for their normality, for not recognizing that such an essential part of the world had just slipped away.

Tears pricked the backs of my eyes, and I felt that

strange, otherworldly sensation of being hugged that
came over me whenever I thought of my mother.

"Is everything all right, dear?"

I looked up to see that the neighbors had descended
their front steps and come over to stand by me on the
sidewalk. Preceded by a subtle fog of expensive per-
fume, the two women looked to be in their early sixties, blond, well coiffed, and attractive; one tall and
lithe, the other petite but with torpedo-style surgically
enhanced breasts. Both were dressed in chic pantsuits
in understated tones of cream and beige. Both had that
well-preserved, polished sheen of people willing and
able to spend a considerable chunk of their time and
fortunes on personal trainers, masseuses, and nutritional
counselors.

"I'm Celia Hutchins, from next door," said the taller
of the two, the tennis bracelet and solitaires in her ears
glittering in the bright afternoon sun. Her voice was
husky, her tone refined. "This is my good friend Meredith; she lives across the street. We couldn't help but
notice the ambulance."

Time to pull myself together.

"A man was injured—" I began.

"I have to say I'm not surprised," inserted Meredith,
neatly plucked eyebrows raised and manicured hand
fluttering up to her cheek. She kept rocking up on her
tiptoes, then back down. Lots of nervous energy. "The
party seemed to be getting out of hand last night. That
house . . . It's just one thing after another. . . ." She
trailed off with a shake of her head and a shrug of her
slim shoulders.

"I don't suppose either of you heard gunshots, or
anything else out of the ordinary?" I asked.

"It was loud, lots of music and laughter, but nothing like gunshots, good heavens, no." Celia shook her head. "Was someone shot?"

That was a tough one to answer without getting into gruesome details.

"I'm not sure . . ." I evaded.

"Is Matt all right?" Celia asked.

"Yes, he's fine."

"Matt really is a dear; he invited us over, but I must say, it wasn't really my kind of party. I hire people to do that kind of thing. Speaking of which, is this your car?" She gestured toward my boxy red Scion, which had magnetic TURNER CONSTRUCTION signs attached to the front doors. "You're . . . a builder?"

"We specialize in historic homes," I said with a nod. Celia's gray-green eyes swept over my colorful, low-cut dress. The men I worked with were accustomed to my wardrobe, but when first meeting with clients I usually took care to wear a conservative outfit consisting of a blazer and tailored slacks. Physically, I was a throwback to the pinup-girl era, with what my father's cohorts would call a va-va-va-voom body. An extra fifteen pounds or so only intensified this effect. It was an extravagant look largely out of favor these days, most popular with long-haired bikers and truck drivers.

"How darling that you're a woman," Celia continued. "I've been wanting to have a room redone for our club meetings. We're simply desperate for a good contractor."

"Are you a lesbian?" piped Meredith.

"*Meredith*. Just because a woman is doing a nontraditional job doesn't make her a lesbian." Celia leaned toward me and spoke in a low voice, as though in confidence. "Not that it would be a problem if you were.

My niece is gay and she's a darling girl. An artist. Very creative."

The last thing I wanted to do at the moment was to talk about my sex life, much less sweet-talk a client. Still, in my line of work one did not alienate Pacific Heights homeowners. I reached into my jacket and dug for a business card.

"Could I come back and take a look at your project tomorrow?" I said. "I'd be happy to give you an estimate, but this isn't really the best time."

"Of course," Celia said, tucking my card into the front pocket of her fine linen slacks. "You know, Meredith and I weren't at the party last night, but for the sake of appearances I sent my son, Vincent, over in our stead. He only stayed for a short while, but perhaps you'd like to speak with him."

"Did he mention seeing anything odd?"

"He left when things started getting rowdy." Celia's gaze flickered down to my left hand. She smiled and met my eyes. "You're not married?"

"I . . . uh . . . No, not at the moment."

"I like your dress," interrupted Meredith.

"Thank you. A friend of mine designed it."

Meredith smiled. Her dark eyes watched me intently for a moment before shifting to look over my shoulder. I turned to see Nico and his two nephews muscling the grand piano down the front steps.

"What's going on?" Meredith asked.

"Matt wanted to put a few things in storage," I responded. "We're removing the piano so it won't get damaged."

"I remember when Gerald brought in that piano. Do you remember, Celia?"

Celia nodded. "Gerald was an ... interesting neighbor."

"Have you lived here long?" I asked.

"Nearly thirty years—since my Vincent was just a boy. How time does fly."

"I've been here twenty-five," Meredith told me, gesturing to an elegant, multicolored Victorian a few doors down.

I watched as the portly police officer hurried down the stone steps after the movers, rushed over to his radio car, lifted his hand toward us in a brief salute, and left. As simple as that.

I've had very little interaction with the police in my life, so I'm not familiar with the standard process of inquiry. Still, it seemed as if there should be more to an investigation of such serious injuries, especially since there was no way in hell Kenneth had done such things to himself—was there? After all, he might be a creep, but he wasn't a superhuman pain freak.

I felt another pang deep in my gut; I had never liked Kenneth, but he had seemed so defenseless, so very human, when I held him in my arms.

After agreeing to return the next day at noon to check on Celia's project, I excused myself from the women. All I could think about at the moment was getting home and taking a long, long shower.

As I approached my car, my heart sank. The last place I remembered seeing my satchel was on the second floor, when Matt and I were confronted by Kenneth. I procrastinated for a moment by looking in the mailbox and gathering the letters and papers I found there: store circulars and several notices from the city. I tossed the junk mail in the recycling bin, put the rest of the mail in my car to pass on to Matt, and finally forced myself to enter the house.

I mounted the circular stairs with trepidation.

A blood trail stained the threadbare, gruel-colored carpet on the landing. I took a deep breath, pausing a moment, before giving in to ghoulish curiosity. Careful not to step on any evidence, I picked my way along the hall and entered the den.

A thick plastic tarp protected the floor and held building supplies: a small pile of two-by-fours, boxes of latex gloves and safety masks, a couple of bags of Fixall patching compound, and a stack of half-inch sheets of wallboard. The homemade fireplace formed an imposing presence along the far wall, otherwise covered in cheap paneling . . . and marred by a faint spray of red-black specks. Kenneth's blood, I presumed. I swallowed, hard. A multipaned French door leading out to a fire escape also showed evidence of blood spatter.

Finally I allowed myself to focus on the table saw set up in the middle of the room. The machine was encircled by sawdust and blood, and the round, serrated blade looked as though it had been dipped in dark brownish red paint.

Bile rose to my throat; black spots danced in front of my eyes.

I sank to the floor, squeezed my eyes shut, put my head between my knees, and concentrated on breathing.

After several moments the nausea subsided.

I heard sounds. Scraping, a footstep. The whine of a saw? A distant scream?

I opened my eyes and looked up toward the table saw. In my peripheral vision, I saw someone in the doorway.

Kenneth. Bloodied but standing tall.

Chapter Three

"*Kenneth?* What are you—"
As soon as I looked straight at him, he was gone.

I glanced around. The room was as empty as it had been a moment before.

Pull yourself together, Mel.

Kenneth had just been taken away in an ambulance; he couldn't have been standing here in this room. Had I passed out? Was I dreaming?

I shivered. The air was cold. Frigid, even. So cold I could see my own breath.

A ghost?

I put my head back down on my knees.

Enough. Too many thoughts of death and dying; far too much imagination. Post-traumatic stress, maybe.

Again, I thought of my mother's death. Right after she passed away, while I was driving my father home from the hospital, she appeared in my side window, standing in the middle of the road. She disappeared as soon as I looked over, but I swerved and barely avoided slamming into the car next to me. When I asked my dad whether he had seen her, he told me I was nuts. And I had to agree with him.

Since then she would come to me from time to time, memories and thoughts of her so vivid I would have sworn she was standing beside me or whispering in my ear. Especially in that otherworldly moment between sleep and wakefulness, I could feel the smooth warmth of her hand on my forehead.

I always assumed that my sense of her continuing presence had to do with our closeness before she passed. In stark contrast, the only sort of emotional intimacy Kenneth Kostow and I could claim was a mutual dislike.

Besides, I reminded myself, *he isn't dead, just injured. Gravely injured.*

Grimacing, I looked down at the blood drying on the leather jacket.

Another deep breath.

"*Mel?*" called Nico, his voice floating up from downstairs and yanking me back to reality.

"Up here!" I called. "I'll be right down."

Nico had packed up the crate. I gave him the access code to my storage unit in a facility out near the Port of Oakland, which he noted in the tiny notebook he kept in his shirt pocket. I asked him to take the piano to my dad's house. The garage/workshop was dry and heated, and Dad rarely used it as a workshop anymore, anyway. It was as good a place as any to store the beautiful instrument in the interim.

Waving good-bye to Nico and his nephews, I climbed into my Scion.

Before starting up the engine, I watched the chocolate brown dog joyfully chase a squirrel up a tree as I placed a few phone calls. It was Sunday, but running a construction business meant there was work to be done all day, every day. First I checked in with my foreman, Raul Hernandez, on the job we were finishing up in the posh neighborhood of St. Francis Wood; he assured me everything was set for the walk-through meeting with the clients scheduled for tomorrow morning. Then I returned several calls to subcontractors, addressing details regarding an etched-glass shower panel, a faulty solar-operated attic fan, and a shortage of copper piping.

Finally, I dialed Matt's cell phone, hoping to find out how Kenneth was faring. No answer.

I sat for several more minutes, trying to pull myself together, before starting down Vallejo Street toward the bay. Still, my mind raced. Could Kenneth's injuries truly be the result of an accident? I supposed stranger things had happened on job sites. And one never knew what shenanigans alcohol-fueled amateurs might get up to around power tools, which is precisely why I maintain such strict safety standards on my projects.

Demolition, or "demo," looks like a free-for-all, and in some ways it is. It doesn't take the finesse of finish carpentry, but there is an art to properly taking the walls back to the studs—especially in historic homes where preservation is key. Clearly last night's efforts had been much more free-for-all than finesse.

And then this morning something nightmarish had occurred with Kenneth.

I snuck into the carpool entrance to the Bay Bridge right before official hours and crossed the double span toward the East Bay. Twenty minutes later I pulled up to a once-lovely old farmhouse undergoing renovation in the middle of the seedy but vibrant Fruitvale section of Oakland.

Home. For the moment.

I never thought I'd be the type to move back in with my husband and my mother passed away unexpectedly, I needed a temporary place to land, and my dad needed the company. Though we found each other's political views mutually appalling and had head-butted throughout most of my youth, since Mom's passing Dad and I had both honored a kind of pseudo détente.

A broken flagstone path led around the side of the house to the rear entrance, the one used by friends and family. The door opened onto a tiled mudroom, which in turn led to a roomy, old-fashioned kitchen currently redolent of spaghetti sauce—the kind made with ground beef and sausage and plenty of olive oil. My father had learned to cook as a teenager at an old resort in the Adirondacks, and he wasn't about to change his ways in concession to newfangled health trends, high blood pressure and cholesterol be damned.

Dad stood at the vintage Wedgewood stove, happily arguing politics with his old friend Stan while stirring a pot of bubbling sauce with a long wooden spoon.

"Hey, babe," he greeted me with a nod.

I kissed his whiskery cheek and caught a faint whiff of the twice-a-day cigarettes he secretly enjoyed out behind the detached garage.

"Smoking again, Dad?" I asked.

"Impossible," he blustered. "I have no bad habits."

Though he still loomed large in my imagination, my father seemed to have shrunk since my mother's death, so with my boots on I stood nearly as tall as he. A plain white T-shirt hugged his workingman's shoulders and taut but prominent beer belly; worn jeans sat low on still-lean hips.

"Nico and the boys brought the piano by already," he said. "They stuck it in the garage. I hope to God you're not trying to play that thing. Remember what happened with the flute."

"It was a clarinet."

"Sounded like an injured cat, you ask me."

"And it was in the fifth grade. I think we should move on."

Frowning, he looked me up and down and gestured with the sauce spoon. "What's with the getup?"

By which I gathered my father didn't approve of my wardrobe.

"She's a breath of fresh air is what she is, Bill, you old codger," asserted my father's oldest friend, Stan Tomassi.

"Thanks, Stan." I leaned over to give my defender a kiss.

"I especially like the beads," he added.

"Stan, get Mel a drink," commanded my father in his military voice. My father's version of a martini was throwing some gin over ice. If he got fancy, he'd stick an olive in it and call it good.

"I can get it," I said.

"Let me," Stan winked and waved off my protest as he rolled toward the liquor cabinet. Once hale and hearty, Stan had worked construction with my dad for nearly twenty years, until one terrible miscalculation had resulted in a fall from a roof and two smashed vertebrae. My parents had seen him through several grim months of hospitalization, surgeries, and physical therapy. When

Stan was finally released from a rehabilitation center, my dad built a wheelchair ramp onto the side of the house, widened the downstairs bathroom, and moved him in. Not long afterward, Stan helped Dad cope with my mother's sudden death from heart failure.

Stan—partly out of guilt, partly out of the need for something to do—had elected himself my "chief cook and bottle washer," by which he meant my ersatz business manager, writing up schedules and charming clients with his exaggerated Oklahoman accent and homespun wisdom. I couldn't get him to stop answering the work phone in Turner Construction's home office.

"You okay, hon?" Stan asked as he handed me a shot glass of amber tequila. "You look worse'n a possum the day after."

"Something terrible happened today," I said, taking a fortifying drink before giving both men the rundown of the events at Matt's place on Vallejo Street. As I wrapped up the sorry tale, I asked my father the question foremost on my mind: "Is there any way Kenneth could have done it to himself somehow?"

"There *are* cases of people committing suicide with a circular saw," mused my dad as he sprinkled black pepper into the sauce.

"Seriously?"

He nodded.

I didn't even want to *think* about how that would work.

"Assuming this was some kind of an accident, what's the normal process of inquiry?" I asked. "How should the police treat it?"

"They have to file an incident report, especially in serious cases. On top of everything else, Matt'll need a police report for the insurance claim. If it had been one of our job sites, Cal-OSHA would come in and investigate, though since this was a homeowner project instead of a legitimate contractor, they'd stay out of it. Leave it to the cops."

California Office of Safety and Health Administration, or Cal-OSHA, was the government's workplace watchdog and the bane of every builder. On the other hand, its mere existence saved lives by striking fear into the heart of any employer who wanted to skimp on safety measures.

"You know who you should call?" Stan said. "Graham."

"Graham? Graham *Donovan*?" I asked.

"Yup. He's working—"

"The last thing I need right now is to see Graham Donovan," I interrupted, shaking my head. Graham used to work with my father, and I had a mad crush on him while I was in graduate school until I transferred my affections to my now-ex, Daniel. I hadn't seen Graham since before I got married, which was just as well. I certainly didn't want to open up *that* can of worms.

"Suit yourself," Stan said with a shrug.

"The officer who responded to the call didn't seem to be taking it very seriously," I mused. "Kenneth—the injured guy—said it was an accident, and the cop seemed to believe him."

Dad shrugged and started slicing a fresh loaf of sourdough for garlic bread. "Why wouldn't he believe him? Probably under pressure to be in too many places at one time. Police officers are workingmen—they get points for closing cases, not for asking questions."

"Workingmen and -*women*," I corrected him automatically, leaning back against the counter and sipping my drink. "Dad, I've been thinking. . . ."

"Uh-oh. Serious trouble."

"I told Matt I would take over the remodel."

"From what I read in the papers, your buddy Matt can't afford our services."

Though he had passed the business on to me, Dad continued to take a proprietary interest, reflected in the use of the royal "we." Since I stubbornly clung to a vague hope that he would step back in and take over, I didn't discourage this.

"Luckily he has a friend in the construction business," I said. "And this isn't charity; Matt will cover our expenses, and then we'll take a cut of the sales price. It's Pacific Heights, after all."

"Is this about your ex?"

That one came out of left field. "How would this be about Daniel?"

"He seems to inspire strange ideas. Unless I miss my guess, your plan to run away to Paris was about that SOB."

"Moving to Paris was about *Paris*, not Daniel."

He just snorted and shook a liberal amount of fragrant oregano into the sauce.

I noticed the jar was getting low. My mother used to gather herbs from her lush garden every year, hanging them to dry from the exposed beams in the kitchen. When they were ready, she would strip the leaves and store them in fat little marmalade jars that still sported labels written in her fluid, rounded handwriting. I smiled, feeling her presence for a moment.

My mother's passing was a tragedy for our family. But its aftermath also became a major stumbling block in my attempts to move on with my life, post-divorce. After eight strife-filled years of marriage, travel, and academic striving—Daniel and I were both anthropologists, he a professor at UC-Berkeley, I a lowly contract worker—I had come to the conclusion that, in general, people seemed kinder, more intelligent, and more interesting when I couldn't actually comprehend what they were saying.

So during the last excruciating death throes of my marriage, I had come up with a plan: I would run away to Paris, where they appreciated women of a certain age and where I wouldn't be able to understand anyone. Retreating to an obscure, anonymous pied-à-terre, I would indulge myself in licking my still-tender psychic wounds. From time to time I would emerge to eat my fill of *glacé aux cerises*, stroll along the Champs Elysées, loiter in the galleries of the Louvre, and maybe even take some handsome, monolingual French man as a lover. But otherwise I would return to my Left Bank refuge to continue my exquisitely solitary pity party. I figured if I kept my expenses low by not eating, this sort of behavior could go on for years.

But with my mother's unexpected death, all bets were off.

My father, who had remained strong and resilient through two tours in Vietnam, fell apart. His business languished; clients threatened. Stan took me aside and told me he didn't think my father would be able to resume the responsibilities of the job anytime in the near future. So I had stepped in, fully expecting my stewardship of Turner Construction to be a temporary fix.

Just a few months. A couple more. We were going on two years now.

As my many employment-challenged friends would be more than happy to remind me, being handed a successful, profitable business during these difficult economic times didn't exactly inspire sympathy. But I hadn't asked for this. I wanted to become a hauntingly thin martyr in a tiny Paris apartment; I wanted my ex-husband to feel guilty for as long as possible; I *wanted* to be left utterly alone for a year or ten.

But as the song says, you can't always get what you want.

"I also found some cartridges," I said, changing the subject. "Thirty-eight caliber."

"Was someone shot?"

"Not that I know of. But it seemed odd to find the bullets at Matt's place, what with everything else going on."

"This sort of thing wouldn't happen if we had some form of logical gun control in this country," Stan declared.

I sighed inwardly. The mention of gun control was bound to send my father off on a tirade concerning the Second Amendment, and judging by the wicked smile on Stan's face this was precisely his goal. Stan's paralysis had radicalized him, and with the rare verve of the recently converted, he had become a self-appointed champion of the masses, demanding access to health care and opportunities for all. I imagined that my father, outwardly disgusted at this turn of events, was secretly thrilled. There was nothing he liked better than arguing politics.

Saved by the arrival of two fifteen-year-old boys.

They shuffled in through the back door, dressed nearly identically: jeans sagging low to show off plaid cotton boxers, oversized T-shirts under dark blue UC-Berkeley hoodies, baseball caps on sideways, longish hair falling over their eyes. The only difference was that my stepson, Caleb, was dark, while Dylan—Matt's son—had his father's sandy hair and bright blue eyes.

"Hey," Dylan said to no one in particular.

"Hey," echoed Caleb, lifting his chin in greeting.

The deep, grown-up timbre of Caleb's voice always took me by surprise. Try as I might to move on, I still remembered him as the five-year-old I had come to know and love when I married his father, or as the thirteen-year-old who cried, begging me not to leave when we divorced two years ago. The man-child in front of me was achingly familiar, yet so like a stranger. My fingers itched to pull up his pants and brush the chestnut hair out of his near-black eyes.

Caleb opened the refrigerator's freezer compartment, foraged for a moment, and pulled out two ice-cream sandwiches. He handed one to Dylan.

I waited, but neither said a word, much less offered an explanation of what they were doing here. Caleb knew he was always welcome at my house, but without wheels Oakland was a long haul from San Francisco. He had to take BART—our local version of a subway—and transfer to a bus to get to me. Usually he called first and tried to cajole a ride.

"What's up, Goose?" I asked. "Dylan?"

Both boys grunted and acknowledged me with slight lifts of the chin. In hopes it might improve the tenor of our conversation, I reached over and pulled at the white cords hanging from their ears, releasing the ever-present iPod earbuds.

"What are you guys doing here?"

"Mom's out of town, and I'm not supposed to stay at my mom's house alone." Left unsaid was Caleb's disdain for his father's new wife, Valerie. As long as she was at Daniel's place, Caleb didn't stay there if he could help it.

"I thought you were spending a few days at Dylan's house."

The boys exchanged a significant look. They could be sullen and quiet, and were quick to revert to grunting behavior, but they weren't usually evasive with me. No need. As a former stepmother, I had no legal rights to Caleb; our ties were pure affection. I was in no position to mete out punishment, and they both knew it.

"Can't," Caleb said finally. "Dylan's mom is in Europe, and his dad . . ."

"Is something up with Matt?"

"Yeah. Dad was, like . . ." Dylan said, trailing off with a shrug.

"What?"

"Kind of, like . . . arrested."

Chapter Four

"Matt was *arrested*?"

"I guess."

"For what? When?"

Dylan shrugged and stuffed the last half of his ice cream sandwich in his mouth.

"He might not be totally arrested," Caleb said. "It was sort of, like, they wanted to ask him questions. But they were, like, probably he wasn't gonna be home tonight. I was thinking Dylan and me could stay here."

"Dylan and *I*," I corrected him. "Of course you can. But, Dylan, does anyone know you're here? Matt must be beside himself."

"He called," Dylan said, sticking his hand deep into his jeans pocket and rummaging around. The search process took a while. Finally he brought out a balled-up scrap of paper and handed it to me. "This is his lawyer's number. Dad told me I could hang here with Caleb if it was okay with you."

"Of course it's okay with me. You can stay as long as

you need to. But did your dad say anything about what happened?"

He shook his head, his young brow sketched with worry despite his nonchalant demeanor. Dylan was one of those kids raised in economic privilege but emotional famine. Matt was devoted to him, but Dylan's flighty mom had primary custody, and he was too often left to fend for himself. I imagined he was wondering who would be in his corner if his dad landed in prison.

"I knew that whole do-it-yourself thing sounded like a bad idea," mumbled Dylan. "Some guy died at that house he's fixing up. That Kenneth guy."

"Kenneth?" My voice shook.

"Yeah."

"Kenneth *died*? When?"

Dylan shrugged again and looked away. I tried to meet Caleb's dark gaze.

"We're gonna go watch something, 'kay?"

"Okay . . . sure," I said, temporarily giving up on the hunt for info. "Are you hungry?"

"I guess. Maybe later," Caleb said as they both trailed out of the room.

My dad met my eyes for a long moment before handing me the portable phone.

"I'll put on some more pasta," he said.

A series of phone calls yielded the information that Matt was being held in the prosaically named "Jail Number Two," but that no official charges had yet been filed. His lawyer, a fast-talking New Yorker, arranged for me to speak with Matt at nine the next morning. After a restless night, I tried to act as though I visited friends in the slammer every day while I fed the boys breakfast and drove them into San Francisco.

Halfway across the bridge I rushed to flip the radio off, but not before Matt's name was mentioned as a person of interest in the suspicious death of his "business associate" Kenneth Kostow. I glanced at the rearview mirror to see whether Dylan had noticed. He was looking out at the bay; white strands hung from his ears, and his mouth moved silently, as though reciting rap lyrics along with whatever he was listening to on his iPod. Good.

Unfortunately, Matt's high-profile celebrity status meant that most of the boys' schoolmates would have heard the news by now; we'd be lucky if it wasn't already splashed all over the local newspapers and the Internet.

I dropped the boys off at University High, their exclusive private school in Pacific Heights, not far from the scene of yesterday's terrible discovery. I doled out money for lunch, buses, and BART, and watched as they pulled their laden backpacks onto their young, slouching spines. Worried, I told Dylan to call me on my cell if he needed anything at all.

Then I made my unfamiliar way to the Bryant Street Hall of Justice.

Matt shuffled into the visiting room and took a seat opposite me at the institutional, cafeteria-type table. His square jaw was covered with reddish blond stubble, his eyes even more red-rimmed than when I'd last seen him. Before I had a chance to say anything, he started talking.

"Would you take care of Dylan for me? His mom's out of touch, on a cruise somewhere, not expected back until the end of the month. He'd be happier with Caleb than with his grandparents."

"Of course I will, but—"

"Oh, and keep on with the work at the house?"

"Matt, who cares about the remodel at this point?"

"I've got everything wrapped up in that place. And it's not just me. We owe some people money."

"What kind of people?"

He shrugged. "I'm not actually sure. Kenneth took care of all of that. He was the business side of things; I was just the creative. I've been working with the architect on the plans. Do you know him? Jason Wehr? He's won the AIA Design Award for Excellence in Architecture *twice*. It'll be bloody beautiful when it's done."

"Matt, did you pull official permits on this job?"

"Sure, Kenneth took care of all the paperwork."

"So was there a contractor involved, or was it a homeowner's permit?"

"I guess you'd have to check with the architect on that."

I blew out an exasperated breath and made a note to myself to call Jason Wehr. I remembered the name from the paperwork when I'd done the original home inspection for Matt. Architects were usually involved with the builders on a home they designed; Wehr was likely better informed than the aging rock star sitting in front of me.

"So . . . what's next for you?" I asked, afraid of the answer. "Will you make bail? Can your lawyer get you out of here?"

"We're not sure about bail yet. We don't even know whether they'll file charges." Matt started humming, his long-fingered, graceful hands playing air guitar. "You know, it's so strange. When you told me to find Kenneth's severed hand, I thought you were referring to that Pearl Jam song. You know that one? 'Severed Hand'?"

"Matt, *focus*. This is serious. What reason do the police have to believe you would do this? What motive could you have?"

He shrugged. "Motive's the easy part. Kenneth and I . . . we were partners in the business. There's a lot of money involved."

"Do they have any evidence against you?"

"I need money—that much is true." Matt shrugged again and looked down at his fingers, which were now tracing invisible shapes on the green laminate tabletop, as though writing a secret message.

"Matt?"

"Kenneth told them it was me, right before he died. I imagine that was the part that really struck a chord."

Words failed me. I stared at Matt for several beats.

"What are you talking about?" I finally croaked.

"It was in the emergency room. The doctors were working on him, trying to get him into surgery but he'd lost so much blood. . . ." Matt dropped his face into his hands, rubbing his forehead for a moment before looking back up at me. "Have you ever heard of something called a deathbed declaration?"

I shook my head.

"I hadn't, either," Matt said. "Apparently it's the only exception to the hearsay rule in the American justice system. If someone accuses someone else right before dying, it can be used as evidence. Anyway, one of the nurses heard Kenneth say something to implicate me."

"What exactly did he say?"

"Dunno."

"Who was the nurse?"

He shrugged and shook his head. "I wasn't allowed in while they were working on him. She was South African; that's all I know. Good-looking. She came out to talk to me at one point, and I recognized the accent. She told me she was from Johannesburg."

"Does *anyone* know what she said? Your lawyer, maybe?"

"He's working on it. But listen—that's another reason you need to keep on with the project at the house. I'm going to need access to money; I've got a construction loan to pay you with, but most of what I have is wrapped up in that place. And now, with the condition that it's in after the party, I think it might be worth even less than we paid for it."

"I'll see what I can do. Right now it's probably closed off, since it's a crime scene. But if they give me the go-ahead, I can get my crew on it right away."

"Thank you." Matt's eyes filled with tears. He reached out and put his hand over mine. "I didn't do this, Mel. I would never do something like this. Kenneth was my friend."

"I know."

"Really? You believe me?"

"I do."

And I did.

Yes, he had been drunk, and people have been known to do all sorts of crazy things while under the influence. But despite Matt's flighty behavior and inattention to details, he was a profoundly sweet man. He baked cupcakes for his son's birthday, escorted the kids on field trips, and paled when confronted with spiders. I once witnessed him make the sign of the cross at the sight of a raccoon roadkill.

I'm not naïve. I believe most of us would be capable of lashing out at someone in a moment of overwhelming passion . . . but torture was another matter entirely. To use a nail gun on Kenneth repeatedly, and then to hold the man in front of a table saw . . . It was too horrifying to contemplate.

But contemplate it I did, all the way across town.

I breathed a sigh of relief when I finally entered the posh, bucolic neighborhood known as St. Francis Wood, an early planned community from the 1920s carved out of 175 acres from the old San Miguel Ranch grant. Businesses were banned, utilities were buried, and lots were large by San Francisco standards. Decorative posts at the entrance let you know you are entering the Wood, whose wide boulevards are lined with mature trees and graceful stucco buildings. Two huge water features on St. Francis Boulevard, one a fountain at the intersection of Santa Ana Avenue and the other a cascade built into the hillside, evoke the sumptuous gardens of Renaissance Italy.

Long before I started officially working in construction, St. Francis Wood was one of my favorite walking neighborhoods. San Francisco is a relatively small but highly varied city, perfect for walkers. There are dramatic paths along the rugged coast of the Pacific Ocean, crowded jaunts through Union Square and Chinatown and North Beach, strenuous climbs up the Lyon Street Steps, and the famous stroll across the majestic art deco Golden Gate Bridge. But I prefer exploring the less well-known neighborhoods, especially in the evenings, when the interior lights are on and voyeurism is at its best: I adore inspecting the styles, the decorations, the graceful references to other eras.

So I felt a certain deep-down contentment as I pulled up to the Zaben job, which Turner Construction was wrapping up after nearly a year. The Italianate stucco-and-dark-wood two-story structure was accented with carved balconies, leaded-glass windows, tiled stairs, and wrought-iron banisters—many of which had to be restored, since the originals had been torn off during an ill-advised remodel forty years ago.

This was the first project that I had overseen from start to finish, totally independent of my father, after completing the projects he had begun before my mother's death. I was proud of the results. So proud, in fact, that my heart skipped a beat.

"Morning, Mel," called my foreman, Raul, over the loud whine of an electric drill.

"Good morning," I said as I climbed from my car. "Everything ready?"

"Good as near."

I wasn't sure what that meant, exactly, but I was sure it was positive. A small, wiry man with black hair and eyes, Raul was attentive to detail and demanded the respect of our workers and subcontractors through a quiet, almost solemn, authority. He was scheduled to take his general contracting exam soon, and I imagined he'd be moving on to open his own business. As happy as I was for him as a friend, I didn't look forward to that day. Good foremen are pure gold.

"Why you dressed like that?" Raul asked, dark eyes traveling up and down my wool slacks and blazer. "You look good in your dresses."

"I'm trying to look respectable."

"Why? The Zabens already know you are."

"Yes, but . . ." I didn't want to mention I'd had an appointment to see a friend in jail this morning. "I'm meeting with a potential new client later."

"Oh. Okay," he said, still sounding doubtful.

I smiled at the thought that people now expected me to dress inappropriately—so much so that when I didn't, it threw their days off.

Raul's black Lab, Scooter, trotted up to welcome me. Scooter was a fixture on the job sites or in the cab of Raul's truck. Construction folk are dog people.

My mind cast back to the stray dog hanging around Matt's house—his bedraggled coat and red bandanna had made him seem like a construction pup, and I wondered whether he had wandered off from some job site. If so, I hoped he'd meandered back to his people by now.

"The landscaper's due to begin on Wednesday—we should be sure to get this yard cleaned up, make a run to the dump," I told Raul. "Did you call Nico?"

"I tried earlier," Raul said, "but I haven't been able to get hold of him. Must be out of town."

That was odd. Nico *always* answered his phone. I assumed he showered with the device within easy reach, just in case. Sort of like me.

"He did a job for me yesterday, so he's around," I said. "I'll try him again later."

"Good. Thanks."

Just then the clients, Mark and Joanne Zaben, pulled up, their two young daughters in tow. We did a thorough walk-through of their nearly finished home to draw up a final punch list, an inventory of small details to attend to before Turner Construction officially left the site. The last thing anyone wanted was for the clients to move in all their worldly possessions—which tended to be *expensive* possessions—and then for us to have to come back and work around them. The walk-through was the clients' chance to ask for last-minute changes: The bookcases in the study need extra shelves; there should be another mirror in the bathroom; the wall color in the entry is too pale, the stain in the pantry too dark.

In addition to the clients' requests, Raul and I had developed our own punch list of leftover construction tidbits . . . of which there were always many.

But overall, the Zabens were thrilled, as was I.

It was exhilarating to rescue a home suffering under the abuses of a 1970s remodel and bring it back to its historical glory, inch by painstaking inch. My father had been flipping houses—buying fixer-uppers, living in them while he remodeled, then selling them for a profit—since long before such a scheme had a name, much less its own devoted cable TV following. After a childhood spent tripping over compressor hoses and dining on plywood counters, my two older sisters now lived in brand-new, cardboard-and-spit condos, vowing never to come near another do-it-yourself project. I was the only one of the brood to catch my father's rebuilding fever.

I spent days sifting through salvage yards in Richmond, Berkeley, and Oakland to unearth doors, moldings, and hand-pounded hardware original to the era and style of whatever house I was working on. In addition, over the years my father—and now I—had developed a long list of local artisans and specialists who could restore or re-create the handiwork of yore: plasterers, carvers, skilled finish carpenters. A local business named Victoriana reproduced intricate plaster ceiling medallions; Metro Lighting in Berkeley blew its own glass and poured metal to re-create molded bronze lamp fixtures; and I could have wood trim remilled with a custom knife cut at Beronio Lumber to match the original design.

As the Zabens, Raul, and I finished up our tour of the house, I brought a package out of my satchel and laid it on their new kitchen island—which was tiled in authentic bottle green glazed crackled ceramics from a small outfit in San Luis Obispo that had started reissuing original Craftsman-style tile designs.

"This is a small memento from Turner Construction," I said. "So you won't forget us."

The fat scrapbook was labeled *The Zaben Home*.

Joanne eagerly flipped through the pages, exclaiming over the before-and-after photos. The girls, ages eight and ten, crowded in to peek at the album.

"This is incredible! Remember how awful it was?" Joanne said to her husband, pointing at a particularly egregious example of harvest gold linoleum in one of the home's four bathrooms.

"How about the pseudo-psychedelic wallpaper in the downstairs office?" Mark chimed in. "That was my personal favorite."

Because Turner Construction specialized in renovating historic properties, each project included a good deal of research on the history of the house. We studied old photos, references in letters or newspapers, anything we might find in the attic or walls. Often we even interviewed neighbors and local historians. My mother had started the tradition of putting the before-and-after photos, articles, and any other relevant ephemera together in a big scrapbook and presenting it to the clients

as a souvenir of many months—sometimes years—of
hard work and patience.

And at the back of the album, I always included a
group photo of everyone who had contributed to the
building effort. All of them, from the highest-skilled car-
penter to the lowliest sweeper, left a little of themselves
with each project. They deserved recognition.

As I watched the Zabens look through the photos, my
mind wandered back, again, to Kenneth's tragedy. Matt
had mentioned that Kenneth hired a photographer for
their demolition party. What was the name again? Zach
something? I wondered whether the police had already
spoken to him, and whether the photos had revealed
anything. Could the investigators honestly have enough
evidence to file charges against Matt? Surely a deathbed
declaration, by itself, wouldn't be enough—would it?

After the Zabens left, Raul and I went over the final
finish schedule.

Then I started in, making and returning calls. As a
general contractor, I spent half my life on the phone. I
soothed clients, scheduled subcontractors, pleaded with
city inspectors, harangued overdue creditors, and as-
suaged vendors. If I didn't answer my phone, I was either in a meeting, in the shower, or driving. Probably
by the time I made it to Paris I'd be working on a brain
tumor from all the gamma rays.

After talking to a few subcontractors and confirming
plans with the landscaper, I tried Nico. It kicked over
to voice mail. I asked him to call me back as soon as he
could.

I also called the two MIA mothers, Caleb's and
Dylan's. I left my number on Dylan's mom's voice mail
and told her that Dylan would be staying at my house

for a few days. Not knowing whether she was up on Matt's current arrest drama, I didn't mention why their son was with me. Frankly, I doubted she would care.

Caleb's mother, in contrast, cared deeply about her son. Angelica was in Chicago for a weeklong financial seminar and talked with Caleb daily; he had already informed her he was staying with me. Originally from Brazil, Angelica was open and friendly and too smart to have married someone like Daniel. Of course, she said the same thing about me. One night not long after I married Daniel, she and I had bonded over margaritas and our mutual love for Caleb. Though he tried to deny it, I could tell it bothered Daniel that Angelica and I were friends; in his worldview, we should have been natural enemies.

Finally finished with my phone calls, I headed to Vallejo Street in Pacific Heights, pulling up in front of Celia Hutchins's house at noon on the dot.

Next door, Matt's run-down construction site was now cordoned off with crime scene tape. Two police cars and several unmarked vehicles crowded the driveway and street. Clearly they were taking yesterday's incident more seriously than the officer had yesterday. . . .

But what did this mean for Matt? Would a thorough investigation prove his innocence, or implicate him further?

Alongside the cop cars a Cal-OSHA truck sat in the drive, vulturelike. As a builder, my knee-jerk response to Cal-OSHA was one of defensiveness and dread: The agency inspectors were empowered to write citations, impose fines—or, worse still, shut down a job site. Contractors learned to tread carefully.

Still, though my father enjoyed railing at the

"bleeding-heart liberals and the goddamned government" who wrote and enforced our intricate workplace safety codes, most of them were in place for good reason. Exploiting the health and safety of workers was not only morally abhorrent, but bad for business on all levels. My mother used to say, *Happy workers build happy houses.*

Trite but oh so true.

Cal-OSHA would get involved in the investigation at Matt's house only if the incident was considered to be a construction-site accident. Which meant that Kenneth must have filed an official building permit with the city. Was he working with another contractor? If so, why hadn't Matt mentioned it? On the other hand, Matt didn't seem exactly up on the paperwork side of things. Perhaps the architect would know more.

I hesitated, wondering whether I should stop and offer to talk to the police at Matt's house. But after all, I had given my statement to the responding officer yesterday. They had all my information and knew how to get in touch if they wanted to interview me again. Plus, it would make me late for my appointment with Celia Hutchins, and I was never late for clients.

Nice rationalizing, Mel, I thought to myself as I mounted the stone steps to the front landing and rang Celia's doorbell.

"How lovely to see you!" Celia gushed upon opening the solid oak door. "Do come in. Good heavens, what in the *world* is going on next door? Is it true what they say on the news, that Matt has been arrested?"

"He's being questioned. I don't believe any charges have been filed. I'm sure it's all a mistake. Have the police spoken to you yet?"

"The police? My Lord, no. Why would they?" Celia asked as she led the way into the entry hall.

I felt a sense of déjà vu as I stepped over the threshold. The facade of Celia's house was distinct from Matt's, but inside, the building had exactly the same layout, though its mirror opposite. The same octagonal entry with a sweeping circular stair leading upstairs; same carved limestone fireplace in the front parlor, flanked by bookcases; same dining room and short hallway leading to a spacious, recently redone kitchen.

But there the similarities ended. Celia's home had undergone a remodel or two over the years. Though the woodwork—baseboards and doorways and crown moldings—was of similar design to that in Matt's house, it had clearly been remilled. It had none of the dings and dents intrinsic to any historic structure, the traces of everyday life through the years. A coat closet had been improvised in one corner of the entryway, and the basement stairs leading off the hall were accessible through an open arch rather than closed off by a door as in Matt's place.

In addition, the classic Beaux-Arts architecture—featuring broad, elegant arches and massive scale—had been modified with the addition of details in the Spanish, Moorish, and Craftsman styles. The overall effect was lovely, with lots of intricate tilework, white stucco, concrete tracery, and tall arches reminiscent of the Zaben home. I even recognized the artisan tiles on the stair risers from the ones I had used in the Zaben kitchen.

"The man who was taken away in an ambulance yesterday passed away," I said, by way of explanation.

"Oh, good heavens! What a terrible thing. I'm . . . stunned. Though I have to say, that house has always been a bit . . . jinxed."

"Jinxed?"

"Would you like some tea?"

"I'd love some, thanks." I wondered why she thought the house was jinxed, but I didn't want to push. "You have a beautiful home."

"Thank you. We love it. Did you know this house was built at the same time as Gerald's? Well, I mean Matt's house, now. They're twins."

"I can see that, yes," I said.

"I think they must have been nearly identical once, though the details are different, and of course there have been a number of additions and alterations over the years. Come out to the atrium."

She led the way through a pair of French doors to a glass-ceilinged garden room, furnished with vintage wicker chairs and love seats. A fountain tinkled; caged canaries chirped. It was charming.

"I'm going to be working on a conservatory addition for a home in Piedmont in a couple of months," I said. "This room is inspirational."

"Thank you again. I'm so very lucky, in so many ways. Please, do have a seat while I go for the tea," Celia said with a wave of her manicured hand.

I sat on a down-pillow-bedecked love seat. Celia's sandals clacked loudly as she hurried down the tiled hall.

Several minutes passed. Celia was taking her time. As though I were a two-bit actress in a bad movie, all I could hear besides the birds and the fountain was the ticking of a grandfather clock down the hall.

Feeling awkward, I got up and started to peruse

the bookshelves. They were filled with generic curios and antique leather-bound books that no one actually read—the kind interior designers bought by the linear foot to use as decoration. This phenomenon of unread books was depressingly common in the homes of the wealthy. I couldn't fathom not needing every inch of bookshelf space; the to-be-read stack near my bed was so high that I used it as a perch for drinks, as though it were a precarious bedside table.

Only one shelf here was filled with newer-issue volumes. I leaned in to read their titles: *Ghosts and Other Uninviteds*; *Voices from Beyond: Hoax or Hope?*; *Our Journey after Death*; *Practical Tarot*; *Fun and Facts with the Ouija*—

"Ever get the feeling you're being set up?"

Chapter Five

I jumped, startled at the sound.

A man lounged in the doorway: tall, broad-shouldered, light brown hair falling artfully over a tanned brow. Somewhere between thirty-five and forty, I guessed. He wore fine gray slacks and what looked like a cashmere sweater. Good-looking. *Rich*-looking.

"I'm Celia's son, Vincent. Vincent Hutchins."

"Nice to meet you." I put out my hand. "I'm Mel Turner."

His hand was warm and strong as he shook mine.

"A pleasure."

"'Set up' for what, exactly?" I asked.

"My mother is matchmaking. It's only fair that you be warned."

I looked him up and down.

"You mean . . . you and *me*?" I asked. "I'm not that much of a prize."

He grinned and took a seat in a wicker chair, stretching his long legs out on the ottoman and folding his hands over his stomach. "She's nearly given up hope for me and now thinks I'll only be happy with a woman who presents a challenge. I imagine she thought you fit that bill."

"Why would she think that?" I asked as I slipped into the seat opposite him.

"I hear you run a nontraditional business."

"I'm hardly the first woman to work in the trades."

"True enough, but she also liked the dress you were wearing yesterday. She described it in some detail."

"My friend Stephen designed it. He's quite good." Stephen had recently been turned down for a position as a costumer with the San Francisco Opera, so I tried to encourage him by wearing his creations about town. "Still, somehow I find it hard to believe you need help getting girls."

He gave a nonchalant shrug and smiled again. I studied him for another moment. Rich, handsome, well-spoken . . . and *single*?

In San Francisco, that was code for gay.

"I hope you're not dying for tea." Vincent sat up and peered through the doorway and down the hall. "At this rate it will be a while. You might not see my mother again until we have the wedding invitations printed up."

I laughed.

"Has she talked to you about what work she wants done?" he asked.

"Not really. She just mentioned a club room. . . ."

"Again, I feel I should warn you, but it's hard to know where to begin. Maybe it's best if I show you."

He rose and led the way out of the garden room, down the narrow hallway, and to the basement stairwell. As we descended, Vincent asked, "What's your stance on alternative lifestyles?"

"As long as everyone's a consenting adult, I'm good. Why do you ask? Does your mother have a hard time accepting that you're gay?"

He stopped short and looked back at me.

"Do I seem gay to you?"

"In my experience it's often hard to tell. It's not like any of us walk around with signs on our foreheads."

"I meant 'alternative' as in seeing the world a little . . . differently."

Just then he flipped on the lights to the basement.

"Wow," I said.

It was like my childhood conception of a haunted house: pure faded Victoriana. Thick Persian rugs covered the floor and heavy velvet drapes lined the groin-vaulted, curved brick walls. Hanging pendant lamps were trimmed with beads and colored glass, and several gold-framed mirrors graced every wall. Though it was tidy and the air carried the perfumed aroma of scented candles, a slight musty, mildew smell let you know you were still in a basement.

But what really caught my eye was the round table in the center of the room, ringed with six chairs covered in deep red fringed brocade. A huge crystal ball was set out next to a Ouija board and a dog-eared set of tarot cards.

It was the setting for a séance.

"Are you dismayed?" Vincent asked.

"Frankly, I'm relieved," I said as walked around, perusing the space. "In this town, you never know what you might find in someone's basement. Especially when referring to 'alternative lifestyles.' "

There aren't a lot of basements in San Francisco, at least not usable ones. In many older homes, ground-level, open pass-throughs from the street to the back-yard were dug into the ground and once served as open areas to keep livestock. Most of these had been closed up over time and converted to garages and storage spaces.

But this was a genuine windowless, claustrophobic, musty basement.

"The bricks worry me, though," I said.

"The bricks?"

"If your house is sitting on a brick foundation, you'll be in trouble during the next big quake," I explained.

"I believe my parents addressed the foundation some years ago when they bought the house. The brick faces were replaced over the reinforced concrete, just for show."

I was impressed. That was the sort of thing Turner Construction did, an unnecessary—but aesthetically pleasing—attentiveness to period detail. Rare.

"Any idea what was down here originally?" I asked.

"Not really. I do know it only had a dirt floor until my folks poured the new foundation. The two houses, this one and our neighbor, now Matt's house, used to be connected through here." He gestured toward one curtained wall. "A single family owned both homes. The access was bricked off years ago."

I picked up a poured-resin pyramid, with a seated Buddha and rose petals trapped inside. On a cherry demilune side table was another stack of books about the occult and more tarot cards. Bundles of herbs hung from a series of decorative hooks under one shelf, and white candles were placed on just about every doily-covered surface.

"I have to admit, when your mother mentioned this was her 'club room,' I was imagining something more like needlepoint. Or bird-watching."

Vincent laughed, a deep-throated rumble.

"Some of those bird-watchers are pretty edgy, you know." He paused and ran long, graceful fingers along the tasseled edge of a tapestry panel. "I know it's sort of strange, but she's convinced that if she tries hard enough, she can make contact with . . . the beyond. I try not to judge. Since my father's death a few years back, she's been . . . 'searching,' I guess is the best word for it."

"I understand."

"Follow me. I have something else to show you."

Vincent led the way up the steps and outside into the garden. Though the homes in Pacific Heights were built on a massive scale, their lots are not large; the yards tend to be compact, though highly manicured and designed. Celia's was a well-tended English-style foursquare garden, flowering copiously despite the season.

Next door, a young, fresh-faced police officer was doing his best to make his way through Matt's garden, apparently peeking under the brambles for clues; the once-elegant layout was overgrown with weeds and vines, virtually impassable. A small garden pond decorated in bright mosaic held murky brown water. A number of statues, crumbling with age and green with moss, stood at the corners of the yard, giving silent testimony to a more refined era.

Truth was, I sort of loved it; I enjoy decrepit symbols of the past. But I wondered what Celia had thought all these years, having to look upon that eyesore right next to her tidy pastoral splendor.

One other thing marred the beauty of Celia's garden:

An incongruously shabby shack sat on the line dividing the small yards. Painted a faded forest green, it had a narrow little porch and a cedar shingle roof.

"Have you seen one before?" Vincent asked.

"A, um, garden shed?"

"Actually," he said as he held the door open for me, "it's one of the cottages the city built for the refugees displaced by the 1906 earthquake."

I entered, my shoes clomping loudly on the aged fir boards. The structure was a simple single room. Other than two weather-beaten straight chairs and a small wood table, it was devoid of anything but history.

"When thousands of people were displaced by the disaster, the city hired carpenters to build these cottages as temporary housing in the refugee camps," Vincent explained. "After the camps closed, people hauled the shacks to private lots to live in while they rebuilt. Some people cobbled several together to form larger homes, or simply kept them as garden shacks."

"I've heard of these, but I've never actually seen one."

"Interesting little slice of history, isn't it?"

"Very." More than a century later, many of these "temporary" structures still stood: a testament to the care and craftsmanship of the age.

"My mother mentioned you were a history buff."

"How would she know that?"

"She said you specialized in historical restoration—I assumed the love of history."

"I used to be an anthropologist. I guess curiosity is part of the package. When Turner Construction takes on a historic remodel, we do a lot of research to figure out how to restore the structure to its original state. We dig up photos, descriptions in old letters, original blueprints, that sort of thing. It's amazing what a person can turn up with an hour or two at the California Historical Society."

Or when digging around behind old walls, I thought to myself. I suddenly remembered what I had seen behind the wall in Matt's house, right before Kenneth came in, bloodied and dying. What could it have been? I hadn't seen anything clearly enough to know. . . . Was it a package of some sort? A box? An old lunch pail? Most likely it was not anything of particular interest, nothing related to the terrible crimes against Kenneth Kostow.

Still, I wondered whether the police had come across it in their search. They would have had to be thorough to find it; I had accidentally knocked it down into a well between the joists, so it was no longer visible from inside the room.

"I'll bet you enjoy your work." Vincent's words startled me. He was standing near me, gazing down with blue eyes. The sunlight made them sparkle; he was even better-looking out in the sunshine. What was his story? How in the world was a grown man like him letting his mommy find him women?

"I do, yes. Very much," I said, avoiding his intense gaze. "How did this cottage come to be here?"

He shrugged. "It was here since before my parents bought this place. The fellow who originally built both of these homes, Walter Buchanan, was a prominent businessman and banker, way back in the day." Vincent stood with his hands in his pockets and rocked back slightly on his heels. "There was some sort of family tragedy—he died fairly early on. But the family kept both homes for a while, and they survived the 1906 disaster more or less intact. They donated money for some of these refugee cottages to be built. My guess is they wanted a souvenir of their good deeds."

"Clearly this was before your old neighbor Gerald's day?"

"Indeed, though Gerald was the original builder's great-grandson, I believe. The family sold off our house at some point, but his was one of the few homes around here that has remained in one family since it was built. Until Matt bought it, that is."

"How well did you know the former owner?" I asked.

"Gerald? Not well. He was a real recluse; my whole life, I think I could count the number of interactions with him on one hand. And he never let anyone in his place. I think he lived off family money, frugally—old fortunes don't last as long as they used to. The only thing I could tell you about him was that he had his groceries delivered, he played the piano very poorly, and he was a tinkerer; you could hear him working on projects at all hours."

"Yes, I think I noticed one or two of his art projects in the home," I said, thinking of the mosaic pond in the garden next door and the light fixture Matt hadn't seen fit to save.

"We returned from vacation last fall to find he had suddenly sold the place and was moving to an assisted-living facility with the proceeds. Apparently he passed on within a few months. He was quite elderly."

"I've got a really strange question for you," I said as we walked along a mossy brick pathway back to the main house. "Have you ever heard rumors about the house? About it being ..."

"Haunted?"

I nodded.

Vincent smiled. "Yes, I've heard the stories. In fact, I think I did my part to create them. When we were kids . . . well, the place was pretty overgrown, and always in need of paint, with trim and whatnot hanging crookedly off the building. What can I say? I used to watch a lot of horror movies, and I was wildly curious about the old man I never saw, and the house that was sort of a twin of ours, and yet not." Vincent reached around me to open the back door, and waved me in. "My friends and I used to ratchet each other up, talking about it being a haunted mansion. I once charged my schoolmates a dollar apiece for a 'tour' where I snuck them into the backyard to look in the windows."

"I'll bet the reclusive Gerald Buchanan just loved that."

"Yeah, well, I'm sure I drove him further into hermit mode. I wasn't a mean kid, but . . . kids can be thoughtless."

"And does any of this have to do with your mother's séances?"

Vincent looked surprised. "To tell you the truth, I never really thought about it. But I don't think so. She's probably heard the haunting rumors just like everyone else in the neighborhood, but she never discovered my boyhood antics. I don't think there's any connection."

We walked through the spacious redesigned kitchen. Kitchens are the one area where period authenticity usually cedes to practicality, even in the most careful historical restorations. Original kitchens in fancy homes—like the one in Gerald's house—were set up to accommodate staffs consisting of several people. Stoves used to be heated with wood, making maintaining a consistent oven temperature a dicey procedure at best. The only refrigeration was provided by a chunk of ice inserted in a little door at the back of the kitchen, in what was quite literally an icebox. Furthermore, since kitchens were considered servants' areas, they were cut off from the living areas of the house.

Modern design, in contrast, usually incorporated the kitchen as one of the most-used family rooms in the home. Celia's kitchen, for instance, opened onto a bright room overlooking the garden, lined with comfy-looking couches and featuring a breakfast nook.

"My mother mentioned you were asking about Matt's party the other night," Vincent said. "I did drop by, but I left when things started getting rowdy. I'm not much of one for working with my hands; just wanted to help out. Plus, I was curious to finally see inside the house."

"Did you notice anything out of the ordinary? Anything suspicious?"

"Nothing I can think of."

"I don't suppose the police have questioned you about it yet?"

"No . . ." he said. "Do you think they'll want to?"

"A man was injured sometime after the party; he passed away at the hospital. I thought someone might be canvassing the neighborhood, looking for witnesses. But then, my knowledge of police work is primarily gleaned from mystery novels."

"Not *CSI*?" Vincent asked with a smile.

"I'm not a big TV watcher," I said. "I never seem to find enough hours in the day as it is."

"Mel!" Celia's smile was as bright as her blue eyes as she joined us in the front hall. "I see you've met my handsome son. Vincent, I hope you've been keeping

Mel entertained. I *do* apologize—I had to take a phone call, long distance, you know. I forgot all about the tea!"

"Please don't bother," I said. "I took a quick look at the basement room, but I should tell you that Turner Construction specializes in historic restoration, taking homes back to the style they were in when they were originally built. For your purposes, we might be overkill."

"Nonsense—I'd love to hear your ideas. It's rather dreary down there, don't you think? What I'd like to do is make it feel more integrated with the rest of the house. I find myself spending a lot of time there."

"Are you working with an architect?"

"Do you think it's necessary?"

"It's helpful on a redesign," I said. "I have several names I could give you if you'd like."

"Have you ever seen that two-story library in *My Fair Lady*?" Celia asked. "I've always fantasized about something like that! Perhaps we could get rid of the floor here, make it a two-story room, lined with bookcases?"

This from the woman who didn't have enough books to fill her current shelves.

"I do know that movie," I said, "and I've always coveted that library. But something like that would involve major structural issues. You'll definitely need to include an architect in a project of that scale. I can put some preliminary numbers together for you, but they'll depend on engineering reports and the final drawings."

I had the sense that Celia's true agenda had more to do with her son's love life than construction, but I still felt obligated to work up a proposal. We descended into the basement, and I took measurements while we talked further about what she envisioned. I jotted down some notes and sketches on my clipboard, took a series of photos with my small digital camera, and promised to send the estimate soon.

Vincent saw me to the front door as I left.

"So, I have to say, I think my mother has good taste. Could I take you out for a proper dinner sometime?"

"I . . . I'm flattered, but . . ."

"You don't date clients?"

I don't date *anyone*.

"Actually, I don't. But I appreciate being asked. Thank you."

"Consider it an open invitation. And don't think my mother will give up this easily. She seems sweet, but she has an iron will. You wait—she'll come up with another scheme soon enough."

The police were still milling about next door when I emerged from Celia's house.

I couldn't justify hopping in my car and leaving without at least offering to talk to them. Besides, I wanted to ask when I might be allowed to start construction. This being my first crime scene, I had no idea how long it would take to process the place for evidence. A day? A month?

I waited outside on the sidewalk while a uniformed cop went into Matt's house to fetch the detective in charge. I was just as glad that I wasn't invited in. I wasn't ready to go back inside what I now thought of as Matt's House of Horrors.

I hoped my trepidation would die down soon; it would be difficult to give my all to a construction project with that kind of attitude.

The man who came out of the house to talk to me had the puffy, ruddy look of a heavy drinker. He was a large man, the kind who might once have been attractive but had gone soft over the years: a high school football star heading for his fifties and fighting it the whole way. He seemed right at that pivotal point when he was about to start the dramatic slide down.

"I'm Inspector Brice Lehner," he said without preamble. Chewing gum with a vengeance, he fixed me with pale, intense eyes and demanded: "You the Turner Construction on the permit?"

"On the permit? I'm not—" I began, then hesitated. I didn't want to get Matt into any more trouble. But how could Turner Construction be named on a permit? Conveniently for me, Inspector Lehner wasn't waiting on my answer.

"I'm just sayin'," he interrupted, "seein' as how your name's on the work permit, you could be held liable in this situation if it's ruled a workplace accident. Hope your insurance is paid up."

My heart raced. A homeowner ignoring safety codes could plead ignorance; a contractor deals with fines at best . . . or at worst loses her license and faces a lawsuit. But this was crazy. I hadn't filed any permits with the city. For the moment, though, I thought discretion the better part of valor.

"Did you see the statement I gave the responding officer?" I asked. "And get the cartridges I found?"

"Yeah, I got 'em. But Kostow wasn't shot with a regular gun. Just nails."

Lehner's eyes kept moving around, looking at just about everything but me. He chewed his gum double time and had a habit of flicking his chin whiskers with his thumb. He was a twitchy guy.

"Surely this couldn't have been an accident, though, could it?" I asked.

"We're investigating all possibilities, including suicide."

"But Kenneth couldn't have—"

"Look, lady, we're looking into it, okay? Just because your ass is on the line doesn't mean I'm declarin' it a crime if it wasn't one, get me? Anything else you want to add to your previous statement?"

Again I hesitated. I should tell Inspector Lehner about seeing something behind the wall. But it was probably nothing, some unimportant little bit of the house's history. There must be some other kind of explanation for what happened to Kenneth. Besides, there was something about the inspector that seemed . . . impatient. Uninterested. *Off.*

As that thought crossed my mind, I saw someone standing in a second-story window, gesturing. When I looked up, he disappeared, but when I focused on the inspector in front of me, I could still see him in my peripheral vision.

It wasn't a cop or other crime scene investigator.

It was Kenneth Kostow.

Chapter Six

I took a deep breath and tried to ignore the apparition.

"Matt Addax would like me to carry on with the renovation work," I said. "Is that possible, or is this considered a crime scene?"

"We're processing it now. Gotta tell you, place is a mess. We got blood, prints everywhere. Still, it should be released soon. I'll let you know." Lehner looked off in the distance. "I gotta be straight with you, Ms. Turner. This is a sensitive investigation."

"Sensitive?"

"Things like this don't happen in this neighborhood. Bring everybody's property values down. We don't want to upset anyone unnecessarily. I'd appreciate you speaking only to me about it, otherwise keeping mum. And that includes talking to the neighbors or anyone else."

"Does 'sensitive' mean you're not going to investigate it as a murder?"

"Look, lady, our shift caught three homicides this week. We held your friend Addax mostly because of the accusation from the deceased, but the investigation is still going on until we press charges or decide to drop the case. Okay?"

"But if Cal-OSHA is here, does that mean you think it was an accident? Isn't that what Kenneth told the officer originally?"

Cold eyes flickered over me. "You know anything more about this whole mess, you tell me—and only me. Otherwise you keep out of it, get me?"

He didn't wait for my answer before climbing into his beige Ford sedan and taking off.

I remained where I was, rooted to the spot.

My loyalties were at war. If it was an accident, Matt would be off the hook. But if Turner Construction was really listed on the permit papers, that could mean we were in big trouble.

And on top of everything else, I kept seeing Kenneth's ghostly visage in the second-story window. Every time I looked at him directly, he disappeared, but when I looked away I could see a wavering visual of him out of the corner of my eye. It was incredibly frustrating—in addition to being creepy. I couldn't help but think of seeing Kenneth standing in front of me, injured but still alive, in that blood-soaked den yesterday.

I did the math. According to what Matt's lawyer had told me, Kenneth had already died at the hospital by the time I had "seen" him here at the house.

And now he was standing in the window, looking down at me. Gesturing. I could almost feel his yearning, as though he wanted—*needed*—to tell me something.

I tried to shake it off, closing my eyes and turning my face to the warm sunshine. Weren't ghosts supposed to come out at night? They didn't appear in broad daylight, did they? But assuming I wasn't seeing Kenneth's ghost . . . was I having some sort of breakdown?

"Sorry I'm late."

The man approaching looked to be of Indian or Pakistani origin, with dark hair and eyes, but his accent was native Californian. He wore khaki chinos, a pale blue polo shirt, and shiny brown leather loafers.

It took me a moment to realize he was talking to me. I imagined it was the effect of the clipboard still cradled in the crook of my arm. When you hold a clipboard, people tend to assume you're in charge, or at the very least know what's going on.

"I—" I began.

"Is Kostow inside?"

"You were supposed to meet Kenneth Kostow?" I asked.

The man glanced down at a huge, expensive-looking gold watch encircling his slender wrist. "Ten minutes ago. I'm Philip Singh. What's with the cop cars?"

Well. This was awkward. Other than when my mother passed away, I had never been in the position to inform people of someone's death.

"Nice to meet you. I'm Mel Turner. I—"

"I'm the buyer." He sounded impatient, as though I should have recognized his name. He looked past me and back over his shoulder as though searching for someone else to consult. He was out of luck. The uniformed officer I had spoken to earlier had disappeared inside; we were the only ones on the sidewalk.

"Are you working with Kostow on this?" Philip Singh struck me as the type of man who did not usually have to ask twice. "I'm running late today. Why don't we start the walk-through without him?"

"I'm sorry; you're the buyer of what, exactly?"

"The house."

"*This* house?"

He looked at me as though I were an insect. An annoying insect.

"I don't believe the house is for sale," I said, suddenly weary of the conversation and his attitude. "And even if it were, you'd have to contact the owner directly. Matthew Addax. He's . . . indisposed at the moment, but I'm sure he'll be available soon."

Singh's expression shifted ever so slightly, from distracted to angry.

"Look, all the details have been worked out," he said. "I was supposed to meet Kostow today to finalize the agreement."

I blew out a frustrated breath. "If you want to give me something on paper, I'll pass it on to the owner when I see him next," I said while trying to brush past him. "That's the best I can do."

He stepped in front of me. "You're not trying to cut me out, are you? Where the hell's Kostow—"

"Is there a problem here?"

We both turned to see a man descending the steps with the grim, determined air of an avenging angel. A pissed-off avenging angel.

Graham Donovan, in the flesh . . . and in a Cal-OSHA work shirt, faded jeans, and work boots. A clipboard in one hand, battered brown leather briefcase in the other.

"Graham," I breathed.

"Mel." He acknowledged me with a quick nod before setting his briefcase down and offering his hand to Singh. "How's it going?"

"Um, okay . . ." He was taking in the uniform.

"I'm Graham Donovan, Cal-OSHA inspector and, at least for the immediate future, manager of this particular accident scene. Is there something I can help you with?"

The man looked down at Graham's hand, aghast, then back to me. "Accident scene?"

I nodded.

"What is this? First the lien, now this? You guys can't cut me out—"

"The lady said she was done talking to you." Graham stepped forward so that he was standing just a little too close to the man, staring him down.

"But—"

"I have some anti-harassment pamphlets in the truck if you need some clarification. The State of California takes this sort of thing seriously."

Philip Singh's furious gaze dropped back to mine.

"This isn't the end of this," he hissed before turning on his heel and stalking off.

Graham and I watched as the man climbed into his late-model Lexus and slammed the door with an expensive-sounding *thunk*.

"What was all that about?" Graham asked in a quiet voice.

"He said he was buying the house."

"*This* house?"

I nodded.

"It's for sale?"

"Not that I know of."

Our eyes met, and anything else I was going to say fled my mind.

The decade that had passed since our last encounter amounted to more than ten years. It was a lifetime.

A few specks of silver shone in his dark brown hair, there were signs of crow's-feet at the corners of his long-lashed brown eyes, and a small white scar bisected one eyebrow. But Graham Donovan looked great. Really great. Better than I remembered, even. I glanced down at today's boring outfit and wished I looked half as good.

If only I'd thought to dress provocatively for this particular homicide investigation.

"You're with Cal-OSHA?" I finally managed.

"Obviously."

Graham used to dream of owning and operating his own business specializing in "green" construction. How had he wound up working as a glorified bureaucrat?

My dad always referred to OSHA as "a protective coating made by half-baking a mixture of fine print, red tape, split hairs, and baloney—all applied at random with a shotgun." None of that sounded anything like what I knew of Graham Donovan. But then, my own dreams of becoming a world-class anthropologist had seeped away while I attended to real life as well. . . . Still, I was doing my best to blame that on my ex-husband.

"I was sorry to see Turner Construction come up on our radar," Graham said. "Your dad's always run a clean site."

"It's not my dad's site; it's mine."

"So I hear."

"Actually, it really isn't mine, either. I—"

"Let me stop you right there. You might want to consult with a lawyer before talking to me. I'm obligated to turn over any and all evidence to the SFPD."

"I wasn't involved in any of this, Graham. Not at all."

"Says here you did the original presale inspection."

"Um . . . okay, that's true."

"Are you a licensed home inspector in the state of California?"

"Not exactly. I did it as a personal favor."

"Why didn't the prospective owners hire a licensed inspector?"

"I don't know."

"Did your inspection satisfy the mortgage requirements?"

"I assume so. They were able to buy the building."

"And why is your name on the building permit?"

"I have no idea."

His mouth set in a hard line and there was a cynical look in his eye—familiar to me despite the years that had intervened.

"Look, Mel—" When he spoke, the words seem to cost him a great effort. "I tried to get off this case when I saw that Turner Construction was involved, but we're shorthanded at the moment and this was supposed to be a quick handover to the SFPD. But let me be clear: I'm not your buddy, much less your knight in shining armor. Any . . . 'connection' I have with your family will have no bearing on this investigation. Is that clear?"

"As a bell."

"You might try to explain it to your father."

"I'm sure he understands."

"I wouldn't be so sure. He called me last night, said you were talking about taking over this remodel. He asked me to talk you out of it."

"He did?"

"Little does he know I'm the last man to talk you out of anything."

His eyes fixed on me, and just that easily I was twenty-eight again.

One week before my wedding to Daniel, Graham had taken me for a drive through the lush gardens of San Francisco's Golden Gate Park. Perhaps spurred on by the drama of a sudden rainstorm, he staged a kind of romantic intervention, running down the list of reasons why I shouldn't marry Daniel: He was too old for me, he only wanted me because I was young and talented, he would derail my budding career. Graham declared that Daniel was incapable of being faithful to any woman, perhaps incapable of love. He also insinuated that I was being swayed, in part, by Daniel's money and globe-trotting lifestyle—and the huge diamond ring he had given me—which blinded me to the kind of man he was deep down.

Graham's unprecedented emotional outburst was followed by a kiss that started out oh-so-sweet but soon turned wild and out of control, the memory of which still made something flutter deep in the pit of my stomach. Afterward I refused to return his phone calls, and a week later I was married to Daniel, as planned, in a lavish ceremony at the Palace Hotel.

Though Graham had stayed in touch with my dad, I hadn't laid eyes on him since that day. I imagined he still despised himself for having said what he did . . . just as I resented him for having been right.

Graham cleared his throat.

"I was sorry to hear about your mother. I was out of town, or I would have come to the memorial service." There was a slight softening of his expression. "She was a remarkable woman."

"She was. Thank you."

"You've had a rough couple of years."

Tears stung the backs of my eyes. The frank sympathy

in Graham's deep voice was enough to push me over the edge. *Terrific*. I'm in the man's company for all of ten minutes and I'm ready to fall apart.

I shrugged. "A lot of people go through a lot worse."

He just nodded, eyes still on me. I looked around at anything but him.

Unfortunately, I saw Kenneth again. He now stood, plain as day, right behind Graham. I saw him out of the corner of my eye, but as before, when I looked directly at him he disappeared.

"What is it?" Graham asked.

I shook my head and tried for nonchalance. "Nothing."

Graham looked over his shoulder, where my gaze kept fixating.

There were faint lines in the cement sidewalk and a barely noticeable indentation in the wall.

"Good call," Graham said. "Looks like that used to be an entrance. Were you planning on restoring the original floor plan?"

"I don't have what you'd call 'fixed plans' at this point," I managed to say. "I haven't even seen the blueprints. I need to talk with the architect."

I swallowed, hard. Maybe I really *was* losing it. Truth was, I had felt displaced for the past two years, and recent events certainly hadn't helped, much less this current blast from the past. Just two weeks ago, on what would have been my mother's sixty-seventh birthday, my sisters and I had scattered her ashes over her favorite lake. I hadn't been myself since.

"You sure you're all right?"

I nodded. "Thanks, I'll be fine. I'm just tired. And a little . . . Finding Kenneth yesterday was pretty traumatic, I guess."

"I can imagine."

Our eyes met again.

"So, are you ready to give a statement?" Graham asked, back to business.

"Statement?"

Opening his briefcase, he brought out several detailed documents, and I spent the next forty-five minutes writing things down. Chief among them was that I had no idea how my name wound up on the permits and that I'd had nothing to do with the site, other than the original inspection, before yesterday's gruesome discovery.

"That'll do for now," Graham said as he stashed the paperwork in a file, placed the materials neatly in his briefcase, and returned his pens to their case.

"I asked the officer earlier, but I was wondering, since you mentioned you're in charge of the scene and all . . ." I thought I might as well try my luck with Graham. "Do you have any idea when the scene will be released? I'd like to be able to tell my client when we'll be starting work."

"I thought you just told me you weren't in Addax's employ?"

"I wasn't. But he just hired me to take over."

"This is the man up on murder charges?"

"I don't believe they've issued any charges yet. Isn't that partly up to you?"

He gave a curt nod.

"Matt Addax wouldn't hurt a fly," I said.

"That's not for you to decide."

"But you wouldn't be here unless the police thought it was an accident, would you? They must be unsure that it's murder, right?"

"I can't discuss this with you, Mel. You should know that."

Graham was just about as open and informative as that laugh riot Inspector Brice Lehner. But as he said himself, he wasn't my buddy, much less my knight in shining armor.

Kenneth appeared behind Graham again. A sense of longing and need emanated from him. I felt a sudden, overwhelming desire to get as far away as possible.

"I'd better be going."

Graham nodded again. I felt the heat of his eyes on my back as I crossed the street to my car and took off, grateful to be gone.

Chapter Seven

Hoping Matt's architect would have a handle on what was going on with the building permit—and maybe even an insight into what had happened to Kenneth—I looked up his address on my BlackBerry and called ahead. Jason Wehr was in, and invited me to drop by his office downtown.

Unfortunately, I'm what my friends call "parking-challenged," famous for pulling up to a space right behind the person who gets it. Finding a parking spot for my little Scion took me longer than the entire trip across town.

To my surprise, Jason Wehr's Market Street address led me to a cavernous discount fabric and craft-item store, the kind that sells wholesale to other stores as well as to the public. When I asked whether I was in the right place to find the architect, a young Asian woman at the register pointed me to a set of stairs on the left of the main shop floor.

Upstairs, in what was essentially an open storage loft,

with cardboard boxes stacked six high along the walls, I found Jason Wehr huddled over a large drafting table, studying drawings.

He was a small, scholarly-looking man in his early forties, with light brown hair graying at the temples, a neatly trimmed beard, and wire-rim glasses. He wore a tweed jacket over a crisp new pair of jeans. No surprise there. Architects are the academics of the construction world—for good and for ill. Often harboring artistic temperaments, they were known amongst builders for their flashes of brilliance right alongside unrealistic expectations and temper tantrums. They rarely knew the ins and outs of actual hands-on construction and tended to insist that their creations be built exactly as drawn, without checking in with the people responsible for bringing those designs to life: the builders.

"Melanie Turner, at last! Good to meet you," Jason Wehr said as he stood and shook my hand.

"Call me Mel. Nice to meet you as well," I said. "Matt can't stop singing your praises. What's all this?"

On a table to the side was an intricate model of a building and its surrounds, complete with miniature lichen trees and tiny little cars. Architects, especially the old-school type trained before the widespread use of computer-aided design programs, were expert model makers. Some verged on an almost maniacal attention to detail, along the lines of miniature railroad enthusiasts. The miniconstructions were often beautiful little worlds, and they offered clients a physical perspective that was lacking in a two-dimensional drawing.

"That's my Eden," said Jason.

"It's beautiful."

"Isn't it?"

"Where are you building it?"

"In my mind, at the moment," Jason said with a self-deprecating laugh. "It's my dream, really. It's a completely green building. Check this out."

The building was built into the hill, with a sod roof.

"I would use sheep to mow the lawn. They'd keep it short, while providing essential nutrients to the soil with natural fertilizer."

"So you could literally fall asleep counting the sheep overhead."

"Oh, it's so well insulated you'd never hear them," Jason said, completely serious.

"I was just kidding, actually," I said, but Jason had already moved on to show me the windmill, the passive solar potential, the cistern below the building, and the system of gutters to catch and divert the rain to fill it.

"Very impressive," I said.

"You know, the thing about historic buildings," Jason said, "is no matter how well-intentioned, you can't go green the way you can in new construction."

"I disagree," I said, though I knew from experience that this argument was futile. I love the idea of green buildings, myself, but in my opinion their proponents overemphasize new construction over restoration. "What about embodied energy?"

"In what sense?"

"'Embodied energy'—all the energy it takes to build a new building. Hauling things back and forth to the dump and the store, for example. The electricity used to run power tools. The manufacture of new products. A lot of people forget to take all that into consideration when they speak about building new 'green' homes. It takes thirty-five years for the average home to recover its carbon use from being built; historic homes have filled that bill long ago."

"All I know is my Eden will allow its people to live off the grid entirely." Wehr's eyes shone as he stared at his creation.

I had to hand it to him: He was an artist, with a devoted passion to his design as great as any Renaissance painter's to his portrait. Hanging on the wall near his desk was a brass plaque denoting Jason Wehr as winner of the AIA Design Award for Excellence in Architecture. It brought out my envious side: I coveted the AIA Award for Historic Preservation and Innovation in Rehabilitation. One of these days—soon, I promised myself. I just needed the right project. The perfect project. And the perfect architect to join forces with wouldn't hurt, either. I had even entertained the notion that Jason Wehr might be that person, but after our green vs. green discussion I had the sense that Jason Wehr and I weren't going to be creating award-winning projects together anytime in the near future.

"Speaking of Matt," Wehr said as we both sat down in white molded-plastic chairs, "how is he? Do you know? What's going on . . . ? Is he honestly being held for Kenneth's death?"

"No charges have been filed yet," I said. "But everything's still up in the air. Have the police spoken with you?"

He shook his head.

"I take it you weren't at the party?" I said.

"Actually I was, earlier in the evening. I left by ten or so. Things seemed to be getting rather out of hand, and as a professional I felt obligated either to put an end to it . . . or to leave."

"And you chose the latter option?"

"I spoke to the bouncer at the door, and was under the impression that he would take care of it. Then I left."

"What was going on?"

"Lots of drinking, people carousing . . . all in good fun but with the added element of power tools. . . . It's a bit like that old saying about running with scissors: You're bound to lose an eye eventually." He shook his head and pushed his wire-rim glasses higher on the bridge of his nose. "I guess poor Kenneth is a sign of what can happen when that sort of thing goes amok, right? I really can't believe it."

"Do you know anything about the house being for sale?"

"They were going to sell it after the remodel."

"But not before, right?"

"Of course not. They were flipping it for a profit."

"That's what I thought. Ever heard of a man named Philip Singh?"

"Doesn't ring a bell."

"He said he had an agreement with Kenneth to buy the house."

"That's impossible, unless he had some informal agreement to buy it afterward. But as you know, we haven't even started with construction. The design process ran over schedule."

"Why's that?"

"Matt and Kenneth had a hard time agreeing. They fought a lot. . . . There were times when, if I didn't know better, I would have sworn Kenneth was delaying the project intentionally. Plus, we wanted to remain true to the original design. It's a beautiful structure, with a lot of history. As you know. You did the original inspection, didn't you?"

I nodded.

"I thought I recognized the name. You were the contractor listed on the permits, right?"

"Did Kenneth say that?"

He nodded. "He said you and Matt were old friends and you were giving them the friends' and family discount."

"Really."

"It was all spelled out in the prospectus."

"Prospectus?"

He opened a file cabinet and brought out a file, extracted a thin, bound sheaf of papers, and handed it to me. I'm not great at high finance, but this much was clear: It was an agreement to a private investment, a share of the final sale price of the house.

"You're an investor in the project?"

"I am, yes. There were several of us. Kenneth didn't want to use a bank to get a traditional mortgage, so he sold shares in the finished product instead."

"He didn't use a bank at all?"

Wehr shook his head. "I don't believe so."

I must have looked dubious.

"I assure you it's perfectly legal."

"Weren't you concerned about their ability to flip such an expensive house?"

"On the contrary. The housing woes that hit everyone else don't really apply to a neighborhood like Pacific Heights. Just as your high-end remodeling business is probably recession-proof, by and large—am I right?"

He *was* right. There was a whole stratum of very wealthy clients who were insulated from the swings in the markets. I had always been unclear on where their funds came from, frankly. Though my folks did okay, I was unfamiliar with the concept of family money. As my father always said, Turners work for a living.

"Bike messenger's here," came a woman's voice from downstairs.

"Excuse me a moment," Wehr said to me. "I just have to run these down to him." He grabbed a large manila package and a roll of blueprints from atop his desk.

I looked over the little ledge and watched him hurry down the stairs. He handed the items to a strapping bald fellow wearing a messenger bag slung over broad shoulders. Bike messengers were usually lithe, with nerves— and *thighs*—of steel, especially in a hilly town like San Francisco. Then again, I imagined drivers would think twice before hitting such a beefy guy. I only saw him from the rear, but he seemed nearly as big as one of Nico's nephews.

Which reminded me. I tried Nico again. Still no answer.

I'm now officially worried, I thought as I watched the messenger pull on a red motorcycle helmet.

Oh, *that* kind of bike. That made more sense.

Now my mind went in yet another direction. Back in the day, Graham Donovan had a red-and-black motorcycle helmet—it matched his red Ducati. The other guys used to tease him: Construction workers rode in huge trucks, not on bikes ... of any type. Graham bragged about the fuel efficiency, though I suspected he harbored Marlon Brando fantasies. He had been brash, confident to the point of arrogance, with the bold know-it-all stance of youth. Judging from even the brief nature of our recent interaction, though, he seemed to have mellowed with age. Was he married? Did he have children? Was there some way I could ask Dad or Stan without being too obvious? Maybe I could work the conversation around by asking about . . .

". . . save a fortune on delivery." I realized that Jason Wehr was talking to me.

I nodded as though I had been listening.

"So, where were we?" Jason asked as he sat down behind his desk again.

"Do you know who the other investors in the house project are?" I asked.

"No idea."

"How much money are we talking here?" That house and lot were worth millions, remodel or no. "Do you mind my asking?"

"I don't know about the others. . . . I was putting in my design time, waiving my normal fees, of course. And on top of that I put in two hundred fifty thousand."

"A quarter of a million dollars?" I gasped. All wagered on a project coming in on time, on budget, and then selling the home for a sweet profit. No wonder Jason Wehr was conducting business out of the loft space rather than a proper office. Kenneth must have been one excellent fast-talker . . . or maybe I just didn't share whatever vision it took for people to dump their fortunes into an uncertain situation. I was the safe, simple, savings-account type; if I got fancy, I might try an interest-bearing money market. I shopped at resale and consignment shops, put it down to my love of all things old and historical, and called it good. My tightwad attitude used to drive my ex-husband insane. He always told me it takes money to make money.

Yet another reason to move to France, where, I'd been told, buying at flea markets and in thrift stores was considered chic and savvy . . . rather than just cheap.

"There's a fortune in that house, and Matt seemed

optimistic that we would get our money back, along with the profit, within six months," Wehr added. He sat bolt upright. "Wait, with Kenneth gone—what does this mean for the project?"

"Matt asked me to keep working on it. As soon as the police release the scene I'll shift my guys over from a project we're wrapping up now in St. Francis Wood. We should be able to begin soon. In the meantime I can get up to speed on your drawings; and it's never too early to start scouting salvage yards and the like."

"Let me know when you'd like to meet. I'm happy to do a detailed walk-through with you, go over what we've worked out so far."

"Do you happen to have a copy of the permits I could look at?"

"Afraid not. Kenneth had all that."

"How about a copy of the blueprints to study?"

"Didn't Kenneth give them to you already? He told me you were on the job."

I shook my head. "I'm new to the whole thing. Trust me, that do-it-yourself demo party wasn't exactly my style."

He rummaged through a container of cardboard tubes until extracting one labeled KOSTOW/ADDAX and handing it to me. The tube was deceptively heavy, indicating a fat roll of blueprints within.

"How soon can you finish?" he asked.

"I haven't even studied the drawings yet, Jason. And I can't guarantee a turnaround in six months—that would be virtually impossible." I bit my tongue before adding: *as you well know*. A professional in the building trades should understand that a project of this scale couldn't be finished so quickly.

Yet another trait architects were known for amongst builders: Unrealistic Optimism.

"But I'll do my best. Another project of mine has been delayed, so once I get the go-ahead from the police, I can get a lot of workers on the job and expedite things."

"Thank heavens," he breathed, relaxing back into his chair. It was only early afternoon, but Jason Wehr looked like a man who needed a drink. "I'll need a return on that money soon, or I'm in trouble with a capital T."

By the time I got back to my car and checked my phone, there were four calls to return, and Raul needed me back on the Zaben job. I phoned home to tell Dad I was going to work late to make up for the time I'd spent with Matt, and now the architect.

"I picked the boys up from BART an hour ago," he said. "I'm making Turner Steak and baked potatoes for dinner."

"Ah, your signature dish. Sorry I'm missing it. Hey, Dad . . . thanks for looking after the boys."

He snorted. "By their age I was hitchhiking my way across the country, alone."

"Yes, but they're studying things like calculus and organic chemistry," I pointed out. "Whereas you probably maxed out at geometry."

"It would do them more good to learn how to swing a hammer," he grumbled. "I should take 'em up to Stan's cabin to help me build that wheelchair ramp."

"By all means, put them to work. Just remind them to finish their homework first. You might offer to give them a hand with their quadratic equations."

He groused some more, we hung up, and I went back to work at the placid, incident-free St. Francis Wood work site. The Zaben home was scrumptious; it was at that tipping point in a project where the home takes on its new—and, in the case of historic homes, its original—character. Saving beautiful structures from the ravages of time, nature, and bad previous remodels was addictive.

We were completing the final finishes: painting and staining and gilding. In addition to the housepainters, a small army of faux finishers had arrived. I double-checked their sample boards before giving them the go-ahead to begin re-creating a parchment surface with Venetian plaster in the living room, a Gauguin-inspired mural in the playroom, and clouds on the blue ceilings of the girls' bedrooms.

Besides answering questions and giving instructions, I concentrated on helping Raul to whittle down the construction punch list. Wood can swell and shrink depending on the environment, and it wasn't unusual for newly installed doors to stick or fail to close properly. I removed several doors from their frames, shaved a tiny bit of wood off the top and bottom to ensure a good fit, then rehung them. After that, I corrected a small tiling problem behind the toilet in the powder room—this was the sort of thing the subcontractor should do, but it wasn't worth it to bring him all the way back here for a five-minute fix. Finally, Raul and I installed a dozen special-ordered wrought-iron heating vents in the baseboards throughout the house.

The work was absorbing, and given what had happened at Matt's yesterday I was glad to be able to focus on the restoration of beauty and grace. My mother used to tell me that gardening was her way of connecting with simple, straightforward work—making things beautiful, feeling the earth in her hands and witnessing the miracle of growth. I felt that way about building: I orchestrated people coming together, giving of themselves and their skills, to create a structure that was much, much more than walls and a roof.

After all, a beautifully restored home was the stage for the play of life.

It was after nine by the time I headed east on the Bay Bridge toward Oakland. The route home was so familiar that I drove on autopilot. Unfortunately, this allowed my mind to pursue an annoying, repetitive loop: I fretted about Matt (*Will he be released? What will happen with poor Dylan?*), pondered what really had happened to Kenneth (*murder or accident?*), wondered what I should do about it (*if anything*) . . . and daydreamt about that long-ago kiss with Graham (*It seems like freaking forever since I've felt that way about a man. Does he still like me? Why did I wear this stupid outfit today of all days?*).

Over and over and over.

"*Mel*. Can you hear me?"

Said the ghost sitting in the passenger seat of my car.

Chapter Eight

"*Holy crap!*" I yelled, careening slightly before recovering full control of my vehicle.

As soon as I glanced over, he disappeared.

"I *thought* you could!" Kenneth said, reappearing in my peripheral vision when I looked back at the road. "Hey, watch the driving, though, or you'll be joining me in eternity, as they say."

Resisting the urge to squeeze my eyes shut, I took a deep breath and counted to ten.

He was still there.

"*What* is going *on*?" I gasped.

"I was hoping you might be able to help me with that one. It's been the damnedest experience," Kenneth said, shaking his head and looking out at the lights of the tankers on the San Francisco Bay, shining through the darkness. Just an average everyday ghost out for a drive.

My heart pounded. If I hadn't been driving, I would have covered my face for a moment to regroup. I couldn't pull over on the bridge. . . . Should I exit at up-coming Yerba Buena Island?

Was this thing out to kill me? What did it want?

Did I even *believe* in ghosts?

I tried to force my academic sensibilities to kick in. My anthropological training taught that all human cultures, throughout time and across the globe, have developed a concept of the afterlife—and thus have theorized that spirits of the dead cross over to our earthbound exis-tence from time to time. Sometimes to harm, sometimes to help, often to bring closure to unfinished business.

On the other hand, modern psychology would say that I must be suffering from some sort of mental break. . . . Maybe I really *did* have a form of PTSD.

Clearly I needed to talk to someone. Might as well start with the one at hand.

I swallowed, hard, and took another deep breath.

"Okay, you're . . . Are you a spirit of some sort?"

"What the hell do you think I am? I *died* yesterday, remember? Or did it already slip your mind? Criminy, woman, you held me in your arms and everything. I thought we had a moment."

"Of course I remember. It was a terrible tragedy. I'm so sorry, Kenneth." *I'm consoling a ghost*, I thought. *Or I'm completely insane. Or both.* "Okay, so you're a ghost because you died yesterday."

He made an impatient motion with his hand, rolling it as if to say . . . *And then? "Yes*, I'm a ghost. Frankly, I al-ways thought you were a little more on the ball than this."

"Who *did* this to you?"

"That's the problem. I have no idea." He held up his injured arm. "And where the hell's my hand?"

Good question. "In the trash, I would imagine."

"The *trash*?"

"Biowaste."

"That's disgusting."

"You're telling me."

"You're saying I have to go through eternity without my right hand?"

"Like I would know the answer to something like that. Don't *you* know?"

"How would *I* know?"

"You were there, after all."

"I can't remember a thing."

"Aren't there, like, spirit guides around you, or someone to give you a hand?" I winced at my unintentional pun. "So to speak?"

"That's not funny."

"Sorry. Is there someone—or some*thing*—to help you understand what's going on?"

"I must have missed the orientation meeting. I really don't know what the hell's happening."

"At the very least they should have a handbook."

"Again with the sick jokes?"

When we drove through the tunnel at Yerba Buena Island, Kenneth's image flickered like a weak broadcast signal.

"That's interesting," I said. "Like my cell phone."

"You're not as funny as you think you are."

"Okay, so why are you bugging *me*?" I cast about in my mind for some way to interpret this turn of events. "You can't rest until you find justice?"

He snorted. "Like I know. I keep telling you, it's not exactly clear."

"You don't remember who killed you?"

"I can't remember a damned thing."

"The cops said you told them it was an accident, at first."

He held up his bloody arm. "You think *this* was an accident?"

"And then at the hospital you blamed Matt."

"Matt?" Kenneth sounded genuinely bewildered. "Matt wouldn't do something like this. Would he?"

"No. I can't believe it of him." We reached the foot of the bridge and I veered south toward 880. "But assuming this was no accident, what are you telling me? You're a ghost and I'm supposed to find your killer to let you rest in peace?"

He shrugged and looked out the window.

"Kenneth?"

"I don't know. I really . . . I haven't known what in the world's going on since I got here. The people here aren't exactly friendly."

"*Here*, as in where? There are other people with you?"

"It's all pretty fuzzy. . . . Yeah, there are other people, other ghosts, I presume. But no one will talk to me."

"Could be your sparkling personality."

"Nice. I'm dead and that's all the sympathy you can muster."

"I'm just trying to wrap my mind around all of this." I pondered for a moment. "Wait—if you're a ghost, aren't you supposed to haunt wherever you died?"

He shrugged. "Dunno. For some reason you're the only thing that makes sense. I remember you were holding me. I remember that." His voice dropped slightly. "You were talking to me. It was really . . . decent of you."

I shrugged, not knowing what to say.

The freeway was miraculously light on traffic, so we

zipped along until I took the Fruitvale exit. A few more blocks east and to the north, past bustling taquerias, check-cashing venues, and discount stores full of colorful piñatas, we pulled up in front of my dad's old farmhouse.

"Listen, Kenneth, I have to go deal with real live people now. So could you . . . disappear, or go wherever it is you go?"

I got out of the car before he could respond. Or before my subconscious, or whatever it was that was making me see things, could come up with a response.

The cool night air hit me like a slap in the face. I hoped it would wake me up, snap me out of it. Could I have fallen asleep while still driving? I hadn't slept well last night. . . . Could I be that tired?

I hurried into the house, blessedly ghost-free.

Dad and Stan were in the living room, watching a game on Dad's new big-screen TV.

"Leftovers in the fridge if you're hungry." Dad spoke without looking up.

"Thanks, I grabbed a burrito off the truck earlier."

"That stuff'll kill you one of these days."

"Night, Dad. Good night, Stan."

"Night, babe."

"Night, Mel," said Stan.

I left before they thought to ask me about Matt. I wasn't sure I was up to that discussion tonight, especially the part where Kenneth's ghost followed me home.

The boys had set themselves up in Caleb's room, each working—or more likely playing—on his notebook computer.

"Did you see my dad?" Dylan asked, not looking up from the screen. Seemed to be a male trait.

"I did. I saw him this morning. He said you should stay here for a few more days until they get things sorted out."

Now he looked up at me, worried blue eyes of an old man in a young boy's face. "Is everything gonna, like, be okay?"

"Your dad would never hurt anyone," I said with conviction. "The police just need to figure a few things out. And no matter what happens, you're going to be okay."

He had already turned his attention back to the electronic device in front of him. I wanted to say more, but I wasn't sure what. Besides, I doubted he was still hearing me. Unable to help myself, I embarrassed each boy by kissing him on his head, then did the mom thing, haranguing them about doing their homework and telling them to get to bed by ten.

"Remember, it's a school night."

They grunted in response.

As I walked down the hall to my bedroom, I noticed Kenneth following close on my heels, lurking like an ethereal shadow.

Great.

I stopped in my tracks. If he'd been corporeal, he would have bumped right into me; as it was, I felt a second of searing cold. I shivered, feeling goose bumps break out on my arms and a tingle on the back of my neck.

"What do you think you're doing?" I asked him through clenched teeth as I resumed walking to my room.

"I thought I made that clear. I have no idea what I'm doing."

"You're not sleeping in here with me."

"Come to think of it, I'm not actually sure I even need to sleep."

"Oh, goody. This just gets better and better. Well, go haunt the neighborhood or something. Go on down to the taco truck in the Goodwill parking lot. You ought to be able to stir up plenty of trouble there."

"I want to stay with you."

"You don't even like me."

"I don't?"

"You never used to when you were . . . you know . . . alive."

He seemed genuinely perplexed.

"You mean I never made a pass at you?"

"More than once. But believe me, you were not the kind of man who needed to *like* a woman in order to make a pass at her."

"No?"

"You honestly have no recollection?"

"It's strange. I'm just wherever I am, with only the vaguest sense of the past. And the future . . ." He made a gesture like a poof in the air and shook his head. "Nothing."

"Sounds rather Zen," I said. "Maybe all the Berkeley types have been right all along? It's best to live in the here and now?"

"I wouldn't go that far. I don't exactly feel contented."

I crossed over to my bathroom and started to brush my teeth.

Glimpsing up at the mirror in front of me, I realized that by using the glass, I could look directly at Kenneth's reflection, which was a relief. That peripheral vision thing only added to my sense that I was off, askew . . . crazy.

Kenneth's blue eyes were haunted. Was it any wonder?

"Go away," I said around a mouth of toothpaste foam.

He didn't move.

I rinsed my mouth and wiped my face with a hand towel, taking the moment to regroup. I may well be going insane, but . . . this had been a man. A live man. Once again I flashed on the memory of holding him in what turned out to be some of the last moments of his life.

I glanced in the mirror again to see Kenneth watching me intently over my shoulder.

"I have to take a shower," I said, hoping he'd take the hint.

No such luck. When he was alive Kenneth was pretty obtuse; as a ghost, he seemed even more so.

"Shoo."

"Where?"

"I don't know. . . . How about the attic? Don't ghosts like attics?"

"I'm not a bat."

"The guest room, then."

I led him down the hall. A light fixture hung limply, awaiting the electrician, and the wide-planked hallway was bare wood, stained with paint and in need of sanding and a new coat of varnish. There were cracks in the original plaster walls and ceiling. Patches of paint evidenced the effort to try to decide on wall paint colors. A huge multipaned window above a window seat was missing two panes, filled with cardboard in the meantime. My dad tinkered a bit here and there, but he never seemed to get much done anymore. Stan had accomplished a number of things downstairs, but had no wheelchair access to the second floor. And I ... Well, Chez Turner was a classic example of the cobbler's children having no shoes.

"This place is a wreck," Kenneth whined as he followed me. "And I don't like the way that woman looks at me."

"What woman?"

There were no women in this house other than me— on the contrary, it was all testosterone, all the time. After growing up in a house with two sisters and a mother, I often felt as though I was living in a twisted fairy tale. My current life was filled with my father, Stan, Caleb, and my almost exclusively male cadre of employees. And now Dylan, and a decidedly masculine ghost.

"She looks like an older version of you. Has your eyes, anyway."

A wave of grief and shock washed over me. "*Mom?* You can see my mother?"

"That's your mother? I don't think she likes me."

"She probably wants you to leave me alone," I said, my voice sounding hollow to my ears. Suddenly I was on overload—I simply couldn't think about death, my mother, or ghosts anymore tonight.

"Look, Kenneth," I continued. "I have *got* to get some sleep. Since you're probably just a figment of my imagination, I won't be seeing you again. But it's been ... interesting. And I really do wish you all the best."

The arms of the old-fashioned alarm clock glowed green in my dark bedroom. Five a.m. on the dot.

I squeezed my eyes shut. I had hoped to sleep late this morning, figuring I needed the rest, but I was a creature of habit. Alarm or no, five was my usual wake-up hour and my internal clock seemed to rouse me no matter what.

Construction workers are early birds by vocation; we begin our workday at seven, and are often off the job by three or four. This is in part due to local noise ordinances and partly to an effort to get as much work in during daylight hours as possible. Today, though, I wanted to take the boys to school at eight . . . and after what I had seen and heard last night, I was beginning to seriously worry about myself. I had been hoping extra sleep might improve matters.

I wasn't good at asking for it, but this much was clear: I needed help.

Every time I closed my eyes, I saw Kenneth. In my arms as he lay injured, or looking down at me from the window at the Vallejo Street house. And then there was the exceedingly bizarre apparition of the chatty, confused Kenneth in the passenger seat of my car. Was I going insane? And if I was going to be haunted by a ghost, shouldn't he at least know something about his own murder, or what was happening with Matt, or . . . something?

Every time I opened my eyes, I feared I would see Kenneth for real.

I lay in bed for several minutes, listening to the familiar early-morning sounds of the neighborhood: Our next-door neighbor revving up his Pacific Gas and Electric truck for the early shift; stray cats mewling and whining at one another; someone poking around in the recycling bins, amassing their humble treasure one redeemable aluminum can at a time. Finally I gave in to inevitable sleeplessness and kicked off the covers. I dressed in a relatively tame—for me—short and stretchy black skirt, black thigh-high tights, and a colorful V-neck sweater over a pink tank. And my work boots, of course.

Avoiding the squeaky floorboards so I wouldn't wake up the boys, I snuck downstairs to the home office, started up the computer, and flipped on National Public Radio for the morning news.

So far, so good. No Kenneth. I let out a deep breath and got to work.

One thing about running your own business: You always have something to do in the case of insomnia or worry. Too bad I hadn't been able to lose myself in my academic dissertation the same way; when married life became miserable with my ex-husband, Daniel, the last thing I wanted to do was sit alone in a chair and write. Every time I tried to do so, my mind inexorably wandered back to wallow in the emotional pigsty that had become my personal life.

By managing Turner Construction, on the other hand, I seemed to be able to immerse myself, lose myself in the process of finding the perfect oiled-bronze hinges, or figuring the proper cut for the new trim, or sketching out the precise geometry of the gallery arches.

I rolled out the blueprints for Matt's house on the large drafting table, using paperweights to hold down the curling edges. I studied them for several minutes—there were separate pages with detailed plans for everything from the electrical schema to the suggested finish trim. Jason Wehr might be out of touch with actual building, but he knew his stuff when it came to mandated codes and basic design. He had done a good job. Thorough.

Trying to treat the Vallejo Street remodel as if it were any other job, I started up a file on the house. This included a preliminary schedule and budget based on assumptions of availability and best-case scenarios; the timetable would change—it *always* changed—but I had to start somewhere.

Remodeling begins with the infrastructure. We work from the inside out, the bottom up. The first tasks were to get a thorough engineering report on the foundation structure and complete a *careful* demolition to take the walls back to the studs. Once the walls were open, we would begin redoing and upgrading the electrical and plumbing, heating and air ducts, and installing modern features like Wi-Fi capability and central vacuum. Some of these tasks could be accomplished simultaneously, while others had to be staggered. That was where careful scheduling came in.

Meanwhile, I would assess what trim, moldings, and hardware from the house could be rescued, what would have to be replaced either by scouring junk shops and salvage yards or with new items produced in a traditional way. I used a faux finisher to make new surfaces look old only as a last resort.

I deliberated over the blueprints further as I worked up the calendar. Graham was right—if we were going to do this job as it should be done, we needed to restore the original floor plan. We could look through Celia's twin house for inspiration, though hers had clearly undergone many changes over the years. There hadn't been many alterations to the essential structure of Matt's house, but there were a few details missing in the blueprints, such as the entrance that Kenneth was using yesterday when he was lurking behind Graham and driving me nuts.

Speaking of nuts, I wanted the opinion of a more or less neutral party with regard to my sanity . . . or lack thereof. I placed a phone call to another early riser. Luz

Perez was a dear, trusted friend; more to the point, she was the closest thing I knew to a therapist. She agreed to meet me at Liverpool Lil's for lunch.

Soon afterward I was lured toward the kitchen by an enticing aroma wafting down the hallway: coffee.

"Good morning," I said to Dad and Stan as I entered. Dad had already brewed a pot of French roast and was chopping ham and onion for omelets. He believed in big breakfasts.

"Hey, there, baby girl," Stan said.

"Morning, babe," said Dad, looking up from his task at the cutting board. "Hungry?"

"No, thanks." Morning was just about the only time of day or night that I *wasn't* hungry, so I never had anything but coffee. Still, the habit of thirty-eight years didn't keep my father from offering—and then looking disappointed by my answer—each and every morning. Day after day after day. I tried to interpret Dad's persistence as a demonstration of paternal love, but the daily interchange set my teeth on edge and made me fantasize about moving out. Presuming that Paris wasn't anywhere in my near future, I might need to make other living arrangements, and soon.

I poured coffee into my favorite cobalt blue travel mug, emblazoned with a BERONIO LUMBERYARD logo, leaned back against the counter, and took a sip. Reveling in the aromatic steam and the promise of caffeine, I noticed Stan and Dad exchanging significant looks.

"What?" I asked.

"About that late-night guest you had," Dad said. "He comin' for breakfast?"

Chapter Nine

"Guest? What guest?" I asked.

Again with the exchanging of glances.

"Look, babe," said my dad, "I'm only too aware that you're a grown woman and you can tell me to go jump in a lake. But . . . with Caleb and Dylan here, maybe you should be a little more discreet."

"I just remembered I have to be . . . somewhere else," interjected Stan, wheeling himself out of the kitchen without a backward glance.

"Dad," I said, chuckling at Stan's obvious ploy, "there's no one here."

"We heard you talking to someone last night," Dad said, breaking eggs with a single hand into a bowl.

"Last night? Did anyone answer?" I almost hoped for corroboration. At least it would mean I wasn't insane. "Did you hear a man's voice?"

"Just yours, come to think of it. But then who were you talking to?"

"Um . . . no one."

"No one?"

There was a long pause while our gazes held.

"I seem to be developing a bad habit of talking to myself, running through thoughts aloud. I'll try to keep a lid on it." I cleared my throat. "So, I saw Graham at the Addax job site yesterday. Why didn't you tell me he was Cal-OSHA now?"

"Stan tried, but you didn't want to hear it, remember?"

"It's hard to imagine him working for a government bureaucracy."

"A man has to do things he doesn't want to, from time to time. He needed benefits, more than I could give him."

"Why?"

"Long story. I'll let him tell it."

I watched while Dad dumped the chopped veggies into the eggs, then poured the whole mix into his favorite omelet pan. The concoction sizzled and popped, filling the room with the scent I associated with big family brunches on Sundays when I was young. I had scoured that skillet once when I was ten, thereby learning my lesson about never washing a cook's "seasoned" omelet pan. I still wasn't quite sure what that meant, but I was happy to leave the cooking of eggs—and cleaning up after them—to my father.

"Hold on here a minute." Dad looked over at me. "When you say 'the Addax job site' it makes it sound like you opened a file on the job."

"As a matter of fact I did. I told you I was going to."

He slapped the spatula in his hand down on the cutting board.

"For cryin' out loud . . ."

"Before you go too far with that attitude, *Father*, you should know that this is entirely your fault. You're the one who passed your house-flipping zeal on to me."

"Last I heard, Matt Addax was in the hoosegow for murder."

"Keep your voice down, Dad," I scolded in a loud whisper. "Matt hasn't been charged with anything yet. He could be released anytime. In the meantime, he's got everything he has wrapped up in this place, and the job needs to get done. Our Marin project has been delayed while they work out the hillside engineering issues, and the Piedmont job is still in the consultation phase. Our employees are going to be out of work soon if I don't get them on another project, and this one happened to fall into our lap."

I paused, then added, "And on top of everything else, it's an incredible house. It's been abused. It needs us."

Usually appealing to my dad's sense of duty worked. Not this time.

"Sounds like a damned waste of time to me. Especially after what happened there. Doesn't sound safe. What you need to do is get out on the town and find yourself a husband, and quick, if you want to give me grandchildren. You're not getting any younger."

"Gee, thanks. Anyway, my sisters have provided you with plenty of grandchildren. And I already have a son. Remember?"

"He's a loaner."

"He's mine."

Bought and paid for with innumerable PTA meetings, never-ending homework sessions, countless lunches packed and boo-boos kissed and tears wiped. I had left my husband without a backward glance, but his son was a different matter altogether.

"And by the way," I added, "I don't appreciate you calling Graham Donovan behind my back, asking him to talk me out of this remodel as if I were a child. In case we're not clear, *I'm* running Turner Construction these days. As soon as you'd like to step back in and take over, I'll happily bow out."

I topped off my coffee and moved toward the hall that led to the office. "At the moment I've got to bring Stan up to speed on Matt's job and have him draw up the contracts, and then I have a million other things to do today, not the least of which is trying to figure out what's up with my most recent client. Otherwise you may have inherited yourself yet another stepson."

As if on cue, Caleb shuffled into the kitchen. He'd never been what one might call a morning person, and now that he'd come down with a bad case of teenagehood, the before-school sullenness had only gotten worse. But in his own way he was trying.

"Hey, Mel. Hey, Bill," he rasped before reaching into the fridge and pulling out a carton of orange juice.

"Morning, kid," my dad answered. Not unfriendly, but not with the warmth of the typical grandfather. My ex-husband was one of my dad's least favorite people, and it was hard for Dad to separate Caleb from his father.

Dylan trailed in a moment later and helped himself to some juice.

"Sit down, both of you, and have a hot breakfast before you go," Dad said.

"We're pro'lly gonna be late," Caleb muttered.

"Eat."

Both boys sat down at the table like well-trained recruits. They responded to Dad's innate air of authority, just as I always had when I was young. I looked at my father with fond exasperation.

The man was well past his prime, but once a marine, always a marine.

My father always said that being a general contractor was like leading an orchestra in which every member belonged to a different union. I just thought of it as a constant juggling act. After dropping the boys at school, I returned more phone calls, met with some new clients and their architect, then checked on a paperwork snafu at city hall.

While I was there, I looked up the permits I had supposedly filed for Matt's house. There was "Turner Construction," listed on the paperwork as plain as day, with all of our pertinent licensing information. I supposed anyone could have lifted private business information from a similar permit from any other job. My signature had been forged. I made a copy for our files, still wondering whether I should make a stink over the forgery or just let it pass.

I should have gone by Matt and Kenneth's business office to look through their paperwork, but it was located in Matt's house in Mill Valley and I had no time or desire to schlep all the way out there. Not this morning, anyway. Maybe I could swing by later, after lunch with Luz.

The rest of the cold, foggy morning was spent on the job site in St. Francis Wood, making sure everyone was still on schedule and riding herd on the final subcontractors. This was the fun stage, though, where the countless details started adding up to a polished jewel of a home. Unless I was mistaken, once the Zaben home was properly furnished it would be yet another Turner project ripe for *Sunset* magazine, or even *Architectural Digest*. Or maybe that AIA award. One of these days . . .

It worried me that Nico still wasn't answering his phone and hadn't called me back. I considered dropping by his house later to make sure everything was okay. Among other things, as soon as the scene was officially released I wanted to start on Matt's renovation. Nico and his nephews were my go-to demo guys, the first in on a job of this magnitude.

To my great relief, Kenneth was nowhere to be seen this morning. So maybe it really *had* been some sort of temporary insanity. Still, I was looking forward to talking to a trusted friend about it. Just in case she needed to take my car keys and admit me to the SF General psych ward for my own good.

My phone buzzed.

"This is Mel," I answered.

"Melanie Turner?" asked a gruff voice.

"Yes."

"Inspector Lehner here. I wanted to let you know the Vallejo Street house is open—you're free to do whatever it is you do."

"Already? That's great."

"You gonna start the job right away?"

"That's the plan."

"Okay, good. Let me know if you find anything else."

"Find anything? Like what?"

"Anything at all that might seem like evidence. We did a pretty comprehensive search, but you'll be in and out of every corner of that place, am I right?"

"Wait, Inspector—does this mean Matt's off the hook?"

"Let me know if you find anything out of the ordinary." He hung up without answering my question.

I guessed Lehner's call meant that SFPD had its evidence . . . or acknowledged the lack of it. I tried Matt's lawyer again, but the phone went immediately to voice mail; I left a message.

Then I rushed to meet Luz at Liverpool Lil's, at the edge of the Presidio, right down Lyon Street from Matt's house. The old-school restaurant was modeled after a genuine British pub, but its clientele reflected the tony residents of the Pacific Heights/Cow Hollow neighborhood. Most people eating lunch were wealthy and over the age of sixty; the others were trendy sorts who sought out the haunts of late, lamented local editorialist Herb Caen.

I had chosen it because Luz really liked the hamburgers there . . . and because I doubted anyone I cared about would be able to overhear what I had to say.

Before I even had a chance to sit down, Luz brought out a neatly labeled three-ring binder full of pictures she had clipped from magazines, alongside paint swatches and catalog entries. She had recently bought a condo in a 1920s-era building and was redoing it in an energetic fit of first-home-ownership pride. She asked my opinion on some lighting fixtures for her media room, and then we discussed her tile choices for the master bath and the paint color in the guest bedroom. I tried to save her a little money by buying whatever items I could with my contractor's discount, and I lent her some of my guys from time to time to help her with small jobs.

After the waiter brought our food, I gave Luz an abbreviated rundown of what had happened with Kenneth.

"A nail gun *and* a circular saw?"

I nodded.

"Okay, *that* is just about the most disgusting thing I've ever heard," she said in the slightly inflected, husky drawl that always made me think of a Latina Marlene Dietrich. She put down her bacon cheeseburger as though she had lost her appetite.

"Unfortunately, that's not the worst of it."

Luz leaned back in her chair, crossed her slim arms over her chest, and raised one neatly plucked eyebrow.

"I saw him."

"Him who?"

"Kenneth."

"You just told me that. You said you held him until the paramedics got there."

"I mean after he . . . died." I picked at the turkey on my Cobb salad.

"You saw his body?"

"I saw his ghost."

Pause.

"You did not."

"Oh, right, because I'm making this up to make myself look sane."

"You're saying you think you saw this Kenneth person's *ghost*?"

I nodded.

"Seriously."

I nodded again.

"Really, though."

"*Luz*, please." I rearranged my knife and spoon. "It's not like I haven't gone over this a thousand times in my own mind. Could I . . . Do you think . . . After a traumatic event, a person could suffer from PTSD, right?"

Luz and I had become friends six years before, when

she attended a summer course I offered in anthropological methods. Though she aced all the tests—she was
a whiz at theory—she wasn't as gifted with fieldwork.
She ended up pursuing sociology instead, where re-
searchers can keep a safe distance from their subjects
and don't have to get their hands dirty. She went on to
get her PhD, and now taught potential social workers at
SF State; she still was more comfortable teaching others
than actually dealing with clients in need.

"Ye-e-ah," she said, sounding doubtful. "PTSD usually has to do with living through some immediate
danger to you, though, rather than just witnessing something gross."

"'Gross.' Is that a technical term?"

"Sure. Like 'crazy as a loon.'"

"Funny. So if it's not post-traumatic stress, what do
you think's going on?" I asked.

"Well, it would more likely be diagnosed as CISS, or
STSD."

"What are those?"

"Critical incident stress syndrome, or secondary
traumatic stress disorder. We see them sometimes in
ER workers, cops, first responders of all types. People
who deal with the aftermath of traumatic events, or who
deal with the people who were involved with aforemen-
tioned traumatic events."

Luz dug back into her hamburger. Speaking of the unexplainable, I would never understand how the woman
managed to consume what she did and still maintain her
lithe figure.

"Maybe that's it," I said, stealing a couple of her fries
and dunking them in ketchup spiked with Tabasco. "Do
you think that's it?"

Still chewing, Luz looked suddenly serious, her therapist vibe coming through.

"What I think is that you've had a rough couple of years, and this trauma has triggered those feelings of loss."

"Okay, I get that part. But why in the world would my mind invent a ghost, of all things? And if I'm suddenly seeing ghosts, why is it of someone I don't even like?"

"An obnoxious man in your life. Gee, let me think of where I've heard that before."

"You're saying Kenneth is a stand-in for my ex-husband?"

"It's possible. This guy, Kenneth, was an arrogant thorn in your side, right? The subconscious tends to transpose parallel characters in dreams, so why not in waking life?"

"But it's more than just seeing him. I feel like he wants something from me. I get the sense I should find his killer, bring him to justice. Isn't that what ghosts need? Unfinished business and all that?"

"Again, I think maybe you're fixating on this as something you might be able to solve, since you're feeling out of control in your own life."

I pondered that. Companionable silence reigned for a few moments as we both turned back to our food.

"Hey, guess who I saw yesterday," I said.

"I'm hoping you mean somebody alive," Luz said.

"Yes. Very. Graham Donovan."

"Who's Graham Donovan?"

"I told you about him. He used to work with my dad, and I had a crush on him when I was in grad school."

"Oh, right! Biceps gleaming in the sun, echoes of that famous Diet Pepsi commercial."

"Trust you to remember the visuals."

She shrugged. "Don't have much else to go on. Wait! Was this was the guy who tried to derail your wedding?"

I nodded.

"Sounds like a smart man."

"Yeah. And I rejected him. Thanks for the reminder."

"Is he still gorgeous?"

"I didn't see him with his shirt off."

She cast me a Look.

I gave a rueful smile. "Older. A few more miles on him. But yes, gorgeous."

"Where'd you see him?"

"He's investigating me. Or the scene, anyway. Of the—" Was it a crime or an accident? "The incident at Matt's house."

"The *incident* that resulted in the supposed ghost that followed you home. Uh-huh." She stirred half a packet of Splenda into her latte before fixing me with a compassionate yet challenging stare. "Lots of stuff going on lately, is all I'm saying."

I nodded and considered Luz's interpretation. It was true that my emotions were all over the place. It had been a rough couple of years—and Kenneth's death really *had* been traumatic.

"Remember my brother, the one who's a Realtor in Danville?" Luz said.

"Tim?" I asked. I had a hard time keeping Luz's six siblings straight.

"Manuel. He's got this colleague. . . . I always assumed she was a whack job, but apparently there's a lot of that going around."

"Again, I love the sensitivity of the mental health professional."

She rooted around in her huge, expensive, designer bag. I know my fashion sense isn't shared by many, but I really don't understand those purses. Humongous buckles, multiple pockets, gold lamé ... To me they seemed like the sort of things we would all make fun of in a few years. And on top of being garish, they cost a month's rent.

"I met Manuel in his office last week for lunch," Luz said, "and this woman practically forced her card on me. She's a shameless self-promoter, but nice enough. Ah! Here it is."

Luz handed me a glossy, full-color business card. It stated that the pretty blond woman pictured, Brittany Humm, specialized in "The Sale and Acquisition of Haunted Houses throughout the Bay Area."

"Humm's Haunted Houses," I read aloud. "Cute."

"Give her a call."

"You're kidding me, right?"

"This from the woman who spent the last ten minutes telling me about being stalked by a ghost. I'm just saying, maybe she could shed some light on this. Otherwise, I don't know what to tell you, *amiga mia*. Ghosts scare me."

"Nothing scares you."

"Uh-huh. Nothing but ghosts." She gave a little shiver. "Oh! And clowns."

I smiled. "Luckily, I haven't seen one of those. Anyway, I thought you just said you didn't believe in ghosts."

"Sure I do. I just don't necessarily believe *you've* seen a ghost. As with most unusual events, best to weed out the logical explanations first. Like the fact that you've been working too hard for, like, a couple of years now. You need to sit on a beach somewhere and have some fine young man bring you drinks with umbrellas in them. For at least a month or two. As your best, most devoted friend, I volunteer to accompany you."

She consulted a slim gold watch on her wrist and gestured for the waiter to bring the bill.

"It's Tuesday, right?" Luz continued. "I've got an hour before my office hours. You wanna go by the house really quick?"

"Matt's house? Seriously?"

"I'm thinking you're probably feeling nervous about going back in. I'll be your backup."

"The investigating officer did call not long ago to say I could have access. As of yesterday it was still a closed crime scene."

"Well, no time like the present, then," Luz said. "Let's go check it out."

I let out a breath I hadn't even known I was holding and paid the bill.

"Thanks, Luz."

"Anytime."

The stone stairway to the mansion's front door was no longer roped off by crime scene tape. There were no police cars, no Cal-OSHA presence, and given the ramshackle appearance the house always sported it gave no indication of being the scene of a recent murder.

On the other hand, it wasn't much of a stretch to imagine the neighborhood kids making up haunted house rumors about the place, à la the young Vincent Hutchins.

I dreaded going in. I hadn't seen Kenneth all morning, so I was keeping my fingers crossed that he was, indeed, some figment of my imagination born of the stress of the last couple of days. Or weeks. Or years. Now, standing in front of the house, I was afraid that going back in might trigger yet another ghostly visitation.

Luz came around the car, noticed my hesitancy, and raised her eyebrow in mute challenge. We walked side by side up the front steps. I scrounged around in the bottom of my satchel to find the front-door key Matt had given me.

No need. The door was not only unlocked; it was slightly ajar. I pushed it in warily.

"Hello?" I called out.

Nothing.

"The cops probably forgot to lock up, that's all," said Luz.

I nodded and walked in. I felt a strong frisson upon entering, a feeling of déjà vu. I couldn't help but think back to the day before yesterday, when I'd had no idea what lay in store for me besides a hungover ex–rock star.

Things looked much as they had last time I was here. Trash everywhere, walls bashed in here and there, dust, and broken windows.

"Check this out," Luz said, immediately distracted by the architecture. She ran her finger along the edge of the chair rail in the dining room. "I love this kind of detail. What's this called again?"

"Which part are you referring to? The dado, or the bullnose?"

Luz laughed. "Is it just me, or does the whole builders' vocabulary sound just a little bit dirty?"

I joined her, laughing at myself as much as at her comment. Luz was right; there was nothing to be afraid of. This was a historic home, the kind I loved, a house that needed me. There was no sign of Kenneth, no sign of death. I was suddenly eager to get to work—I felt like grabbing a broom and starting right away. Without even thinking about it, I started composing a mental to-do list.

Luz wandered into the kitchen, and I followed. In marked contrast to Celia's, this kitchen was essentially unchanged from its original layout. It was huge, and the walls were tiled up all the way to the ceiling in muted pistachio green four-by-fours. The cabinet for cold storage still had its little sliding door at the back that opened to the outside for the ice block. An aged refrigerator stuck out awkwardly into the room—traditional kitchens had no enclosures built for such things. A narrow, chipped gray marble counter along one wall had probably been used for making pastries and the like, back in the day. A massive wood-burning stove must have once stood against the wall where a cheap gas version now sat—the chimney for the old smokestack and flue was still evident. Someone had stuck an old coffee tin in the round opening to close it up. Open shelves had been emptied of their contents but not washed; they were grimy with grease and accumulated dust.

Luz opened the door of what looked like a small cabinet next to the refrigerator.

"Oh my God, a dumbwaiter! When's the last time you saw one of these?"

"They're not that uncommon in the old homes of this neighborhood," I said.

"I wish *I* had a dumbwaiter. But then, I guess they're not as cool without someone on the other end of it to cook stuff and send it on up."

She started turning the crank. It squeaked in protest. I was noticing that every wall in the place had been gouged open, not in a systematic way of replacing wallboard but more as though someone was opening walls, looking for something. . . .

"Um, Mel," Luz said, her voice sounding hollow. "You might want to check this out."

I came to stand next to her. On the little lift lay a revolver. A Smith & Wesson .357 Magnum. My father had one just like it; we had fired it at the shooting range. I remembered him explaining that he didn't like the rebound from the .357s, so instead he used .38 specials to load it.

Luz and I stared at it.

"A gun," Luz said. "Why would there be a *gun*?"

A loud thump came from overhead.

Together we froze and looked at the ceiling, as though we might be able to see through it to the floor above. The kitchen was directly under the "den," where the tools and equipment had been set up. Where Kenneth had lost his hand.

"What was *that*?" I whispered. *Please don't be Kenneth please don't be Kenneth please don't be Kenneth.*

"Maybe the cops are still here after all," Luz suggested.

"Maybe so."

Heavy footsteps.

Angry voices.

More thumping, a shout, and a crash.

Or maybe Kenneth wouldn't be so bad after all, I thought. *At least he didn't seem bent on hurting anyone.*

"*Let's get out of here*," I whispered.

Luz looked at me with some disdain.

"Ghosts may scare me, but vandals I can handle." She snatched up the gun, waving it in my general direction. "Does this thing work?"

"*Luz!* Put that *down*!" I said in an urgent whisper, grabbing her arm and pulling her out of the kitchen.

"I'm not going to *shoot* anybody. I'm just going to scare them."

"Because that philosophy worked so well during the arms race."

"What do *you* suggest we do?"

"Run outside and call the police."

"They're probably just some kids fooling arou—"

I yanked Luz back behind the dining room wall just as a body tumbled down the circular stairs.

Chapter Ten

The grunting and thumping came to a halt with a sudden thud.

There was a brief moment of silence. In the distance we could hear the clatter of a fire escape.

Luz poked the barrel of the gun around the edge of the doorway. Gingerly, we both peeked out.

"*Oooow.*"

A young man sat on the landing, his back up against the wall, large hands massaging his ankle. His short-cropped golden brown hair was either intentionally tousled or attractively mussed from the fall. He had a lean, muscular swimmer's build and wore a thigh-length black leather jacket over faded jeans and a black T-shirt. Low-heeled black boots topped off the coordinated outfit. Just a tad better dressed than your average vandal.

He spotted us, put his hands up, and smiled.

"*Whoa*, don't shoot. I'm not armed, I . . ." He trailed off as he looked around him, patting his chest as though searching for his keys. A horrified look came over his handsome face.

Without saying another word, he scrambled back up the steps.

"Let's go after him," Luz whispered.

"We're not going *after* him!" I exclaimed. "What are you, Wonder Woman all of a sudden?"

"I have a gun."

"I realize that, Luz, but maybe he went back upstairs after *his* gun. Did you ever think of that? Let's *go*!"

"Too late."

We hunkered back behind the wall as the stranger began descending the steps, still favoring his right ankle. Hanging around his neck was a bulky black and silver camera with a huge lens. He inspected it with the tender concentration of a father checking his newborn for all ten toes.

I reached over, gingerly pried the heavy, cold Smith & Wesson from Luz's hands, and flipped open the revolver to see if it was loaded. It was. Fully. Six chambers, six cartridges.

My father had taught me never to use a gun as a bluff; if you held it on someone, they had to know you were willing and able to use it. Though my heart fluttered, my hands were steady and I felt strangely centered. There's nothing like standing in a house of horrors facing an unknown intruder, with a friend at my side, to clarify issues.

"Stop right there," I ordered, stepping out from behind the wall and leveling the weapon at him. Assuming the stance.

"*Damn*, Mel, you're a regular Charlie's Angel," murmured Luz as she rose to stand by my side.

The stranger froze on the second-to-last step. His

gaze alighted on the barrel of the gun before rising to meet mine. He gave me a long, thoughtful look with light, sherry-colored eyes that seemed, somehow, too old for his face. Then he smiled again.

"Sorry about that. I had to go back for my camera." Moving slowly, he lifted the massive specimen off his broad chest as evidence. "I'm a photographer. Zach Malinski. You don't need that weapon."

"Why don't you tell us what's going on?" The gun did not waver.

"A couple of kids broke in, I think. They were probably just looking around, but you never know." Malinski spoke in a measured, oh-so-casual tone, as though he encountered gun-wielding women off their meds on a daily basis. "They went out the fire escape off the study."

"Uh-huh." Other than his eyes, he didn't look much older than a kid himself. A really tall, broad-shouldered, good-looking kid. "And what—"

"This is private property, pal," Luz interrupted. "We're well within our rights to just shoot you here and now."

"Actually, you're not," he said, not seeming particularly perturbed. "In California you're not supposed to shoot people without provocation. Gotta love the Golden State."

"You're provoking us," Luz snapped.

"*Luz*, enough already," I said.

"The door was open," mentioned the photographer.

"You walk right into every open door you find in the city?" I asked.

"I'm a friend of Matt's. I was at the party the other night."

What had Matt said? A new photographer from the

paper ... who looked like a young Antonio Banderas. Zach's coloring was a little lighter than the movie star's, but I guess I could see it.

"Look, I just wanted to capture the look of this place post-party, pre-remodel. I'm supposed to be documenting the thing for Kenneth and Matt. But I guess I was a little late. Looks like things were already cleaned up."

"Cleaned up?"

"Just the workroom up on the second floor. Where they set up the saw and all the equipment."

"Must be crime scene cleaners," said Luz. "I saw that show on TV."

"I didn't call any crime scene cleaners," I said.

"Crime scene?" Zach said, no recognition on his handsome face. "What kind of crime scene?"

"You didn't hear?"

"Hear what?"

I exchanged a quick glance with Luz.

"The police haven't spoken with you?" I asked.

He shook his head.

"What time did you leave the party the other night?" I asked.

"About three in the morning."

"Did you notice anything odd—?"

"Everything okay in here?" Graham Donovan interrupted, standing in the doorway. His calm eyes took in the gun in my hand, flickered over to the young man on the stairs, then came back to me.

"Everything's fine." I lowered the gun. "We were just ... startled by Zach."

"I take it you're 'Zach'?" Graham said.

"Zachary Malinski," he said with a nod, moving

across the entry toward Graham and holding out his hand to shake.

Graham did not take it.

"What are you doing here?"

"I was taking some pictures. Kenneth Kostow hired me to document the process of demolition."

"Uh-huh. So you were here during the demolition party?"

He nodded.

"Have you given a statement to the police?"

"You're the second person to ask me about police in the space of a minute." He shook his head and looked at us, one after another. "What's going on?"

"Kenneth was injured sometime after the party," I said. "He died of his injuries at the hospital."

"Seriously?" Zach asked.

I nodded.

"What happened?"

"That's what we're trying to figure out."

"We'll need your contact information," said Graham. "The police—or I—might need to talk with you further."

Zach reached into his jacket pocket, and my hand with the gun rose again.

"Whoa! You are jumpy, aren't you? I was just going to hand you my card."

"Sorry," I said, relaxing.

He pulled out a small leather case and extracted business cards, which he handed to Graham, Luz, and me.

"So what are you three, then? Investigators?"

"I'm just an innocent bystander," said Luz. "I came along for the free lunch."

"I'm the contractor on the job," I said.

Graham gave me a pained look. "*I'm* the investigator."

"Uh-huh," Zach said, sounding rather unsure of our little gang. "Give me a call if there's anything I can do. I left the party before anything violent took place, but if I can clarify anything, I'm happy to."

"I imagine SFPD homicide will be in touch soon enough," said Graham.

Zach nodded but still studied me. His sad, long-lashed eyes held mine for a beat too long, making me wonder whether he was trying to seduce me, or convince me of something . . . or whether it was just his way.

Finally he nodded to us all and left through the still-open front door.

"*Damn*, girl," Luz murmured, sizing me up with a crooked grin. "You see the way he was looking at you?"

"Men are intrigued by women holding guns," I said. "Don't ask me why."

"Mmm," she murmured, raising an eyebrow. She looked at Graham. "You, too?"

"I find anyone holding a gun more frightening than intriguing, regardless of gender." He glanced down at the gun, then up at me. "So, Mel, you're packing heat these days?"

"No, we just found it . . . and then Zach startled us. I guess it was a reflex reaction."

"You 'found' it?"

"In the dumbwaiter." I nodded toward the kitchen.

"Could I have it, please?" He held his hand out to me. I laid the weapon in his palm.

With his other hand, he whipped a plastic bag out of his satchel.

"You're collecting evidence?" Luz asked.

Graham didn't answer.

"You're a cop?" Luz continued.

"Not exactly. I'm with Cal-OSHA."

"Aaah," she said with a smile and an obvious glance in my direction. "You must be the famous Graham Donovan, in the flesh. What a pleasure. And I mean that."

Graham ignored Luz's blatant insinuation, but I imagined he noticed my burning cheeks. I could feel his eyes on me. Despite everything, despite ten years, part of me still felt like a gangly young woman in front of him.

"What are you doing here, Mel?"

"I was in the neighborhood and I heard the scene had been released. Since the crime tape was down . . ."

"You just waltzed on in."

"Seems to me that if it's no longer a crime scene, I have more right than you to be here," I said, awkwardness ceding to irritation. "After all, this is private property and I've been contracted by the owner. So the real question is, what are *you* doing here?"

"I wanted to check out one more detail for my report. And as far as I know, the scene has not been officially released."

"Inspector Lehner called me a couple of hours ago to tell me it was."

"Lehner called you? Directly? I find that a little hard to believe."

"What, you think I'm making this *up*?"

Graham didn't answer, but I could see a muscle working in his jaw as though he were biting back words. Our gazes held a beat too long.

"*Well*," Luz put in, "guess I should be running along. Let you two professionals work out the details of construction schedules and murder investigations and whatnot." She turned and held her hand out to Graham. "Graham, great to meet you. I'm Luz Perez, by the way. L-U-Z, rhymes with 'juice.' It was a real pleasure. I'm sure I'll be seeing you around."

As she walked toward the door she turned back toward me, rolled her eyes over toward Graham, then held her hand up to her ear in the universal sign for a phone while mouthing, *Call me*.

Unable to stifle it, I returned her smile.

"You want to tell me what's going on?" Graham asked.

"I wish I knew. Is it . . . Do you know whether the cops have decided as to whether they think it was accidental or intentional?"

"I can't discuss it with you, Mel. We've been over this already."

"But you'd only still be here if they thought it might be accidental, right? Wouldn't SFPD homicide just take over if they were putting together a murder case?"

He gave me a curt nod.

"And since you're still here . . ."

"I'm unclear on what part of 'keep out of it' you're not understanding."

"The part where a friend of mine is in jail for a crime he didn't commit. The part where you're still here investigating as though it were an accident, while Matt is sitting behind bars pending homicide charges. So was it an accident or murder? And what are you doing here if the police have released the scene?"

"I just wanted to take one more look before it's cleaned up."

"Apparently you're a little late."

He gave me a questioning look.

"Zach said it was cleaned up already."

"By whom?"

"Maybe the police?"

Graham shook his head. "They don't do that in private residences. It's up to the homeowner to call in a crime scene cleanup service, or just do it themselves."

"Oh. Right."

"How sure are we that that Malinski fellow wasn't cleaning it up for his own reasons?"

"Zach? He's just the photographer."

"That's a guarantee of innocence these days?"

"No, but . . ."

"Ever think that you might have caught him red-handed and he made up a quick story?"

"Actually, it never occurred to me."

"If you're going to hang out with criminals, you should start thinking like one."

"I *don't* hang out with criminals, by and large."

"So this case is an exception to the rule?"

"Very much so."

"Good. Keep it that way."

"Do *you* hang out with criminals?" I couldn't help but ask.

He gave me a scornful look but didn't answer. "I'm going to take a look upstairs. I suggest you go do something useful—as far from here as possible."

"I'll come with you," I said, and trailed him upstairs.

Not only was I curious as to what the hell was going on; not only did I want company while in this possibly haunted house . . . but I was also beginning to remember how much fun it was to pester Mr. Stick-in-the-Butt Donovan. Maybe ten years had not softened his know-it-all mien after all.

Also, I enjoyed the view as I followed him up the stairs.

I paused when we reached the second-floor landing, steeling myself before going into the room that had held the saw and the bloody evidence of Kenneth's fatal injuries.

Graham paused in the doorway and swore.

"What a god-awful room," he murmured.

"Hadn't you seen it before?" I asked as I joined him.

"Sure, but that was with the tarp down, the saw set up, and blood everywhere. In its own, less macabre way, this is even worse."

I smiled. Those of us into home design found truly ugly rooms as painful as an off-key concert was to a trained musician.

My amusement faded as I heard the rattle of a newspaper, clear as day. In the room with us. I glanced around. Nothing.

But I saw that the room had indeed been cleaned up.

The circular saw had been removed, along with the other construction-related items; the blood spatter had been washed from the walls and fireplace. A dark reddish brown stain on the rug was the only evidence of what had gone on; otherwise, the room looked as it had the first time I had seen it during the original inspection: an old-fashioned "man cave." A worn, dirty Oriental rug was set out in front of the monstrous, lumpy fireplace made of river rock, shells, and tumbled glass; a blackened railroad tie served as a mantel. Built-in bookshelves were flanked by the kind of cheap mock paneling bought at home improvement stores.

"Do you smell something?" I asked Graham.

"Yep. The overwhelming scent of Pine-Sol cleaning solutions."

I smelled that, too, but what surprised me was fresh pipe smoke. I had the sensation that if I turned around fast enough, I would spy someone relaxing in a faded club chair, indulging in an after-dinner smoke. I glanced around, paying special attention to my peripheral vision, just in case. Still nothing.

"Any decent professional crime scene cleanup team would never have left a bloodstain like that on the rug," said Graham.

"They can get that sort of thing out?"

"If not, they'd dispose of the rug. They even take up floorboards if the blood has soaked in too far. They're supposed to get rid of all traces of what went on."

"Do you hear paper rustling?"

He paused to listen, then shook his head. "Must be the neighbors."

"It sounds like it's right here in the room with us."

"This place probably has rats. I wouldn't be surprised."

"Maybe," I said.

"Where did you see Kenneth?"

I whipped around, expecting Kenneth's apparition, before realizing that Graham was referring to the other morning when Matt and I found Kenneth, still alive. I took a deep breath; I was feeling a bit jumpy.

"We were in the room down the hall. . . ."

"According to your statement," Graham prompted, "Kenneth came after you and Matt Addax with a nail gun?"

"He managed to squeeze off one round, but that was it. I think he was out of his head by then. Blood loss."

"Show me."

We walked down the corridor to the next room, which was a shambles. Much worse than the day after the party. Wallboard was ripped off the walls every which way; even floorboards had been taken up here and there.

"Matt and I were in here, but it didn't look this bad."

Graham nodded. "I went through this whole place yesterday. Someone's been in here since then. So, the crime scene room has been cleaned up, but this room has been torn apart. Almost as though someone was looking for something, as well as covering up a crime scene."

"I take it you're not buying the 'Kenneth did himself in' argument?"

"Tell me what happened with Kenneth when you found him."

"I wrote it all in the report."

"Indulge me."

"Matt was standing about where you are," I said as I moved toward the wall where the wallboard had been hung crooked. "I was over here, crouched down."

"What were you doing?"

"I thought I saw something in the wall."

"Something? Like what?"

"I couldn't really tell. It looked like a box, but I couldn't reach it. Probably nothing. You know how old houses are—some worker's lunchbox, maybe. Maybe just a bundle of old newspapers."

"Did you mention this to the police?"

"Frankly, it didn't occur to me. It sort of slipped my mind, given . . . the situation."

He moved over to the spot. We flipped on our respective flashlights and crouched to peer into the large hole in the wall.

"I don't see anything," Graham said.

"I know. I dislodged it when I tried to get to it, and I managed to push it so it fell down through the joists."

"Let's open this thing up so you can crawl in there."

"Me? Why don't *you* crawl in there?"

"You're smaller. And you're the one who forgot to mention this to anyone. And besides," he added quietly, "now that I'm Cal-OSHA, you have to do what I tell you."

Chapter Eleven

"You say that as if you were the embodiment of the whole agency. You're not *actually* Cal-OSHA, you know. Much less God."

He smiled. "Close enough in your world," he said as he grabbed the edge of the wallboard with both large hands and pulled.

In the old days, wall surfaces were created by nailing thin slats of wood, called lath, to two-by-four studs and topping these with thick layers of plaster—a kind of cement mixture blended with binders such as horsehair, straw, and sand. Old-school plaster is *tough*. In contrast, modern wallboard—in which powdery gypsum is pressed between two pieces of heavy paper—is about as difficult to cut through as a slice of toasted focaccia. That was why people could put their fists through modern walls in fits of anger—it was akin to Captain Kirk picking up those huge cardboard "boulders" on the old *Star Trek* television show.

Graham snapped half the board off the studs, then

kicked off several other large chunks, leaving a gaping opening in the wall.

I held my miniflashlight in my mouth and crawled into the dark space beyond, balancing on the joists rather than on the surface at their base, which made up the first-floor ceiling. The lath and plaster ceiling wasn't meant to be walked on; the plaster would crack at best, or one's foot could go right through to the room below.

"Anything?" Graham asked.

"Umm mmfingmm," I answered around the flashlight. So far, nothing but the cobweb-strewn recesses typical of the inner walls of any house. But toward the outer wall of this house, the ceiling fell away along the contours of the tray ceiling below, creating a well. I lay on my stomach, trying to balance on the beams.

I took the flashlight out of my mouth.

"Hold my feet," I said.

"Don't hurt yourself," he said, reaching into the wall and grabbing my ankles.

I thought of my short skirt and hoped I wasn't giving him an obscene show. At least I was wearing tights. Then again, they were only thigh-highs. At least I was wearing *underwear*. I nearly laughed out loud at the ridiculousness of the situation. I haven't seen the man for a decade, we snipe at each other over a crime scene, and now I'm flashing the poor guy. *Oh, well*, I thought, *what's done is done*. No sense backing out before I grabbed what I was after.

I peered down into the well, stretched, and finally managed to grasp . . . a box.

"Mull nee ow," I said around the flashlight.

He pulled.

I crawled backward the rest of the way, then handed him the treasure.

We both sat on our haunches and studied my find: a big wooden cigar box, nailed shut.

Graham pulled a blade out of a Swiss Army knife and pried open the top. A red leather-bound book and a sheaf of documents were tucked snugly inside, yellowed and brittle with age.

Graham gingerly pulled the papers apart. They looked like old-fashioned checks, but they were imprinted with an extravagant flowing script declaring them to be legal tender, issued by *The Imperial Government of Norton.* The stack of ten-dollar notes amounted to several hundred dollars.

"Have you ever heard of the government of Norton?" Graham asked.

"Never. But I studied anthropology, not history."

"Surely we would have heard of an 'Imperial Government of Norton,' though, wouldn't we?"

"Seems like. Unless it was one of those archipelago situations. I never could keep all those islands straight." For a while it seemed every wealthy European adventurer and his brother were declaring themselves emperor of this or that island, handily ignoring the people already living there.

"Me neither," Graham said.

I picked up the book and turned it over in my hands. The old leather cracked as I cautiously opened the cover to peek inside.

Feminine, delicate handwriting. There were lists and household accounts, plus intermittent stories about the antics of the writer's two young sons. I flipped through quickly, giving it a cursory once-over—it would take some time to decipher all of the old-fashioned cursive handwriting. The woman noted how happy she was when her parents moved in next door, and she wrote of being proud of her husband, the banker. She recorded family visits, balls, and social events.

About three-quarters of the way through the journal, the handwriting changed. It became blockier, perhaps a man's hand. This script started out hard to read before deteriorating to the point of illegibility.

I handed the journal to Graham, feeling vaguely disappointed. Normally I would have been beyond excited to dig such things out of the walls, to be able to hold and study the remnants of former inhabitants. But this time I had hoped to find some sort of explanation for what happened with Kenneth . . . a hidden treasure so profound that it would have inspired a person to torture and maim another human being. These papers were a fascinating relic from another time, but they were hardly an explanation for such brutality . . . were they?

"Do you think the Norton notes could be worth a fortune? Like early AT and T stocks?" I asked as I looked at the yellowing documents.

"Somehow I doubt it. They had a bunch of gold rush–era schemes back in the day, lots of investments in mines and the like. It probably pertains to something like that. Still, I'd feel better if we had an expert opinion. Don't you know some folks down at the historical society?"

"I do, yes."

"Why don't you take them down there and have them take a look?"

I glanced at my watch. "They close in half an hour. Better make it tomorrow."

He nodded.

"Or . . . do you think we should turn this stuff over to the police?"

Graham hesitated.

"There's something strange about this case," he said softly.

I turned to look at him but remained silent.

"First Kostow says it's an accident; then he accuses Matt Addax? And it's a supposed homicide investigation, but the house is left wide-open to crime scene cleanup and vandalism?"

"And they kept you on the case."

He nodded. "That, too. If homicide is interested, they usually have us write up a report and leave. In this case, they seemed to *want* me to declare this either an accident or suicide. But even if Kostow was suicidal, what are the chances he'd make it all the way through bone and tendon? He'd just slice himself, not completely take the hand off. And then the nail gun on top of it? Please."

"Then what could be going on?"

"I have no idea. The investigators are probably overwhelmed with other homicides and want to close this case as soon as possible. Apparently Kostow didn't have any immediate family, no one to raise a stink about a less-than-thorough investigation. And there are always neighborhood pressures; it's much nicer to say it was an accident, or even suicide, rather than murder. Different statistic."

Graham replaced the notes and the diary in the box and handed it to me.

"Take it to the historical society, and find out whether there's anything valuable. If so, we'll contact the authorities. It's doubtful, but I feel as though if we hand it to the police now, it will just get lost in the shuffle."

"There's something else. . . ."

"What?"

"We removed a crate from here the other day, things Matt had packed into a container and asked me to store out of the way."

"Things? What kind of things?"

"He said they were valuables from the house, lamp-shades and the like that he wanted to keep safe. But I never looked inside."

"Did you happen to mention this to the police?"

"Sort of. I told the responding police officer before I had it removed. He seemed to think it was fine." I cringed at the dawning realization that I hadn't thought to tell the homicide inspector. Did that make me look guilty somehow? This was the sort of thing that made me want to crawl into a pied-à-terre in Paris.

"Where is this crate now?"

"Out in Bayside Storage, near the Port of Oakland."

I looked up to see Graham watching me, his dark eyes inscrutable. Was he concerned? Annoyed? It was hard to tell.

"Let's lock things up here, and then I'll follow you to the storage unit. I want to take a look inside that crate."

"Is that your dog?" Graham asked as we emerged from the house.

The brown dog was lingering near the trash again. He gave me a quick wag of the tail, then hung his head.

"I think it's a stray. Poor thing was here the other day as well."

I approached him, holding my hand out to let him sniff me before I stroked his head. He seemed to accept my attention with patience, if not a lot of enthu-siasm. His long snout and feathers were reminiscent of an Irish setter, but he was a pure chocolate brown with a single white patch on his chest. I glanced up and down the street. Could he belong to any of the nearby houses? His hair was matted in places, and with the ratty red bandanna around his neck, he didn't look like he belonged in Pacific Heights any more than I did in my dusty black attire.

I felt under the bandanna for a collar, but the cop who first noticed him had been correct: no collar, no identification. When would people learn to put tags on their pets so they could be returned if lost? My family had dogs all through my youth—my dad's last pound puppy, a springer spaniel, had passed away about six months ago after enjoying a very long life and rarely leaving my father's side. I kept expecting Dad to bring another pooch home one day; this was the first time in my life I had known him to be without a canine companion.

I dug around in my satchel until I found an abused packet of shortbread cookies left over from my last plane trip. Ground mostly into dust, it was the best I could do. I tore open the bag and poured the contents into the palm of my hand, holding the crumbs out to the dog.

He gulped them down and looked eagerly for more. I splayed my hands and let him inspect—there was nothing edible left.

"Feeding him is as good as naming him, you know," Graham said, patting the dog on the back. "He's yours now."

"Oh, no, he's *not*. I'm not in the market for a dog."

I opened the passenger-side door to set the box we'd found on the floor, and threw my bag in. The dog pushed past me, jumped in, and sat down in the passenger seat.

Behind me, I heard Graham chuckle. "Looks like the pooch has other plans."

"C'mon, pup," I said, patting my thigh and then pointing to the sidewalk. "Get out of there—now."

He thumped his matted brown tail in response. Huge brown eyes lolled over toward me for a moment, then stared straight ahead through the windshield.

"I think you've got a new dog, whether you want one or not."

"No way. A dog does *not* fit in with my game plan."

"What's your game plan?"

"I'm moving to Paris."

"Really. What's in Paris?"

"Solitude."

"A lot of rude people and expensive food, if you ask me."

"I didn't ask you."

"True enough. So when is this move supposed to happen?"

"Two years ago. Or as soon as I can rid myself of the business. Which is why I don't need any more baggage, such as a stray mutt. Come on, now." I tried again, patting my thigh. "Out of there, dog."

The dog yelped and jumped into the back of the car, huddling against the door on the driver's side, as far as possible from the apparition that had just appeared in the front passenger seat.

Kenneth's ghost.

Chapter Twelve

"You're giving my seat away to *dogs* now?" Kenneth demanded.

I glanced over my shoulder at Graham, who stood exactly where he had been before, giving no sign of seeing or hearing the phantom in the car.

"At least he's in the back now," Graham said with a half smile. "I think that's the best you're going to do. I'll follow you."

He climbed into his Cal-OSHA truck.

I blew out a breath, exasperated. Kenneth, Graham, and now a dog. Had I done something in a former life to deserve all these male interlopers in my current life?

Giving up on evicting the dog, I climbed in the car, started the engine, and headed toward the bay.

Careful to look straight ahead while speaking so Graham wouldn't notice that I'd become mentally unhinged, I said to Kenneth, "I thought you'd gone away."

"Where would I go?"

"*Away.* To wherever it is all the other spirits hang out.

Did you find out ... Do you know what you're doing here yet?"

"Not really. I'm not exactly making inroads with these people."

"What I don't get is why you're bugging *me*." We traveled down Scott and turned left onto Bush Street, headed east. "Isn't there someone else you could haunt? Someone you hated in life? Someone, you know, sort of obnoxious like you were?"

"I should have tried to scare the crap out of you. Maybe I'd get a little more respect."

"Too late. Whining is a lot more annoying than scary."

"Marlowe's ghost never had to put up with this kind of thing."

"As in Christopher Marlowe?"

"No. You know, *A Christmas Carol*. The ghost of Marlowe visits Scrooge."

"Okay, first of all that was *Marley*, not Marlowe."

"I thought Marley was a reggae singer?"

"That's Bob Marley. But in *A Christmas Carol*, the ghost of Scrooge's old business associate, Marley, comes back to haunt him."

"Hey!" Out of the corner of my eye I saw Kenneth sit up, excited. "Maybe I'm supposed to show you the ghosts of Christmases past, demonstrate how your life's gone wrong!"

"You'd be a heck of a tour guide to show me how my life has gone wrong—as if I don't know already. Anyway, it's not Christmas, and apparently the other ghosts there won't talk to you enough to cooperate with any sort of character-building exercise for either of us."

Kenneth slumped back down in the seat and remained mute.

"I thought you couldn't remember things," I said. "How come you have such good recall of movies?"

He shrugged, still put out.

I glanced at the rearview mirror to make sure Graham was following in his OSHA truck. Then I shifted my gaze to look at the dog, huddled as far from Kenneth as possible.

"Wait a minute," I said. "The *dog* saw you."

"So?"

"So maybe I'm not crazy, after all."

"Or maybe the dog's a figment of your imagination, too—ever think of that?"

"Very comforting, Kenneth. Thank you."

The thought actually took me aback for a moment until I realized that Graham had seen the dog as well.

The pup looked out the window and panted, long pink tongue drooping from the side of his mouth. I might as well face it: It was going to take a harder heart than mine to kick him out, especially since I now felt a certain camaraderie with the unkempt canine. He seemed to be the only living creature besides me who could see—or sense—Kenneth.

He really did look like the kind of dog that might belong to a construction worker. Maybe if I took him around to job sites and supply centers for a few days, somebody would recognize him.

"Are we going home already?" Kenneth asked.

"No. I need to check out something in my storage unit, and then I'm going back to work."

"What about my case?"

"It's not a 'case,' Kenneth. Or at least it's not *my* case. Unless of course it's a case of crazy, as in I'm nuts."

"I thought we were tracking down my killer."

"As a matter of fact, we're going to see if there's anything in the crate I took from the house that might shed some light on your . . . on what happened."

"Good. I'm really put out about my hand. Like he couldn't have killed me with a simple knife wound."

"Yeah. I don't know what to tell you."

"A bullet would have been so hard?"

"Wait a second. Your killer's a 'he'?"

"What? Oh, I don't actually know. Guess I was just assuming. Ever notice how in situations of murder and mayhem, the culprit's almost always male?"

"As a matter of fact, I have."

We crossed over Market and sat in traffic near the on-ramp to the Bay Bridge.

"I hate to tell you this," Kenneth said, "but it looks like your dog is going to hurl."

"What?" I glanced in the rearview mirror, but I couldn't see the dog.

"He's on the floor, rocking back and forth a little. He's about to lose it."

"No way. Dogs love riding in cars."

"This one looks like it needs Dramamine."

I twisted around when we stopped for the final light before the bridge on-ramp. Kenneth was right; the dog was sitting on the floor, panting loudly.

"This must be your fault," I said.

"*My* fault?"

"You weirded him out, sitting right on top of him like that."

"He was in my seat. Anyway, it was probably the cookies you fed him. I saw the wrapping on those things. How long had those been in your purse?"

"A while," I conceded. "But dogs have strong stomachs, don't they?"

Kenneth looked back and grimaced. "I'm just saying. You might want to get to your destination soon."

Luckily the storage facility was near the Port of Oakland, right at the eastern base of the bridge. Traffic was light, so we arrived quickly.

As usual, the entire port area was deserted. Oakland wasn't great at signage, and I always wondered about hapless tourists who get off at the wrong freeway exit and meander, lost, amongst the huge shipping containers and storage facilities and desolate, uninhabited military housing. The old army post had long since been abandoned; the only parts of it still in obvious use were the outdoor athletic facilities. I remembered taking Caleb to Little League games out here from time to time, where if you forgot to bring drinks and snacks, you were in real trouble—there was nowhere to buy anything at all. Rarely even a sign of life.

At the big gate of the storage facility, I referred to the small notebook I kept in my glove box and reached over to the security pad to punch in the access code.

As I waited for the lumbering metal gate to open fully, I looked over at the office. There was a real live human at the main desk. Even from a distance I could see that he had greasy hair and acne, and if I were to judge him by his looks alone, I would assume he had a generally bad attitude. Then again, if I had to spend my eight-hour workday sitting at a desk out in the nearly abandoned military facility, watching what looked to be a daytime drama on a small TV on the counter, I might be just as grumpy.

I gave silent thanks for my day job. I might complain about the stress and responsibility, but I wouldn't trade it for the world. Except for Paris, of course.

I found a shady spot near the main entrance to the storage building, hurrying to let the dog out. He bounded down and trotted around, sniffing the weeds at the edge of the blacktop, but he didn't toss his cookies.

Graham pulled up behind me and climbed out of his truck.

"Shall we?" he said.

"It's inside," I said. The external compartments facing onto the parking court had been sold out when I rented the space, and I liked the increased security of the internal units. "Let me just put the dog back in the car."

He jumped obediently into the rear seat when I opened the door for him.

To Kenneth I whispered, "Hey, stay here and watch the dog for me, will you?"

Kenneth looked pained. "I'm not really a pet person."

"You're not really a *live* person. Just watch him, in case ... I don't know. In case he needs to go out or something."

"What am I supposed to do about it? I can't open doors."

"You can't?"

He shook his head.

"Okay, well, if he seems like he needs something, come and get me."

"How do I know where you'll be?"

"Good question, except that you've known precisely where to find me every damned time I turn around."

"That's true." Kenneth flashed another wary glance at the dog, who sat patiently in the backseat. "Don't be long."

I patted the dog on the head, cracked the windows, and slammed the door shut.

Inside the building, Graham and I walked down the long corridor, our footsteps echoing in the cavernous, empty concrete-and-metal space. The overhead lights were set on an energy-saving system, so they came on as we walked by but shut off after we passed. Other than a glowing green Exit sign over the door we had entered, the hallway behind us was pitch-black.

I could have sworn I heard a scrape or a footstep behind us. I swung around.

"What is it?" Graham asked, looking back as well.

Could it be Kenneth? Or someone else? Or nothing at all?

"Nothing," I said with a shake of my head. "Imagination run amok, I think."

I had been here before, plenty of times, sometimes as often as once a week, putting things in and taking things out. But somehow now this place seemed spookier than Matt's house.

The last light blinked off as we moved out of range, but the one that was supposed to come on as we passed it failed to light up.

Darkness enveloped us.

Graham yanked a small but powerful flashlight from his utility belt and shone the beam both ways down the empty hall. No one here but us.

"How much farther?" he asked.

"Right here. Number one-eight-four."

Graham focused the flashlight on the combination lock, but there was no need for me to work the dial. The lock hung open on the handle.

I looked up at Graham. His mouth pulled tight in a grim line. He reached down and rolled up the metal security door.

Matt's crate, right in the center of the unit, had been pried open. Amber and red shards of glass littered the floor. There were mirrors, a few framed pictures, window and door hardware, a carved gold gilt wooden chair ... everything strewn around the space, which also held other items from other jobs. Upholstered furniture had been ripped open, stuffing scattered.

"I can't believe thi—"

I was shoved, hard, from behind.

I lost my footing and crashed into Graham. He caught me, but the force of the shove knocked us both off balance and we hit the floor with a painful jolt. I felt splinters of glass dig into my upper arm.

The metal door clattered down, trapping us. Graham pushed me unceremoniously aside and jammed his booted foot under the door just as it slammed toward the floor. Then he tried to shove it up, while someone in the corridor struggled to keep it down.

Graham grunted as the culprit stomped on his foot.

Graham whipped the gun we had found at Matt's, still in its plastic bag, out of his jacket pocket and shoved the muzzle under the door.

He fired.

Chapter Thirteen

The door was released.

"Stay!" Graham shouted at me, flinging out a hand in the universal sign of *Stop*.

I crouched down, my ears still ringing from the blast of the revolver.

The metal door clattered up. Graham was gone.

I heard footsteps running down the dark hallway, but no more shots were fired. Grunts and sounds of a scuffle floated over to me as I rooted around in my satchel for my flashlight. At last, down at the other end of the corridor, an exterior door opened, letting a bright beam of light into the hallway. I saw the silhouette of a man slipping through the opening before the door slammed shut again.

"*Graham!*" I called out, flashing my light down the corridor.

"Here," came his voice. "I'm okay."

My light finally landed on Graham lying on the concrete floor not far from the exit. I ran to him and knelt by his side.

"Are you all right? Are you hurt?"

"It's nothing." He yanked away from the bright beam of my flashlight.

He struggled to his feet, limped to the door, and looked out. There was no way to tell which way our attacker had gone. No sign of life in the parking lot other than the dog in my car, barking crazily.

"*Dammit!*"

In the light I could see that his right eye was already swelling.

I reached up to touch it. He winced and pulled back.

"That looks bad," I said.

"Yeah, well, you should have seen the other guy."

I laughed grudgingly, shaking my head. "You could have been killed."

"Hey, I had the gun."

"Yeah, about that . . . Was using that gun the smartest move on your part?"

"Not really, no. Blame it on the adrenaline."

"I suppose we should report the break-in to the front desk? Call the police?"

"Yeah, about that—" He began to explain, but I interrupted him.

"*Graham*—if they were after something they thought had been in Matt's house, and they knew about the storage crate . . . would they have gone after the piano next?"

"Where's the piano?" he called after me. I was already running to my car.

"My dad's house!"

I was placing a call to Dad even as I ran. No one picked up. Graham jumped in his truck and followed me as I sped toward the freeway. It took only ten minutes to get home; I broke my cardinal rule of never using the phone while driving, redialing my dad, and then Caleb, the whole way. Neither answered.

I saw the smoke the second I crossed International Boulevard.

The panic I was holding at bay shifted into high gear when I made the turn onto our street and saw the blinking red and blue lights of two police cars and a fire truck.

I pulled to a screeching halt and jumped out. The dog bounded after me.

My dad was standing with two police officers, chatting and laughing. He signed a form and handed it back to them, waving at me.

I ran up to him.

"Dad! What happened?" I demanded, trying to keep the panic from my voice.

"Don't worry, babe. Someone got into the garage is all. No big deal," Dad said.

The garage was still sending up whiffs of black smoke. Firefighters had sprayed the structure with water and foam and were already loading up their gear, preparing to depart. Ugly soot marked the tops of the windows and the main door, which had been axed open.

Caleb and Dylan stood by the smoldering ruins, checking it out, excited.

"Graham, good to see you," my dad said with a significant glance at both of us. "You okay?"

Dad looked at me as though *I* was the one who had given the man a black eye.

"I'm fine, thanks, Bill," Graham said. "Long story."

"I'll bet," Dad said. "Sorry, Mel. I'm afraid your friend's grand piano is history."

"And your workshop, too, looks like," I said.

He shrugged. "No one got hurt—that's the important thing."

"What happened?"

"You know how this neighborhood can be."

True, it wasn't the best part of town. But we knew everyone on the block, and with our active neighborhood watch group there had been very few problems in the years my parents had lived here.

"Looks like maybe they tried to get into the house, but Tom next door spotted them and called nine-one-one."

"Everyone's okay?"

"Yup. We weren't even here at the time. The boys were still on their way home from school, and Stan and I were over at the union hall."

The boys came up to us, thrilled, dog in tow.

"What's his name?" Caleb asked.

"He has no name," I said.

"Can we name, him?"

"No." I tried to ignore Graham's know-it-all look. "If we name him, we'll want to keep him."

"Why can't we?" Caleb asked.

"Yeah! I love dogs!" Dylan chimed in. Both boys conveniently forgetting that neither of them officially lived here.

"I have no time or energy for a pet."

"He's gotta have a name, at least," Caleb said.

"Just call him Dog," I said. "Like the cat in *Breakfast at Tiffany's*."

"Wait, what?" Dylan asked, crouching by the animal and petting him with enthusiasm. "What cat?"

"Mel watches old movies from when she was a kid," Caleb said, barely managing to stifle his impulse to roll his eyes. "Don't ask."

"Hey, *Breakfast at Tiffany's* is a classic film," I said. "And for your information, it was made long before my time. I may be old, but I'm not *that* old."

The boys looked at each other, laughed, and started running around on the lawn with the dog.

"Just don't get too attached," I warned, feeling like a curmudgeon of the highest order.

Caleb's and Dylan's real homes didn't allow pets because the boys' parents didn't want hair all over their designer furniture. I couldn't claim that excuse here at the less well-heeled Turner house; that much was certain. But the last thing I needed right now was yet another entanglement.

On the other hand, watching the teenagers roll around on the lawn like carefree kids—rather than in their usual personas as sullen, uncommunicative automatons—was the kind of treat that only a four-legged friend seemed able to inspire.

I walked over to peer into what was left of the garage/workshop.

"Poor Matt," I said as I looked at the remains of the once-beautiful piano. Keys had been ripped from it, the black lacquer finish had bubbled and cracked, the whole top had been hacked apart. One more thing gone wrong.

"Next to what he's facing, I don't imagine he'll care very much about a piano," Dad said. "Let's get inside."

We all tromped into the kitchen, Dog included.

"Guess I'd better start setting the home alarm again," grumbled Dad. "I've gotten pretty lazy about it."

As soon as I walked through the mudroom, I noticed a rifle and a handgun atop the kitchen counter. Fear surged yet again in the pit of my stomach.

"What's going on?"

"A man's got a right to protect his home and family," Dad said.

Stan sat at the kitchen table, cleaning a Glock .40.

"*Stan*," I said, aghast. "I thought you were Mr. Gun Control."

"Aren't they all, until they need to defend themselves and their loved ones," said Dad as he pulled a bag of peas out of the freezer.

He handed it to Graham, who pressed it to his rapidly developing black eye.

"Awesome." Dylan picked up the handgun off the counter.

"*Stop right there!*" I yelled.

I took the weapon from him to make sure it wasn't loaded. It had no clip, but there could always be one round hiding in the chamber. My dad was hyper-conscientious about this sort of thing, but still . . . Something about fifteen-year-olds and firearms did not mesh in my mind.

Something about sixtysomethings and firearms didn't mesh especially well, either.

"These aren't toys," I said, sticking the handgun in the waistband of my skirt.

"I know," Dylan said. "Bill already gave us a training."

I glared at Dad, who avoided my eyes, whistling silently as he scrounged in the refrigerator. He brought out an egg and some leftover rice and hamburger, mixed the ingredients in a bowl, warmed it for a few seconds in the microwave, and set it down for Dog.

"There's a good pup," I heard him say in that quiet, tender voice that he reserved for speaking to animals. His kinder, gentler side. He patted the grateful dog on the back.

Looking around at Stan, Dylan, Caleb, and my father, I could practically smell the free-floating testosterone.

Even Dog was male.

I glanced at Graham, who seemed amused. Hoping he would be the voice of reason, I gave him a "*Well?*" look.

"Bill, Stan, I think you should reconsider the guns," Graham said, stepping up. "Let's let the cops handle this."

"Yes, by all means," I piped up. "Let's let the cops handle this."

"You think the Oakland Police Department has time to guard my place twenty-four/seven?" Dad asked. "I don't think so."

Graham caught my eye and shrugged. "He's got a point."

"Oh, great, thanks so much. Super effort."

"Excuse us for a moment," Graham said to the group, taking me gently by the elbow and directing me down the hall toward the Turner Construction office. He closed the door behind us and started rummaging in the large cabinet by the window.

"Looking for something?" I asked.

"Your dad always used to keep a— Here it is." He held up a first-aid kit, set it on the desk, and started looking through it.

"You need aspirin?" I asked.

"No, it's for you. Your arm."

I looked down to see that there was blood on the upper sleeve of my sweater. It had hurt earlier in a vague sort of way, but I was so caught up in the action that I hadn't noticed.

I stripped down to my pink tank and sat on the edge

of the desk while Graham started cleaning the area with cotton balls wet with hydrogen peroxide. I flinched— there were still a few tiny shards of glass stuck in my skin. He found a pair of tweezers in the box and carefully began picking them out.

Graham's head was bent in concentration, his injured eye swollen and sore-looking. Dark hair curled at the base of his neck; a five o'clock shadow darkened his jaw. He smelled of soap mixed with just the tiniest bit of axle grease and sweat, from the fight, no doubt. Somehow he still managed to smell great, a distinctive scent that was all his. One that I had remembered through the years.

"Just in case what happened at the storage unit is connected to the garage fire," Graham said, interrupting my wayward thoughts, "it wouldn't be a bad idea for them to be on alert."

"Alert is one thing, Graham. The Wild West is another. They're about as likely to shoot each other as a criminal."

"You're dad's ex-military," Graham pointed out. He extricated the last piece of glass, inspecting the area in the light. Then he began to swab it delicately, again, with cotton balls. "Surely the man knows his way around firearms."

"He's . . . not always his old self lately. I don't know how often you see him, but he's changed. Besides, this is the Bay Area, for heaven's sake. Isn't it illegal for kids to handle guns around here?"

"I'm sure your dad has gun permits."

"For himself maybe. That doesn't mean he can take teenagers out shooting anytime he feels like it. You don't know Dylan's mother. She'd go crud-monkeys over something like this."

"'Crud-monkeys'?" Graham asked, looking at me with a questioning smile.

"It's something the boys say to avoid swearing around me." I shrugged. "Probably one of their private jokes."

Graham applied Neosporin to my arm, then brought out a roll of gauze. The sleeves of his blue work shirt were rolled up, and I noticed the way his dark hair clung to the smooth muscles of his forearms. As he wrapped the gauze around the afflicted area, his knuckles grazed the side of my breast. My eyes flew up to his. They were on me, intense and unreadable. I swallowed, hard, and turned my head away.

"The way that blond boy was talking," Graham said, taping the gauze and stepping away from me, repacking the supplies neatly in the first-aid kit, "it sounded as though he'd moved in with you."

"That's Dylan, Matt Addax's son. His mom's off on a cruise somewhere, so he's staying with us for the interim."

"And the other boy?"

"My son, Caleb. My stepson. Ex-stepson. Sort of."

"He lives with you?"

"His mom's out of town as well." Feeling almost naked in my tank, I pulled on a sweatshirt that hung over the desk chair. In need of a distraction, I got up and unrolled the blueprints from Matt's job, spreading them out on the drafting table.

"And his dad?"

"Caleb's not exactly thrilled with his new stepmother, and it's causing a lot of friction between his dad and him. I said he could stay with me until his mom gets back next week."

Graham came over to stand at my side, staring down

at the blueprints with me. "So you're running your dad's business, employing Stan and who knows how many others, sheltering two teenage boys, and now fostering a stray dog." He paused for a moment, studying the drawings in front of us. "For someone who's trying to live baggage-free and move to Paris, you've garnered a lot of obligations."

No kidding. I remained mute.

I was looking at the spot where we had found the box in a recess of the eaves. Could there be more hidden in similar parts of the house?

"Might be worth looking through the rest of the eaves, see if there's anything else to be found," Graham said, as though reading my mind. "Who knew you took that crate from Matt's house?"

"Nico, obviously," I said, realizing that Nico's disappearance coincided with all of this. I hoped to heaven it was merely a fluke. I brought out my cell phone and tried him; voice mail picked up, but I didn't bother to leave another message. I flipped through my phone's contact list. I didn't have Nico's home phone, or numbers for any his nephews. *Darn it.* One of these days I was going to have to get more organized.

"Who else might have known?" Graham asked.

"The responding police officer—I asked whether I could go ahead and take it, and he approved. The neighbors, Celia Hutchins and her friend Meredith. Anyone else who might have been around on the street—I wasn't on the lookout for goons. Hoisting a piano down the steps is pretty obvious. I had no reason to keep it a secret."

"I heard Caleb mention he and his friend are on spring break starting this coming weekend," Graham continued. "Any chance you could talk your dad into taking everybody on a trip somewhere?"

"A trip? Where?"

"A camping trip, maybe? With everything going on, it might be good to get out of town for a few days. Less chance of mayhem with the firearms, for one thing."

"Actually, Dad's been talking about getting up to Stan's family's cabin, building a ramp for the chair."

"That would be perfect. A chance for all of you to get away."

"*I'm* not going anywhere. Someone's got to work the business."

"It wouldn't be a bad idea for you to take a few days off as well."

"I'm all right." Except for the part about seeing a ghost.

"Really, Mel, this whole thing feels fishy. I wish you would stay away from it until I can figure out what's going on. I've got some contacts in the police department; I'll ask around and see what I can dig up."

"I told you, Inspector Lehner called me this morning and told me I could begin Matt's job."

"Starting when?"

"Starting now."

"Like hell."

"Stan already wrote up the contracts. I'll leave a couple of men at my last job to finish up with the landscapers and supervise a few odd jobs, but I'm calling the rest of the crew tonight. We'll start in on Matt's place tomorrow, or the next day at the latest. We need to get things cleaned up, check out plumbing and electrical, make a plan."

"Mel, a man was killed at that site two days ago. And now someone clearly went after the stuff you took out of the house, looking for something. What is it about this that you're having a hard time understanding?"

"How it's any of your business. OSHA no longer has jurisdiction, do they?"

"You don't even have a building permit."

"According to Inspector Lehner, we do."

"A permit you claimed was forged."

"That was when Kenneth's death was called a construction-site accident. Now that we're off the hook, we might as well take advantage of an expedited permit."

"Forward progress, no matter the cost?"

"What 'cost,' Graham? Kenneth's gone; there's no bringing him back. How would delaying the project teach us anything we don't already know?" I shook my head. "If anything, I'm likely to dig up more clues than the cops can find. I'll leave the den intact for now, just in case, but I'll be through every inch of that house, behind walls and in all the cracks. If I find any kind of evidence, anything at all, I'll secure the scene and call you." I paused. "And pardon me for pointing it out, but you're not a homicide cop any more than I am."

"I don't want you going back to that house, Mel."

"Amazing how I haven't seen you for more than a decade but you're still ready to tell me what to do."

"Perhaps if you took my advice more often, you'd be better off."

"What exactly do you mean by *that*?"

"That you're thinking with your heart, not your head. You want to get into that house so you can find something to absolve your boyfriend. But the truth is, you're more likely to get yourself in some sort of trouble. Trouble that your father will no doubt ask me to rescue you from."

"Boyfriend? Matt's not my—"

"Whatever you want to call him." Graham waved a hand in a dismissive gesture. "I was right last time, wasn't I?"

"You are still such an arrogant piece of—"

"Graham—" My dad swung the office door open and stuck his head in. "You're staying for dinner, aren't you?"

"He can't," I hastened to say.

"I'd love to," Graham said.

Later I had to admit that dinner was . . . fun.

Graham was at his most charming, teasing the boys and accomplishing the nearly impossible by coaxing them into actual conversation, with whole sentences. They talked baseball statistics and music while we enjoyed Dad's famous Southern-fried chicken and garlic mashed potatoes. Over Bakesale Betty's apple pie à la mode for dessert, Stan, my dad, and Graham traded stories and memories with the ease of old friends.

I skipped the pie and took refuge in the office for a few moments, feeling the need to lose myself in my work. I called Nico one more time—still no answer. Then I spoke to Raul and let him know about starting Matt's job. I arranged to shift several of our workers over to Vallejo Street tomorrow morning so I could orient them. Before we hung up, I asked him whether he'd gotten through to Nico yet.

"Not yet. He hasn't answered my messages."

"You don't happen to have any alternate numbers for him, do you? His home, maybe?"

"No, sorry. It does seem strange that he hasn't called,"

Raul said. "By the way, Katy says she has to take some time off for finals."

It frustrated me that I had only one woman on the job these days. Katy was a good worker and I was hoping she'd stay with us a while, but she was a student, with an erratic schedule. I had lost the last woman in my employ to the trades—she was now a journeyman plumber, working union jobs in big housing developments, mostly—and the one before that to motherhood. Not that I blamed women for wanting to start families, but it was tough to break out of the men-only construction tradition when females were the ones who got pregnant. The job site was a dangerous place to gestate.

I would love to have a whole team of women working on my sites. In my experience they tended to be conscientious, clean, and organized, like the best male employees. The only problem was their general desire to be anywhere but on a construction site with construction workers. It was something of a Catch-22.

Still, as Luz liked to point out, I talk a big game, but I really like men. Especially the good guys that I worked with. Speaking of good guys . . .

I searched Stan's desk drawers and dug up the old office Rolodex. Finally I hit pay dirt: Nico's contact information card included a number for one of his nephews, who went by the name of Spike. I called him.

"I haven't been able to get hold of your uncle Nico. Is everything okay?"

"Not exactly," Spike said. "He's in the hospital."

Chapter Fourteen

"What happened? Is he all right?"

"Yeah," Spike said. "He got a little roughed up during a carjacking. It's nothing serious, but they wanted to keep him for observation on account o' he has a preexisting heart condition."

"When did this happen?"

"Yesterday."

"Could I visit him?"

"He'd love it. He's at the California Pacific Medical Center on Buchanan; visiting hours start at eleven. Bring food."

"I will."

"Were you calling him about a job?" Spike asked. "Business is slow these days. I'm sort of running things for him while he's out of commission."

I told Spike I needed to schedule a cleanup at the Zaben house, and an interior demo at Matt's house. I gave him the addresses for each.

"I can get some boys over there on both sites first thing tomorrow, if you want."

"That would be great. Thanks."

"No problem. See you tomorrow."

I hung up, feeling slightly nauseated. It might have been due to the ill-advised second helping of mashed potatoes I had eaten at dinner, but more likely it was in reaction to hearing that someone had gone after Nico, and then had searched both places where he had taken things from Matt's house. This was no coincidence.

My father's voice came to me down the hallway from the kitchen.

"Mel, honey, Graham's leaving."

"Good riddance," I mumbled. Charming over dinner or not, I wasn't ready to forgive him for trying to push me around. And on top of that, I was annoyed by my strong physical reaction to his nearness earlier.

I blushed when I looked up to see Graham in the doorway.

"Walk me to my truck?"

"You're scared of the neighborhood?"

"Just walk me to my truck, please. Bring your car keys."

I blew out a breath and followed him. He asked me to open my car, grabbed the box we had found in the eaves, then took it to his truck. He bent down and shuffled around on the car's floorboard for a moment.

"Do I need to be here for this?" I asked.

Graham stood quickly and grabbed me by the front of my sweatshirt. My heart leapt into my throat.

Rather than kiss me, though, he shoved a manila envelope under my shirt.

"What are you *doing*?"

"It's the stuff we found," he said in a quiet voice. "It's probably safest here with you at this point. You're pre-disastered; I can't imagine they'll be coming back here tonight, since they know you're on guard. But just in case anyone is watching right now . . ."

He stood back and made a show of putting the box into his truck.

"Take those things to the historical society first thing in the morning," Graham continued, almost whispering. "And if anyone comes after them before that, just hand them over. None of it's worth your getting hurt over."

I mumbled something noncommittal.

"Be careful, Mel. I'm serious."

"You might want to take your own advice. After all, you're the one shooting at people and getting black eyes."

"Only while in your company, I might point out."

The envelope crinkled under my shirt as I pressed one arm to my waist.

"You really think this stuff is what Kenneth was hurt over?"

"No." He sounded very sure. Then he added: "But I've been wrong before."

That night I sat cross-legged in my bedroom on a plush wool Aubusson carpet that a client threw away because it didn't match his new couch. The muted hues of rose, sage, and ocher made me happy every time I walked into my room. The rest of the house might still be a mess, but my bedroom was not only functional; it was my sanctuary.

I had faux-finished the walls with a subtle parchment treatment, then filled floor-to-ceiling shelves with beloved books and all sorts of strange, mismatched items scavenged from job sites and found in junk stores. Not the froufrou antiques places owned by nice little old ladies who played canasta while their customers perused well-lit aisles decorated with doilies and framed quilts. On the contrary, I sought out gloomy, musty stores run by cranky old folk, the kind who won't let you buy something if they don't like you. I adored the challenge. Everything in my room had a story.

Including, no doubt, the journal and papers that I extracted from the manila envelope. I laid them out on the carpet in front of me, letting my mind dwell, just for a moment, on the feeling of Graham's hands under my shirt. And the almost electric sensations I felt as he held my arm and tended to my cuts. Either he was an amazingly attractive man or I was hard up. Probably both.

Enough of that. My love life—or lack thereof—was the last thing I should be concentrating on right this moment. I looked back at the items from the box. Could any of them provide a clue to Kenneth's death?

Simple murder was one thing, but didn't Kenneth's injuries imply that his assailant was trying to get him to cough up information? Extremely valuable information? Something so important that Kenneth would rather die than tell?

If only my own personal ghost could recall what the hell had gone on that awful night . . . or morning, more like. Kenneth must have been injured shortly before I arrived. Otherwise he wouldn't have been able to come after Matt and me.

I set the Norton notes aside for the moment, focusing instead on the journal. Thumbing through the pages carefully, I didn't see much more than I had earlier: household accounts, domestic stories, and dates of social events. Toward the end of the first section, the author—who I assumed to be the woman of the house—mentioned an exciting venture upon which her husband was embarking. Something sure to make them rich beyond their wildest dreams. Soon afterward, the handwriting shifted and the information was limited to household accounts, lists of purchases, and expenditures.

The journal's aged leather cover creaked each time I opened and closed it, making me worry that I might be cracking the spine. Upon examination, I noticed that the marbled lining on the back inside cover had pulled away slightly near the crease. I ran my fingers along it.

I felt something hidden underneath.

A folded piece of vellum. Gingerly, I pulled it out and laid it flat on the rug in front of me.

It was a large certificate handwritten in a beautiful, flowing script, declaring one Walter Buchanan, of Vallejo Street, San Francisco, to be holder of the deed to a gem field claim full of diamonds, emeralds, and rubies. Was this the venture that was sure to make them rich beyond their wildest dreams?

Below the text was a hand-drawn map, presumably showing the location of the gem field.

As a native Californian, I had been raised on stories of the state's famous gold rush, but gemstones? In my mind, diamonds came from Africa. On the other hand, I knew we had coal in parts of the United States, and diamonds and coal were related, right? But I had never heard of rubies or emeralds—or coal for that matter—being mined in California.

I jumped as Kenneth appeared suddenly in my peripheral vision, sitting on the side of my bed.

He snickered at my reaction. "That's kind of fun. Now I see why ghosts get into scaring people."

"Do *not* make a habit of it," I warned. I didn't know what I could possibly threaten a ghost with, but I'd think of something.

"What's that?" Kenneth asked, looking at the stuff we had found in the box.

"At the risk of sounding like a broken record, I was hoping maybe you could tell *me*."

"How would I know?"

"I found it in Matt's house. Yours, and Matt's, house. Sort of hidden behind the wall. I thought maybe it had something to do with what happened to you."

He came closer and I could feel his cold presence as he peered over my shoulder.

"What's the journal say?"

"I haven't read the whole thing, but it seems to be a book of household accounts. A few personal comments, but mostly numbers. Written by the wife, I would imagine."

"And is that money?"

"Not any kind I recognize. But I think I should take it in and have it assessed."

"By whom?"

"I thought I'd start with the historical society; see what they have to say."

"That's a good idea."

"There's also a deed, with something that looks like a map." I spread it out.

Kenneth glowed.

"What is it?" I asked him.

"That seems like something."

"What?"

"I don't know, but I'm having some sort of reaction. I think it might mean something."

I studied the map. There were no coordinates, no sign of where it was except a reference to the Stanislaus River and an area called Jumping Falls. Otherwise, there was a drawing of a rock outcropping, a reference to a couple of unnamed mountains, a waterfall, and one tiny little dot called Cheeseville.

The Stanislaus River ran through gold rush country, all right. It was only a couple of hours from the little lake where my sisters and I had spread Mom's ashes not long ago.

I jumped again as someone appeared in the doorway. Dylan.

"Were you talking to somebody?" he asked, his big blue eyes flickering about the room.

"Just to myself."

"Um . . . why?"

"I'm just weird sometimes," I said as I shoved the items I was looking at under the bed. "Come on in."

He stepped in and looked around, shy but intrigued. "You like old stuff, huh?"

"I do, yes."

"How come?"

"I guess I like thinking about people who've gone before. You know, all those lives that have passed. But they leave traces."

He nodded. "Cool."

"Did you want to talk, Dylan?"

"Yeah."

"What's up?"

"Dad called. He was, sort of, like, released."

"You mean he's out of jail? That's great news!"

"Yeah." He continued to look at a shelf holding several of my questionable junk shop finds: a wooden shoe mold; a stuffed trout; a paint-by-numbers version of da Vinci's *The Last Supper*.

I knew from my experience with Caleb that the best tack to take with teenagers is to let them speak in their own time, without pushing them. But lately my patience was limited.

"Is there something else?" I asked.

"I was wondering if, like, I could still stay here for a while. Dad's . . . he's, like, dealing with a lot right now? So I was thinking maybe I could stay with Caleb for a little bit. Over break."

"As long as it's okay with your dad," I said. "As far as I'm concerned you're always welcome here, Dylan. Even if you're not with Caleb."

His eyes flew up to meet mine. "Really?"

"Really."

"Awesome. Thanks. Night."

He left.

"Way to rid yourself of entanglements," said the ghost over my shoulder as soon as Dylan closed the door behind himself.

First Graham, now Kenneth. I gritted my teeth.

"Ever hear the expression 'just say no'?" Kenneth continued.

"As in 'no, Kenneth, I won't help you find out what happened'?"

"Hmm, I see what you mean. I take it back. No offense."

"Go away now. I've got to get some sleep."

"What about the map?"

"The map is useless without any other information."
It was probably useless anyway.

Kenneth didn't say anything further, but he lingered
as I brushed my teeth. I could feel waves of forlornness
emanating from him.

Who was I kidding? I wasn't going to be able to go to
sleep in my current mood anyway.

"All *right*, already, I'll go look it up."

I went down to the office and called up the Stanislaus
River on Google Maps. It was a very long river, which
fed into a huge lake. There was no record, anywhere, of
a town called Jumping Falls, no Cheeseville in Calaveras
County or adjoining counties, no *anything* that I could
relate from the hand-drawn map to any real, present-
day map.

I sat at the computer, chin in my hand, for a long moment, just staring at the map and pondering. Graham
was from that area; he used to love riding his motorcycle up in those hills. I remembered him going on and
on about the special magic of gold rush country: Angels
Camp, Copperopolis, Oregon City. If the map from the
box was old enough, a lot of the place-names might have
changed. Even rivers changed course over the years.
Would locals still recognize the old names?

But even if I could find the location the map referred
to, then what? It wasn't as though it was a pirates' map
with the buried treasure marked with an X. Surely any
such gem field would have played out long ago. Would
have been scoured clean.

Moving on, I looked up the California Historical
Society, on Mission in San Francisco. It opened late on
Wednesdays. I would go by after I visited Nico at the

hospital. Then I looked up Philip Singh. Apparently Singh was a common name; there were scores in the phone book, several Philips and many more "P. Singhs."

I called Matt, who said he was exhausted, grateful to be home, and just wanted sleep. He asked after Dylan, then invited me to come by to see him tomorrow. *Right after my research at the historical society*, I thought to myself.

Finally, I called Jason Wehr and left a message on his office voice mail, asking if he could meet me as soon as possible at the Addax job site for a preliminary walk-through, with the plans in hand. Now that I had decided to continue with the project—and had made my insistent proclamation to Graham—I was more than eager to get started. I was itching to save that beautiful historic building from the abuse it had suffered.

As I pored over the drawings, I envisioned what the house would look like when we were done. The Greek key detail in the wooden floor of the parlor should be mimicked elsewhere; the low arches, already present throughout much of the house, could be extended into the bathrooms, and into the kitchen, which would need more renovation than the rest of the house. I stayed up until one in the morning, developing the plans. Feeling my way, in my mind's eye, through the hallways and rooms of the once-graceful house. Losing myself in the work.

First thing the next morning, I went back to the port storage facility and dragged the hapless young man from the office into my unit with me to see the damage. I took digital pictures, then filled out damage claim forms. After that I borrowed a broom and dustpan and cleaned up the shards, taking inventory of what I'd lost. More specifically, what Matt had lost. The light fixtures broke my heart; there were only a handful of survivors. I did find a box full of doorknobs and various pieces of hardware, though. I took one of each to serve as samples—I would need to find or manufacture matching items, enough for the whole house. As the design of each room was decided upon, I would keep a running tally of doors and cabinets.

On the way to Matt's house I stopped at Happy Donuts and bought two dozen assorted pastries. After I pulled into the driveway and grabbed the pink bakery box from the backseat, I saw that Celia and Vincent were standing on their porch, looking over at the dump truck and signs of construction. It wasn't unusual for neighbors to be irked when construction began next door—no doubt about it, it was a noisy, messy proposition.

Celia looked perturbed, but when I lifted a hand in greeting she smiled broadly and waved back. I considered mothers, and their power. It still surprised me that a grown man would be living with his mom, though Celia clearly had plenty of room. Back in Walter Buchanan's day, it wasn't unusual to have several generations living together in these huge old houses. And after all, I lived with *my* father. You just never knew the whole story when looking at the surface.

Spike and several of his cousins were already waiting for me on the front steps, drinking coffee out of paper cups. They smiled at the sight of the doughnut box and set upon it with gusto.

Nico seemed to have an endless supply of nephews, and try as I might I could never keep them straight. I wasn't even sure they were all cousins—I imagined many were friends, and relations of friends—but they were all strong and hardworking, so it didn't make much difference to me.

I gave them a quick tour of the place, then went over my standard demolition speech—respect for the past, for the present, and for their own health and safety.

"If you see anything in the walls that seems out of the ordinary, anything at all, let me know immediately," I continued. "This was a crime scene, and it's always possible the police missed something. And as always, we're salvaging just about everything, from nails to bricks to woodwork."

"You sure you want to save *all* this woodwork?" Spike asked.

"Definitely."

"It takes more time to restore it—it would be a lot faster to replace it."

"Faster doesn't mean better," I said. "That woodwork is original to the structure, and that means something. In some sense, it means everything."

I hated the perfectly smooth, plastic-y look of a brand-new, top-notch paint job. We would fill and sand the worst nicks and dents, but the soft lines of old wood molding were impossible to replicate with new wood, no matter how carefully one mimicked them. Besides, the more we kept and reused, the "greener" the job site would be.

Of course, the more labor-intensive, the more expensive, which is why so much good historic preservation is restricted to the homes of the wealthy. If I could pull off Matt's job, and the new one still in the design process in Piedmont, and I was at least nominated for the AIA award, I hoped to garner enough rich clients to support more pro bono work amongst people without the funds to restore their historic gems.

That was my plan, anyway. And as I knew too well, the best-laid plans . . .

"Okay. I'm just saying, is all," continued Spike. "You could get this stuff new and not worry about stripping the old paint, any of that."

I nodded. "Thanks. I'd like to save it and reuse it. Think of it as my builder's fetish."

I had them start work on the third floor, which had originally been the maids' quarters, instructing them to avoid the "den" for now, just in case the police did need to come back in and check things out. Within moments of their being let loose, music blared, loud voices swapped stories, and tools banged away at walls. Demolition— even supercareful demo—was noisy. *Really* noisy.

I donned my coveralls over today's outfit, which was another low-cut shift designed by my friend Stephen, this one sporting fringe instead of spangles. At least the skirt was short enough to accommodate the coveralls. Before I even had a chance to orient the rest of my crew, Jason Wehr called my cell phone and offered to meet me at Matt's house right away.

While I waited for him to arrive, I started crawling through the eaves around the second story, just to be sure. I squeezed through all the areas similar to where I had found the old cigar box, inching along beams and through tight passages where something might be hidden. Nothing.

At least Kenneth didn't show, and I didn't smell pipe

smoke or feel the forlorn sensations of a suicidal ghost. On the contrary, I felt safe in the house with all the men working, surrounded by the familiar and comforting hustle and bustle of the job site.

I climbed through the attic, poked my head into every recess I could find, but saw nothing more than cobwebs and dust, the usual accumulation through time. The basement door, however, was locked. I had seen it when I did the original inspection—it had been empty other than a massive, nonfunctioning heater. I was about to look for the key when Jason Wehr arrived.

We did a thorough walk-through, discussed his drawings, went through my suggested changes, and assessed a few potential alterations of original walls. He also volunteered to get his engineer out to the house as soon as possible to analyze its earthquake tolerance.

Walking down the stairs, passing by the demo crew, Jason shouted to me: "I'll bet you've found some interesting things in walls over the years."

"Mostly liquor bottles and old newspapers—though I always enjoy looking at the movie listings from the twenties," I said.

"Have you found anything here yet?"

"Not really." I shook my head, surprising myself with the ease of my lie. Best not to take any chances.

"I found a bunch of tram tokens in the last building I remodeled," Jason said. "Did you know this whole area was full of trams at one point? Even the East Bay. It was a terrible day for the environment when they tore those tracks out."

"I'd heard that. I never did understand why they phased out such great public transportation."

"Supposedly the gas and tire companies got together and bought the land or pressured local governments, in order to increase people's dependence on automobiles."

"Seriously?"

"So they say."

"That seems depressingly shortsighted," I said as we reached the bottom of the sweeping circular stairs. "And now they're trying to reinstall the streetcars. I don't imagine your tokens will work anymore, though."

"No, I doubt it," he said with a smile. "The owner agreed to donate them to the Cable Car Museum on Nob Hill." His eyes shifted over my shoulder. He nodded and said, "Hello."

I turned around to see who he was talking to. Vincent Hutchins stood in the foyer, wearing an immaculate charcoal gray suit. I immediately worried about the dust floating all the way down the stairwell from two stories up.

"Hi, Vincent. We were just talking about your house. Do you know Jason Wehr, the architect on this project?"

"Haven't had the pleasure," he said. The two men shook hands.

"Vincent lives next door," I said to Jason. "He's Celia's son. I imagine their twin house could give us some insight, if we need it, for this remodel."

"You're welcome to stop by anytime for a tour," Vincent told Jason.

Jason thanked him, told me he'd work on the changes we had discussed, and left.

"How are you?" I asked Vincent. "I'm afraid I haven't written up the proposal for your mother yet—"

"I expect you've had a few other things on your mind.

I just happened to notice your car out front and couldn't resist a peek. How's it going?"

"We're just barely getting started, but so far, so good."

"Could I ask, do you know what's happening with Matt?"

"I'm not sure yet," I equivocated. "He's been released on bail."

"Ah. Well, that's good, at least. My mother's been worried about him."

"Vincent, you wouldn't happen to know anything about a man who says he was going to buy this house, would you?"

"*This* house?"

I nodded. "His name's Philip Singh?"

"I didn't realize the house was for sale yet."

"Neither did I."

"I thought Matt's plan was to renovate first, and sell later."

I nodded.

"I tell you what, though. My mother would be furious."

"Celia? Why?"

"She was put out when Matt snapped up this house—she had plans to buy it and reconnect the twins. If she realized it had been sold to someone else, again, she'd be irate."

"I'll mention it to Matt when I see him—there's no reason he shouldn't give your mother right of first refusal once he's ready to sell."

Vincent nodded. "That'd be great. I don't suppose you're free for lunch today?"

"I have plans, actually." Tracking down useless clues

to a killing was a time-consuming affair. "But thank you."

"All right, then. Best of luck with the project. Don't get too dirty, now."

"Like my father always says—" I smiled, looking down at my stained and dusty coveralls. "If you don't get dirty, you're not trying hard enough."

At quarter to eleven, I headed for the California Pacific Medical Center.

I found Nico in his hospital room, surrounded by relatives of all ages. They were a tight-knit group who tended to celebrate—and commiserate—with plenty of food and drink. I added two small baskets of farmers market blueberries and strawberries to the mound of edible items stacked on the windowsill.

Nico had been in the hospital only two nights, but already there were cans of Hellaby's Corned Beef, tins of Italian cookies, and, most disturbingly, a Samoan delicacy called *se'a*: the innards of a sea slug, traditionally served in a Coke bottle.

"You remember *se'a*, don't you, Mel?" Nico asked with a huge smile. He had a bulky bandage on his forehead, scrapes on one side of his face, and bruising and swelling along the cheekbone. One arm was in a sling.

"Oh, I remember, all right." I had tried a little *se'a* once on a dare, after consuming copious amounts of alcohol at one of Nico's Samoan-style backyard barbecues. It was not a fond memory . . . which was rather predictable, since, after all, we were talking about sea slug intestines.

"So, what happened?" I asked Nico as I helped myself to the fresh Italian cookies.

"I had dropped the boys off and was headed home. Maybe I wasn't paying enough attention; I was singing to the radio. Two men boxed me in with their SUVs, hauled me out of my truck, and hit me a few times. Then they took everything I had in the cab of the truck and in my pockets." He shook his head and the smile faded from his face. "All these years, people say that area is dangerous but never have I had a problem. It makes a person lose his faith, you know? On the other hand, many people ran to help me. Good people."

"So it wasn't really a carjacking, then, right? They left you the truck."

"Yes, it was just a robbery. Good for me they did not take my truck—that's my livelihood."

"Did you get a good look at the men who did this?"

"The police asked me that." He shrugged. "They were big, and white. Wearing coveralls, like the ones you wear on the job. Beyond that, I can't really say."

As I rose to leave, a thought occurred to me. "Nico, you said they took everything from your pockets. Do you mean money?"

He nodded. "Money, my wallet, even my notebook."

The little book where he had jotted down the information on the storage locker near the Port of Oakland.

Chapter Fifteen

On my way out of the hospital, I noticed a small sign pointing down the hall toward the emergency room. I thought of the nurse who had provided the deathbed testimony, implicating Matt in Kenneth's death.

Would she talk to me? Were there rules about such things? I was here anyway.... It couldn't hurt to ask. I could insinuate that I was Kenneth's sister, just wanting to make contact with the last person to talk to him. Was that smart, or morally wrong? I wasn't sure. All I knew at this point was that I couldn't understand why he had accused his friend. Could I possibly be wrong about Matt?

At the admittance desk I inquired whether I could speak to the nurse who tended to Kenneth Kostow in his dying moments. I was ready to jump in with my story about being Kenneth's family, but to my surprise it wasn't necessary.

A pretty woman standing behind the desk and writing details on cases at a whiteboard turned around and said, in a lilting accent, "That would be me."

"Could I ask you what Kenneth said to you that implicated his friend?"

"He said 'Matt' over and over."

"How clear was he?"

"Not very. Poor man was out of his head, wasn't he?"

"Couldn't he have been calling out for his friend Matt, rather than accusing him?"

"I don't think so," she said. "He was all, 'Goddamned Matt ruined everything.' Excuse my language. Then he said something about how Matt killed him."

As I headed to the California Historical Society I couldn't stop thinking about what the nurse had said. On the one hand it seemed damning, all right; but on the other, couldn't it have been misinterpreted? Kenneth didn't exactly say that Matt had murdered him, did he?

I still couldn't believe it. Call me stubborn, but there was no way I could imagine Matt doing something like that. Period.

I could feel myself relax as I passed through the double doors of the historical society. Given all the time I spent here researching the houses I worked on, it always felt a bit like coming home.

"Why, if it's not my favorite research librarian," I said to the woman at the main desk.

"Why, if it's not my favorite historic contractor," Trish-the-librarian replied.

I smiled. "That makes me sound like someone who lived a long time ago."

She let out a raspy chuckle. Trish Landres was petite and mousy, almost the visual stereotype of a librarian. Tortoiseshell glasses perched on an upturned nose, and a sprinkle of freckles pointed to red hair now gone mostly gray, cut short in a no-nonsense style. Not long ago I learned that Trish loved salsa dancing, had been to Cuba twice, and worked with Pastors for Peace to help finance their shipments of medical supplies to the island nation. It gave her a secret, swashbuckling aspect that one wouldn't suspect from her gray tweed pants and simple blue cardigan.

Unfortunately, right after I arrived, a whole gaggle of women looking into their family genealogies came into the library. I hesitated to bring out the manila envelope in front of them. So in the meantime I gave Trish the rundown of what I was looking for with regard to the family that had originally built Matt's Vallejo Street house.

She spent some time rummaging in the files, then came back with several documents.

"Here's a picture of Walter, Bess, and their children," Trish said, pulling out a paper file with copies of old sepia-colored photos. "They were a very prominent family, so you're going to find more than usual about them, and their home."

It was a staged family photograph, typical of the era. Bess was lovely, with light eyes and dark hair. The children were young and dressed in the formal flounces of the day: the baby in his christening outfit, and the eldest son wearing short pants, jacket, and ascot tie at the neck. Walter was bearded, looked to be a good deal older than his young wife, seemingly stern and capable. Easy to believe he was a bank president.

"Uh-oh, the genealogical research group is calling me over," Trish said. "They're good people, but a tad needy. Why don't you look through these photos and I'll be back as soon as I can."

I always feel a little tingle run up my spine when the history of a house begins to unfold before me. I could practically see these characters within the walls of the Vallejo Street home.

Another photo showed Bess's parents and her "spinster" sister, the ones who lived in the twin house next door, in what was now Celia Hutchins's place. There were more pictures of houses standing side by side, as well as a group photo of the extended family out in front of the residences. I noted a few original exterior details of the house to mention to Jason Wehr.

One more picture caught my eye. It was the front parlor, done up in high Victoriana—and with a central table and a crystal ball. Except for the carved limestone fireplace, the room was the spitting image of Celia's basement séance room—almost as though she had copied it directly.

"Do you know anything about this photo?" I asked Trish when I could get her attention back from the genealogists. "It looks like the setting for a séance, doesn't it?"

"It certainly does," Trish said as she checked the reference. "I wouldn't be surprised if Buchanan signed on to the Spiritualist movement, at least for a while. It was popular in the last few decades of the late eighteen hundreds. Even the most respectable academics of the time were researching the possibility of talking to spirits beyond death, and assessing mediums' abilities to produce ectoplasm, that sort of thing."

"Have you ever heard any rumors about the Buchanan house being haunted?"

"No, but we don't really deal in that sort of thing," Trish said.

"Apparently they have to disclose it in real estate sales."

"What, you mean if the owners think their house is haunted?"

"That's what I hear."

"Huh. Takes all kinds, I guess."

Trish helped me pull up several more resources on the computer before turning back to the genealogists.

I learned that Walter Buchanan, the wealthy and respected president of Western California Bank, married Elizabeth Spenser, known as Bess, in 1864. Walter had the twin homes built as a wedding present to his young bride so that her family could live right next door.

Walter and Bess had two healthy sons, but lost a young daughter to influenza. The family was clearly prominent and very active in San Francisco's nascent social scene. They threw frequent gala events, and Bess was involved with charity work.

But then Walter was involved in a scandal.

In 1872, two men, Charles Nelson and Andrew Giametti, arrived at the San Francisco branch of Western California Bank and deposited several canvas bags full of the bounty from their latest prospecting venture: a small fortune in uncut diamonds, sapphires, emeralds, and rubies. A bank officer, apparently knowing on which side his bread was buttered, alerted his president.

Walter Buchanan had the stones assessed by a local jeweler, who pronounced them to be genuine. He then sent a sampling to an attorney in New York who personally had them appraised by none other than Charles Lewis Tiffany. Tiffany confirmed their value.

Excited, Buchanan contacted Nelson and Giametti, offering them possible financial backing to properly exploit their gemstone claim. The men refused to divulge the secret location of their site, but they took two of Buchanan's trusted employees on a long train trip, blindfolded, then transferred them to mules, in order to show them the gem field. The excited men eventually returned to San Francisco with thousands of carats' worth of rubies and diamonds, describing the field as being "peppered" with gemstones. Conservative estimates stated that the dirt contained five thousand dollars' worth of gemstones per ton, which meant that a crew of twenty-five men could wash out a million dollars' worth of gems each month.

Buchanan put together an elite group of investors, including a senator who was able to cut through federal red tape. They set up the Golden State Mining Company, backed by more than two million dollars of their personal money. Their first order of business was to buy out the two original prospectors for a fraction of what the gem field was estimated to be worth.

A newspaper photo showed a smiling Walter Buchanan, with Nelson on one side and Giametti on the other, holding their entwined hands aloft in a victory sign. The accompanying article heralded the discovery of priceless gems in California. The coveted location of the gem field was kept secret.

The prospectors left town with their money and were never heard from again. But then . . . the anticipated fortune did not materialize.

"The really sad thing is, his wife, Bess, took their children and left, as did the rest of her family," Trish said, rousing me from my reading. I glanced over to see that the genealogists were now absorbed in their own research, flipping through files and reading microfiche.

"Walter remained in the house, *both* houses, actually, all alone. After some months he seemed to grow despondent over his loss of face in San Francisco society, and finally he shot himself in the head, an apparent suicide. The houses sat empty for several years, but eventually his adult son moved back in, and later he sold off the twin house."

"I don't understand—what happened with the gem field?"

Trish shrugged. "Who knows? Played out right away, maybe? A lot of those claims didn't amount to what people hoped, but this case was unusual because it was so high profile. Buchanan made a public proclamation about it, so when the gems didn't materialize, he was something of a laughingstock. There were some people who thought Buchanan had double-crossed his fellow investors and kept the jewels for himself. But with his suicide, I guess he proved them wrong."

Which all begged the question: If the map I had found in the journal really was the map to this gem field, why would anyone be looking for it? Could there still be something there? Or was the map just a worthless piece of paper, valuable only in a historical sense?

I made copies of several of the photographs and articles. This was going to be one doozy of a scrapbook for Matt, assuming he'd still be interested after everything that had gone on.

"I wanted to show you one more thing I found," I said to Trish, bringing out the Norton notes and spreading them on the counter.

"Well, would you look at that?" Trish said. "Aren't they fun? Where did you get these?"

"In Buchanan's house. Do you know what they are?"

"Sure. You mean you've never heard of Emperor Norton?"

"No. Who was he?"

"You grew up around here, and everything." Trish sighed and shook her head. "The way we teach local history in our schools—or don't teach it, more like—really is a scandal. Norton was this fellow who came to San Francisco back in the 1860s. He was an entrepreneur for a while, but then he went off the deep end. He started telling everyone he was the emperor of the United States."

"Emperor?"

She nodded and smiled. "But here's the best part: The locals started going along with it. He'd walk down the street in a costume with a big sword and people would act deferential toward him, sort of playing along."

"Sounds very San Franciscan, somehow."

"Doesn't it?"

"And the notes?"

"He started issuing them himself. In his mind he had his own government, so why not his own money? And the merchants along North Beach went along with that, too, accepting the scrip as legal tender. A lot of people wound up using the notes locally."

"Do you think they're worth a lot?"

She shook her head. "I'm sure they're worth something, but it's only for their historical value. In a case like this, finding them behind a wall, they could be used to help date a house to the 1860s or 1870s, but you already knew that. Anyway, Wells Fargo Bank has a bunch of them in its San Francisco history section. You know the main office with the stagecoach?"

I nodded. I turned one of the notes over to show

the scrawl on the back. "What about this? Looks like a name."

"Does that say . . . Giametti?"

"He was one of the prospectors, right?"

"He was, yes. That's odd. . . ." She checked the others, all of which had a similar flourish on the back. "It's as though someone—can we assume Buchanan?—was treating them like checks, signing them over to Giametti."

"Giametti wasn't from here, either," I pointed out. "Would he have known what this was?"

Our eyes met.

"You think Buchanan tried to buy him off with Norton notes?" I asked.

"Maybe."

"Listen, could I leave this stuff with you? I made copies of it all, but it really belongs here. I'll double-check with the owner, but I assume he'll be happy to donate them to you."

The "hidden treasure" law stipulated that any items found in the walls belonged to the homeowners, no one else. There had been a handful of court cases involving contractors who had found large sums of money or other valuables hidden in walls and other nooks and crannies, and either secreted them away or laid claim to the booty through logic that essentially came down to "finders keepers."

It dawned on me that I hadn't yet mentioned what I had found to Matt. Even so, if it turned out to lead to anything valuable, I was clear on the concept that it belonged to him, not to me. And at the moment he had a few other things on his mind. I still had to break the news to him about his crate of goodies and his now less-than-grand piano.

"Sure. I'll keep them at my desk until he can officially sign them over."

"Thanks for everything, Trish," I said as I helped gather up the articles on the gem field scam. "As usual, you're a gold mine of information."

"I have to say," Trish said, "there's been a whole lot of interest lately in this house, and the gem field."

"Really, from whom?"

"We don't take names, but we had a police detective in here not long ago. And a couple of others as well."

"Could you describe them?"

"Is something going on?"

"I'm just curious."

"A blond woman came in a while back, said she was a neighbor. One fellow was big—chubby. And the other you probably know—he mentioned he was the architect on this house."

"Jason Wehr?"

"Could have been. As I say, we don't take names. Sorry."

Chapter Sixteen

I called Graham and told him what I had learned about the Norton notes, and about the map I had found in the binding of the journal.

"I've never heard of a Jumping Falls, or a Cheeseville for that matter."

"The Stanislaus River is still there," I said.

"Yes, but it was dammed up at one point. And it's gotta be a hundred miles long. No way to figure out the exact location of the map."

"It sounds like something up in that region, though, right?"

"Sure it does. That whole area is rife with gold mines and historic land claims, that sort of thing. But none of that matters much; the map's probably just a memento, as worthless as those Norton notes." I could hear someone in the background shouting to Graham, and his reply that he'd be right there. "Listen, I've got a meeting. But I'd like to take a look at that map. How about tonight?"

"I'd like to, but I have plans with Luz and another friend."

"Tomorrow, then? Wait—Thursday's a busy day for me, back-to-back meetings. It would have to be evening again. Will that work? Thursday dinner?"

"Sure," I said, wondering if this was a date. He was awfully businesslike about it, making sure to mention he was busy during the day, like it was yet another work assignment. *Let it go, Mel*, I thought to myself. If the man was still interested, surely he would have looked me up in the last couple of years? He still spoke with my father from time to time, and I'm certain that nosy old guy had let Graham in on the very public secret that I was available. Repeatedly, no doubt.

Trying to shake it off, I drove across the Golden Gate Bridge toward Matt's house.

Despite his rather high-flying reputation, Matt lived in a humble one-story home at the end of an unmarked cul-de-sac. I wasn't fooled. In Mill Valley, no matter how unassuming a home might seem, prices started at a cool million and climbed precipitously from there. Roads were rural, often unmarked, sometimes unpaved. There were no sidewalks. Eucalyptus and redwoods shaded the twisty lanes. You had to be from here to understand how well-off the laid-back denizens really were.

I parked by the side of the road. Eucalyptus and bay leaves, still damp from morning fog, gave off a heady aroma as I stepped on them.

As I approached Matt's garden gate, a large golden retriever next door ran along the fence, barking at me, making me think of Dog. I hoped he was enjoying his day with Dad and Stan. Given his carsickness, my plan to take him with me from site to site was on hold for the foreseeable future. Instead, I had snapped a photo of him with my digital camera. Maybe I'd find someone who recognized him.

On the other hand . . . now that we'd fed him, and he'd spent the night, and we'd kind of named him "Dog" . . . what were the chances I was going to be able to take him away from Dad, and the boys? Even Stan fawned over the mellow canine. Dad was going to take Dog to the vet today to get him checked out; Stan promised to check in with the humane society and the city pound, in case someone had reported him missing. The boys declared they'd wash him and comb out his hair tonight after school.

Matt was standing in the front doorway, wearing a sad smile of welcome. He had showered and shaved, but his eyes were still red-rimmed and exhausted.

I stepped inside and paused, taken aback. The house was a shambles.

"I've been cleaning up since I got home," said Matt. "Someone trashed the place."

"Vandals? Or did the police come through with a warrant?"

He shrugged. "What's the difference? It's the same mess."

"Could I take a look at the office?"

"That's the worst part."

He wasn't kidding. It was a disaster. Not much chance I would find the answer to my question about the permits in all of this. I picked up a random note that had been written by Kenneth. I wanted to check his handwriting against the forged signature on the permit.

I tried to shake off my feeling of gloom. I was here to cheer Matt up, after all.

His bird, Josephine, called out from the dining room. I went over to scratch her neck and feed her a cracker. Josephine cracked me up. She sang pitch-perfect renditions of Matt's greatest hits, mimicked kitchen appliances, and when she felt ignored she would burst out with a deafening version of the smoke alarm.

"Doesn't Josephine need a companion?" I asked. "I happen to have a dog looking for a home."

"A dog?"

I nodded and showed him the photo on my camera. "Ever seen him before? He was hanging around the job site."

"Which job site?"

"Yours. The Vallejo Street house."

"Oh," he said, shaking his head and leading the way to the kitchen. He had brewed a pot of peppermint tea and put out a plate of finger sandwiches.

"A few days in the slammer and already you're Martha Stewart?" I teased.

"She made it look so good. Actually, my neighbors keep bringing me food. Seems I've only enhanced my celebrity status."

"Probably the most exciting thing that's happened around here in ages."

Matt managed a weak smile. I reminded myself that not only had he endured the trauma of the arrest, but he had just lost a friend—violently.

"How are you holding up?" I asked.

"Truthfully?" He shrugged and shook his head, gazing into his steaming cup of tea as though hoping to read his future. "Could Dylan stay on with you a little longer? He's got spring break coming up, and I'm knackered, trying to figure this whole thing out."

"Of course. He asked me himself last night."

"He did? He's such a good kid. We had a long talk on the phone—I've missed him so much, I can't tell you. I'll pick the boys up from school this afternoon so we can spend some time together. I can bring them by your house later."

I nodded. "Matt, we need to talk about what happened. Do you have any clues, any ideas at all?"

"I've been doing nothing but racking my brain, Mel. Kenneth was . . . Well, there were people who didn't like him all that much, yourself included, obviously. But something like this . . ." He trailed off with a shake of his head.

"Did Kenneth have any family?"

"Not really. He was an only child, and his parents passed away a couple of years ago."

"He wasn't married, involved with anyone?"

"No. He was really well connected, you know, could talk just about anyone into anything when he turned on the charm. But . . . I guess you could say he developed a bit of a reputation as being not quite forthcoming."

"How do you mean?"

"I think people didn't really trust him. He was the life of the party, the guy you invited to openings. But he had a hard time getting close to people. In a way I think I was the closest person to him. Which is sort of sad—he was my business partner, but we weren't exactly brothers."

Silence reigned for a few moments while we sipped our tea, lost in thought. I wondered whether Kenneth's ghost was lingering, and whether he had heard what Matt had said . . . and what he would think of it.

"Maybe we should go about this systematically," I

said. "Do you have a list of the people who were at the party?"

"A list?"

"Some sort of invitation list?"

"Not everyone who was invited came."

"But we could go over the list together, talk about folks."

"I sent out an Evite."

"Let's call it up."

Matt powered up his Mac and typed in a few commands. A moment later we were on the Evite site and he had opened up the list of invitees.

"The police never asked to look at this list?"

He shook his head.

We ran through the names. First Matt told me who had been there and who hadn't shown up, to the best of his recollection. As he himself said, at a certain point his memory failed. And he had invited nearly seventy people, many of whom had brought dates. Tracking down everyone would be an overwhelming task.

I recognized a few of the invited guests: Celia and Vincent Hutchins from next door; the other neighbor I had met, Meredith Montgomery; Jason Wehr, the architect; a few society names; even the mayor of San Francisco.

"Did the mayor show up?" I asked. It was very hard to picture our slick, perfectly attired mayor brandishing a Sawzall.

"Nah. But his cousin was there—Rory Abrams."

"That name sounds familiar."

"He brought the food. Rory opened a new restaurant in North Beach last month. It's kind of a big deal— everyone who's anyone wants to be seen there."

Which would explain why I couldn't quite place him. I wasn't exactly up on the places to go to "be seen."

"Actually, now that I think about it—Rory was a pretty good friend of Kenneth's."

"I don't see Philip Singh on this list anywhere."

"Who's Philip Singh?"

"He came by the house the other day when I was there. He said he was supposed to buy the place."

"Buy it? You mean after the remodel?"

"I'm not sure. . . . I wasn't really thinking clearly enough to ask him a lot of details. I take it you've never heard of him?"

He shook his head. "I don't know anything about that. Kenneth—"

"I know, I know. Kenneth took care of all of that." Or took care of none of it, as the case may be.

"It might explain one thing, though."

"What's that?"

"When I tried to use the house as collateral to make bail, they wouldn't grant it. Said there was a lien against it. Would that be because someone's buying it? But that doesn't make any sense—we just started the remodel."

"You tried to use the house for bail?"

He nodded. "I needed a big chunk of money. The house is my biggest asset."

"How *did* you make bail?" I asked, thinking of him, but also of myself. I had been sloppy, not even bothering to get Matt's name on the contracts before starting the job. Was I jumping the gun? Would Matt be able to pay me? Would I be able to pay my workers?

"Several of my friends stepped in to cover it," Matt said. "A lot of them are pretty well-off, to say the least."

"Well, that's lucky."

"The thing I feel weird about is that a bunch of fans have been sending me stuff as well. When I got home I found a big sack of mail from all sorts of people, sending in their support, five-dollar bills. . . . I feel like such a fraud."

"They like you, Matt. They want to help."

"They don't even know me."

I hated to hear him sound so defeated. I reached out and took his cold hand. "You're a good person, Matt. And your music has meant a lot to people through the years, myself included. Don't disparage that. You'll get through this; you'll see."

"How could anyone think I actually killed Kenneth?"

"I guess we'll have to convince them otherwise," I said.

I couldn't just sit here and watch Matt so miserable and alone. Since the police didn't seem to be doing their job, the least I could do was poke around a little. I'd gotten that nurse at the hospital to talk to me easily enough.

"Matt, the emergency room nurse, the one who heard Kenneth talk about you. She said he said, 'goddamned Matt's fault.' Any idea what he was referring to?"

Matt shook his head. "We fought some over the house design, but it wasn't anything serious. I can't think what he meant."

"And you were asleep on the couch the whole time?"

He let out a breath in exasperation. "Yes, can you believe it? What a time to black out. I swear to God I'll never drink again."

"That's probably not a bad idea. But if you'd been conscious that morning, you might be dead as well. Remember that." It dawned on me that I, too, might have just missed a murderer. Kenneth couldn't have been hurt too long before I arrived. I looked back at the list and pondered for a moment. "Okay, about Zach-the-photographer—do you trust him?"

"Of course."

"How well do you know him?"

"Kenneth hired him."

"So not well, then."

"I just met him the night of the party."

"Then you can't possibly know whether to trust him or not, right?"

He looked bemused.

"Matt, something terrible went on in that house, and you're getting blamed for it. Whether you like to or not, you're going to have to find it in your heart to be suspicious of the people around you."

"I guess you're right. I just hate to think of anyone actually setting out to do something like that."

"So do I. But someone did. Back to Zach. He was in the house yesterday, along with somebody else. He said he found the door open and that there were some kids playing around, but it seemed strange."

Matt just nodded. "I'm going to get myself together, get over to the remodel, and help out. Just give me a day or two—how about I start on Friday? After lunch?"

"Sure, Matt, that would be great. But listen, tell me what you know about Zach. He was at the party that night." I urged him to focus. "Do you think he saw anything?"

"He left in the early morning sometime. The party was still going strong. But I do remember Kenneth was fighting with Vincent Hutchins from next door."

"Fighting?"

"Arguing. Nothing violent."

"About what?"

"I guess Vincent thought we should have sold the house to his mom or something. And I remember this part: Kenneth was being kind of sarcastic, and thanked Vincent for lowering the cost of the house. Which didn't really make any sense. Anyway, I tried to stay out of it."

"You didn't ask him what he meant by that?"

Matt shook his head. "I didn't really get involved in any of the monetary aspects. I just worked on design with Jason. He's amazing. He's won the AIA Design Award for Excellence in Architecture *twice*."

"Yeah, you told me that already."

"Now that I think about it, I guess Jason was sort of, like, friends with Kenneth, too." He picked up a rather anemic-looking finger sandwich and took a bite. "It makes me feel better to think of Kenneth having friends. Last fall the three of us went on a ski trip together, up to Bear Valley. There was a big storm, so we got stuck in a small town at the base of the mountains, called Murphys. Cute place. There was some sort of rock-hound convention in town, so we all had to share a single hotel room—you should have seen the look on Kenneth's face!" He laughed.

I smiled. It was good to see Matt laugh again.

Then he shook his head and the smile fell away. "I guess, now that I think about it, maybe he was just homophobic. Seemed funny at the time."

"Jason mentioned that he was donating his time as part of his 'investment' in this project. He said you didn't have a traditional bank mortgage. Who were the other investors?"

"I don't think . . . They're not people who want their names bandied about."

"I'm not going to 'bandy about' anything. I'm just trying to figure out what's going on."

"I don't even know all of them. There was Rory Abrams, the restaurateur. And there was someone else, but Kenneth never told me his name."

"Why not?"

"Dunno. I probably never asked. Didn't seem important at the time."

I drove away, silently fuming. I cared for Matt as a friend, but he frustrated the hell out of me. With sudden clarity I remembered that I had walked off the kitchen job he and Kenneth and I were all working on, way back when, not only because of Kenneth's obnoxiousness but also because Matt's waffling was driving me insane.

I pulled into the parking lot of Mill Valley's small shopping area, watching self-consciously underdressed Marin folk carry out Save the Earth canvas bags filled with expensive artisan cheeses, free-range organic paté, and locally baked sourdough baguettes while I returned the latest round of work-related calls. Raul had phoned twice: There was a problem with the payroll checks, and the faux finishers at the Zaben house wanted me to check on their progress before they went any further. I talked to Stan and asked him to follow up with our payroll service, then spoke to Raul and promised to stop by this afternoon.

Then my thoughts turned back to the mystery at hand.

Presumably someone knew that Nico had removed items from Matt's house, someone with enough muscle to shake the poor man down for information. They wanted something, badly. If they hadn't found it in the storage locker, or hidden in the piano, could it be in the package that I just left at the historical society? Or were the historical documents just what they seemed: a fascinating glimpse into another time, essentially worthless in any monetary sense?

And why would a lien have been levied against the house? A goods-and-services lien was the ultimate weapon for contractors to use if a homeowner did not make good on payments; I had never had to file a lien against a client, but the threat was always in my arsenal—and included in every job contract. But as far as I could tell, the only official contractor involved in Matt's Vallejo Street house was me. Who else might have done it?

A Realtor might know. And the right Realtor might have some pertinent information about the netherworld as well.

I fished the business card Luz had given me out of my bag.

Brittany Humm sounded excited to hear from me— Luz had sent her an e-mail message about my situation— and suggested we meet for a quick late lunch at the Artisan Bistro in Lafayette. Suddenly starving—those finger sandwiches didn't quite do the job—I agreed. She gave me directions.

The area known as the East Bay changes radically once a person goes through a tunnel or over the mountains. The suburban towns out here seemed to meld together. I wasn't the only one who thought so: Lafayette, Moraga, and Orinda were so similar they were referred to collectively as "Lamorinda." But things got worse as one went on: Walnut Creek, Alamo, Danville . . . they evoked a well-heeled but mind-numbing, soul-crushing suburbanism that set my teeth on edge. Personally, I'd rather live in a trailer park. Of course, the people who lived in these areas pretty much equated living in Oakland—especially the section of Oakland where I lived—with residence in the worst sort of trashy trailer park, so I guessed we were even on that score. I tried my best to invoke my mother's nonjudgmental motto: "To each their own."

Luckily for me, since Turner Construction specialized in historic homes, we rarely worked over here.

The restaurant had been chosen for its cozy, quiet setting; on the outside it looked like a standard tract home, but on the inside it was charming. I found Brittany Humm waiting for me at a table on the garden patio. It was a sunny late-winter day, cool but perfect for sitting outside with the added warmth of standing gas heaters.

I disliked the Realtor on sight: She was young, thin, blond, pretty, well-dressed, and showing off a giant diamond on her left hand. Brittany was like my high school nightmare come to vivid, smiling life.

Why am I wasting my time on this sort of thing when I have work to do? I thought, suddenly frustrated with myself for having come all the way out here to meet with someone who specialized in ghostly real estate. I mentally calculated how quickly I could leave.

As soon as I sat down and ordered coffee, Brittany Humm smiled and leaned toward me over the table, as though I were going to show her baby pictures.

"Luz tells me you've seen a *ghost*."

I glanced around to be sure no one was listening in. I could feel my cheeks burn. "I believe so, yes."

"How exciting!"

"You think?"

"Of course! I've never had the pleasure. It's a real honor."

"It is?"

She sat back and studied me, the smile never leaving her face. "You're worried you're crazy, right?"

"A little."

"I can assure you, you're not. This sort of thing happens more often than you know, but most people who are privileged enough to be conduits are too embarrassed to admit it. It's sad, really. They go through their whole lives denying their special gifts."

The waiter arrived. I felt in need of grease. Since there was no Reuben sandwich on the menu, I ordered a croque monsieur with French fries. Brittany asked for a marinated beet salad and another Diet Coke. No wonder she was thin.

I gave her the rundown of the incident at the house, and then of Kenneth's appearances.

"Here's something I don't get," I said. "Kenneth followed me home—in fact, he turns up all sorts of places. Aren't ghosts supposed to . . . you know . . . stay attached to their real estate?"

"He wasn't actually killed on the premises, though, right? You said he died at the hospital. Did you two have a serious kind of interaction beforehand?"

"He was injured," I said, trying not to think of the intimacy I felt in the moments when Kenneth lay in my arms. "I held him until the ambulance came."

"Gravely injured, I'm guessing."

I nodded.

"That's probably enough to explain it right there. He's latched onto you instead of a building per se. A lot of people who die in hospitals seem to show up back in their homes, since that's where they're most attached. I think hospitals are too cold and clinical to hold all the ghosts of the people who've passed there."

That made sense. I guessed.

"So, assuming he's real, how do I get rid of him? Should I haul out my old Ouija board? Conduct a séance or something?" Maybe I should ask Celia Hutchins for help.

"I'm not sure it's that easy. What has he asked of you?"

"Nothing specific, really. He's pretty unclear. He seems confused."

"Let me ask you something: Have you ever had any other similar experiences, with anyone other than Kenneth?"

I hesitated, sipping my coffee. Finally I decided on honesty. "Only with my mother. She passed a couple of years ago."

"Were you close to her?"

"I was a pretty rebellious teenager, but in the last few years . . . yes. We had grown very close." I was the middle sister, the one who never quite toed the line. Maybe that was why our recent closeness seemed so raw, so poignant to lose.

"And you've seen her?"

"Sort of. Only once, really. But I . . . I feel her from time to time. Do you think it's the same thing?"

"Hard to say. This isn't an exact science."

"I didn't think it was *any* sort of science, actually," I muttered as the waiter brought our food and set it in front of us. In the way of so many trendy new restaurants, the French fries were served with aioli on the side rather than ketchup. I took a big greasy bite of my sandwich.

Only then did it dawn on me that I had just insulted Brittany.

"I'm sorry," I said around the food in my mouth, my cheeks burning. "That was rude."

Brittany tilted her head and studied me, but she did not look offended as much as perplexed.

"I'm always intrigued by people who ask me for advice about the beyond with one breath, then disdain it with the next."

"You're absolutely right. I apologize. I've been … cranky lately." I munched on a French fry. "Actually, according to my friends and family, I've been cranky for the last couple of years."

She reached across the table and patted my hand. Her ring glittered in the sunshine.

"Difficult divorce?"

"I thought you said you weren't psychic."

"I'm not. But it's written all over you—and I should know. I've been through two myself."

"Two? You hardly look old enough to drink."

"I started early." She smiled. "My advice is to move on, live your life."

"I tried to escape to Paris."

"What happened to that plan?"

What happened? My mother died. My father fell apart. The business tanked. I couldn't abandon Caleb.

I shrugged. "You know what they say about best-laid plans."

She smiled again, the sympathy in her eyes shining through.

So much for snap judgments. I decided I liked Brittany Humm, lovely thin blonde or not.

"Did anything happen around your mother's death that was ... odd?" Brittany continued. "Besides just seeing her afterward, I mean. Something more recent? Something that might have had to do with transferring power?"

I blew on my coffee. Tiny ripples emanated out toward the ceramic walls of the mug, making me think of the water on Ralston Pond, where my sisters and I had sprinkled my mother's cremated remains just a couple of weeks ago. My father had been too despondent to join us, instead going hunting with Stan and a few other friends; it was the only time I had ever known him to come back from a hunting trip empty-handed, making me think they went more to drink beer in the woods than to shoot anything.

I remembered the day was cool and still; even the frogs and birds seemed hushed. Fearing that we would feel too emotional to speak at the actual moment, my sisters, Charlotte and Daphne, and I had each written a private letter to Mom. We stood out at the end of the dock at dusk and burned the papers on top of Mom's ashes, saying our silent, final, farewells.

As we stood there, a sudden gust of wind arose out of nowhere, blowing the embers and ashes directly up into the air, and right at me. They didn't burn my skin, but they enveloped me for just a moment. Neither of my sisters; me, alone. After that, the wind died down immediately and the stillness returned.

So, yes, I guess you could say something odd happened.

Chapter Seventeen

"What do you mean by 'transferring' power?" I asked.

"Sometimes, when there's a fairly sudden increase in phenomena such as you've described, it can be related to the passing of a loved one who had similar abilities."

Had my mother had such abilities? If so, she kept them secret. On the other hand, she often seemed to know things she had no way of knowing . . . but I always attributed that to the typical kind of maternal ESP familiar to offspring across all cultures. Mothers always had a sixth sense, didn't they?

"Gorgeous ring," I said in a blatant attempt to change the subject.

"Thank you. To tell you the truth, it seems a bit over-the-top for me. Don't get me wrong—I love diamonds . . . but it's just so huge! My soon-to-be father-in-law is in the business."

"You wouldn't happen to know—were diamonds ever mined in California?"

"I thought we were all about the gold."

"Yeah, that's what I thought, too," I said. "Okay, enough about ghosts. Could I ask you a couple of Realtor questions?"

"Of course."

"Would you consider it legitimate for a group of investors to put money into a house with the intent to remodel and flip it, without using a traditional bank mortgage at all?"

"Sure, if they had the cash at hand. It's not that common in the Bay Area because prices are so high, but in the old days there were people who bought homes with cash, just like you might a car."

I nodded. "How about liens? I know contractors can place liens against homes, but what other kind might there be?"

"There are judgment liens—where a creditor seeks a court order—and tax liens, of course. As you know, the lien against the Vallejo Street house is the standard contractor's lien for goods and services."

"I think we should assume I don't know anything. Who placed the lien against the house?"

Brittany gave me a quizzical look, playing with her salad. "According to the search I ran on the house, you yourself placed a lien against it, for goods and services."

"*I* did?"

"Well, Turner Construction did."

"*I'm* Turner Construction."

"I know that. That's why I assumed you placed the lien."

Not again. Someone had forged my name on documents not once, but twice? "But a lien doesn't mean the owners couldn't sell the house, right?" I asked, seeking clarification.

"Not at all. It just means that if they sell, they have to pay the lien off. But it usually slows things down with a sale, because you have to get assurances that the seller will actually pay those liens. Also, you usually can't get a mortgage for a house with liens against it. Unpaid liens pass on to the new owner of the house. They make things messy, and buyers don't like messy. But that didn't seem to stop the buyer for this house."

"What buyer?"

"According to the search, the house was about to be sold. Didn't you know?"

"Let me guess: to one Philip Singh?"

"That's right. I assumed you knew."

"What disturbs me is that Matt didn't seem to know, and neither did at least one of the investors. The buyer came looking for Kenneth, though, the day after he died."

"Really."

"What could explain something like that?"

"Sounds to me like Kenneth Kostow was selling the house out from under the other investors."

"Selling it?"

"He bought the property with other people's money, no bank involved. Singh pays him for the house, and Kenneth keeps all the cash. He could have made millions off a deal like that, even if the house was in bad condition."

"Could he pull that off without Matt and the others knowing?"

"If you're willing to forge documents, maybe pay off a few people, it would be easy enough."

I sat back, the croque monsieur roiling in my stomach.

"Listen," Brittany continued, "I've only been in real estate for six years, but I've seen one case of renters who impersonated the owners and sold a house, and I know of another where someone stole an identity, bought a house with that person's credit, then flipped it and disappeared with the profit. The worst, though, was a Realtor who acted as his own title company. He managed to sell the same house to three different people on the same day."

"And here I thought real estate might be boring."

Brittany laughed and dug into her salad again.

"One more thing," I said. "I was told the asking price on the Vallejo Street house was lower than normal because the owner had to disclose that the house was known for being haunted."

Brittany smiled. "Exciting, isn't it?"

"Could you tell me how that works? I mean, most people don't really believe in this stuff, do they? How is it a law?"

"There was a court case back east. A couple bought a house that was infamous locally for being haunted, but since they were from out of town they had never heard the rumors. They went to court, contending that their potential resale value was affected by the stories of the haunting. The judge agreed and released them from the contract, setting a precedent that we all now follow."

"So, since the Vallejo street house was supposedly haunted, the price was lowered."

"Yes. But the timing on that was strange," Brittany added. "The house wasn't widely known for being haunted—I didn't have it listed on my Web site, for instance. But right before Gerald Buchanan sold it, there were a flurry of posts about Walter Buchanan's tragic suicide, and then the haunting, almost as if someone was *trying* to lower the price by stoking the rumors."

"Any idea who posted the stories?"

"That's strange, too. It's one of their neighbors, someone who's actually somewhat well-known in our circles for being a medium."

"Celia Hutchins?"

"No, Meredith Montgomery. Do you happen to know her?"

"I met her very briefly just the other day."

"That's perfect, then! Talk to her—I'm sure she could tell you about it. It was just odd to see her online because as far as I can tell, she doesn't really do the Internet thing. A lot of mediums are dead set against it . . . so to speak. They don't trust the electronics involved. But I'll bet she'd be excited to hear about your sight!"

"My sight?"

"You know, the third eye. The ability to see what most of us can't. It really is a privilege, you know." She fiddled with her ring again. It sparkled, dazzling, in the sunshine. "There's only one thing . . ."

"What's that?"

"Suicidal ghosts . . . they tend to be angry, self-destructive. Sometimes they're just sad, but sometimes . . . they can be malevolent."

"Malevolent as in harming someone in the house?"

"Maybe."

"Could a so-called malevolent ghost have had something to do with what happened to Kenneth Kostow?"

"I wouldn't put it past a vengeful spirit. You really should ask Meredith Montgomery about it."

*   *   *

I was so deep in thought as I walked out to my car that it took a moment for it to sink in that the passenger window had been smashed.

Inside was a mess. My toolbox, random newspapers, old coffee cups, the papers in the glove compartment—everything had been tossed, rifled through.

The back of my neck tingled as I cast my eyes around the parking lot and street. I couldn't see anyone . . . but it gave me the creeps to think that someone might have been tracking me. On the other hand, what did I know? Maybe it was a random crime. I was out in the wilds of the suburbs, after all. This wasn't my turf. Maybe this sort of thing happened all the time in Lafayette.

Using an old rag, I brushed broken glass pebbles off the seats, climbed in, locked the doors, and drove to a crowded shopping plaza. I felt the need to have people around. I called Trish at the historical society, but she assured me that no one had been in asking after me or anything I'd left. She promised to lock up the papers in the restricted area.

Then I talked to Dad. He was okay and on guard, and reported nothing amiss. He handed the phone to Stan, who told me that as far as he knew there had been nothing stolen from the office, no evidence of anyone rifling through Turner Construction paperwork at any point. Whoever had filed a construction permit for Matt's house had access to our information so they could fill out the necessary forms, so it was probably someone I'd worked with before.

I looked through the papers in my satchel until I came upon the copy of the forged work permit I had made yesterday while I was at city hall. I'm no handwriting expert, but upon comparing it to the scrawled document I picked up in Matt's home office, I was pretty certain they had been penned by the same hand. Kenneth's hand.

Though it was early for rush hour traffic, there was still a backup of cars sitting at the eastern entrance to the Caldecott Tunnel, the result of four lanes funneling down to two in order to pass through the single bore. There were three bores in the mountain, and the middle one switched directions during the day to accommodate the heaviest traffic flow. Some poor transit worker had to run out and put bright orange stakes in the road at least twice a day to switch the designated direction. Vaguely I wondered how the workers accomplished it without being sideswiped by goal-oriented, belligerent Bay Area drivers.

My broken passenger-side window let in exhaust mixed with the scent of the damp, grassy hills. I caught myself checking the rearview mirror obsessively, trying to figure out if someone was following me.

I used the delay to contemplate. Who had placed the lien on the house, and why? It couldn't have been Kenneth—assuming he was trying to sell the house and abscond with the money, it wouldn't have made any sense. He might have forged the permit, but the lien . . . ?

Someone must have found out about the potential sale and tried to stop it, or at least slow it down.

As I finally made my way through the tunnel, I realized I had just spent an hour talking about ghosts as though they were as real as Brittany, or Matt, or I. Maybe Graham was right: I should take a few days off, go out and breathe some clean mountain air, and stay out of the way of the homicide investigation . . . or what there was of one.

That was what really bothered me. No matter where I went or who I talked to, I didn't seem to be bumping into Inspector Lehner—or any other police personnel for that matter. Why was I more obsessed with this case than professional law enforcement was?

In large part, I supposed, because the victim's ghost kept following me around.

What next? Work, of course. There's always work. There is no real "end" in construction—you complete the main components, then start the long trek to the finish as you whittle the punch list down. Eventually everyone gets tired and so eager to move in that you're done—except you aren't. Not really. For months, sometimes years, the clients call: *The garage door sticks. I want to change out the faucet I special-ordered from Italy. There's a new crack in the garden wall. I'm not sure about the paint color in my daughter's room.*

And it's essential to keep those contractor-client relationships healthy and happy. Despite spending hundreds of thousands of dollars to redo their homes, people still tend to relocate, and often. Luz's Realtor brother once told me that the average American family moves every five years. I would wager that statistic is even higher amongst the very wealthy.

So there's *never* nothing to do.

Meanwhile, I had to keep ahead of the game, making sure there would be work for my employees a week, a month, a year down the line. I subcontracted to people with their own businesses, of course, but Turner Construction kept seven full-time workers, not including me and Stan. They did odd jobs, everything from project management to cleanup to demo to running errands and washing windows. They needed paychecks, and as with many small businesses, there were months when we owners went without our own salary in order to cover payroll. Of course, a happy workforce, in general, led to a profit at the end of the day. I was proud of the fact that other than sporadic temporary shortfalls, Turner Construction operated in the black.

Back in San Francisco I stopped to check on the progress at Matt's house. All was going well, and quickly. The men had not discovered anything unusual in the walls. Spike gave me the happy news that his uncle had been released from the hospital and planned on coming back to work soon.

Before leaving, I found a piece of plastic sheeting and duct tape and did my best to create a temporary passenger-side window in my car. Then I screwed up my courage and stopped by Meredith Montgomery's graceful, well-tended Victorian. There was a long wait after I rang the bell; I was just about to leave when the door opened.

"Oh," Meredith said, her lipsticked mouth making a perfect ring, her big eyes wide with surprise. "I was afraid you'd come by."

"I'm sorry. . . . Is this a bad time?"

"No, no, nothing like that. Come on in. Would you like a drink? Or tea?"

"That would be lovely, if you have a few minutes to talk."

I followed her into the well-appointed kitchen, ringed by cherry cabinets and black granite. She put the kettle on and prepared a china teapot with Earl Grey. I couldn't remember the last time I had been invited for tea twice in one day. Felt downright civilized.

"You said you were expecting me?" I asked.

"Oh, yes. The cards told me. I was hoping they were wrong. But they never are. Never are." A little frown marred her forehead as she fluttered from one cabinet to the next, laying out pastry-shop cookies on a pretty porcelain platter painted with English roses. She then filled a small crystal bowl with picture-perfect deep red strawberries.

I was impressed. Clearly Meredith was the sort of hostess who had such things at hand just in case people stopped by out of the blue. Then again, she had her early-warning device in the guise of tarot cards.

Maybe I should have tried that. My ex-husband always wanted me to be that sort of hostess; I tried for a while, hoping to please him, but I was never much good at it. I was too caught up in my own work or research to care that much about such things. My idea of a dinner party was a group enchilada-rolling event; Daniel would have preferred pheasant under glass. The wonder was that we stayed together as long as we did, or that we had gotten together in the first place. That was what I got for trying to be somebody I wasn't.

Once the kettle boiled, Meredith poured the hot water into the teapot, loaded everything onto an etched silver tray, and led the way to a charming breakfast nook with windows that looked out to the Palace of Fine Arts, the Golden Gate Bridge, and the mouth of the bay.

"I wanted to ask you about your club. About the ... séances."

"I know, dear. I know." Meredith shook her head and poured tea for us both.

"Have you ever made contact with anything, or anyone, or just ... anything?"

"Well, that all depends on what you define as 'contact.' We've had some interesting sessions, especially with the Ouija board. But frankly not as much as one might expect, given the history of the house."

"What kind of history?"

"I believe there is an angry spirit there. I believe he even went after Celia's husband. "

"Would this be the ghost of Walter Buchanan?"

"Oh, no, dear. Someone else entirely."

"And you think that Celia and her husband were haunted by this . . . this ghost?"

She nodded. "Celia tried her best, you know. She thought she could block the access in the basement with bricks. But it doesn't work that way. She even bricked over . . . bones."

"Bones?"

"Don't ask," she said, a hand fluttering up to her cheek again. "Must have been an animal of some sort. Poor thing must have wandered in somehow, got stuck. Like that dog you found not long ago."

"The brown dog?"

"I saw you take him with you. That was kind."

"When did Celia find these bones, and brick things over?" Just the thought made me cringe. Did no one read Poe anymore? These things never ended well.

"About six months ago."

Vincent had told me his parents bricked over the access to the neighboring house decades ago, when he was a child. I wondered which one of them was lying.

"She and Gerald had a terrible row," Meredith continued. "He wasn't invited back into the circle after that. He said our séances had ratcheted things up, tried to take the bricks down with his bare hands. He said the ghosts were angry."

"You're saying that Gerald Buchanan sometimes joined you in the séances? I thought he was a recluse."

"He was, dear. He was. But I believe he was almost in love with Celia, at least for a while. And he was petrified; he claimed his great-grandfather's suicide was brought on by a ghost, and that the family's been under a curse ever since. Funny, though, I don't think he's been happy since leaving the house. Sometimes they need one another, you know, the living and the dead."

"I thought Gerald Buchanan had passed away," I said.

"Oh, no, he's living in Oakland Hills."

"Right here in Oakland?"

"At an assisted-living facility. He tells me he can see the city from his bedroom. We talk on the phone from time to time."

"Could I get his address from you? I'd love to ask him a few questions about the house."

"Just don't mention the haunting," Meredith said as she stood and crossed over to an antique rolltop desk. She flipped through a small address book and jotted the information down on a piece of paper. "He doesn't really like visitors, but I think it's good for him to have company."

"Thank you," I said as she handed me the address and returned to sit at the table. "Meredith, did you post about the haunting on the Internet?"

"Of *course* not. I don't do that."

"Someone did, and they used your name."

"I don't know anything about that." She waved her hand, dismissing the notion. I noticed she wore two large diamond rings on her left hand. I had gems on the brain lately.

"Back to the bones in Celia's basement—are you sure

they belonged to an animal? Could they have been . . . human?"

"Of course not."

"Did Celia dig them up, report them to anyone?"

"Oh, no. She said they were at rest and left them where they were. They were mostly on Gerald's side, anyway."

"Did you have any other guests come to these séances?"

"Oh, we have a few like minds—no one you'd know. Except for Vincent, of course. Oh, and Jason."

"Jason?"

"Jason Wehr, the architect."

"Jason Wehr joined you in the séances?"

"Only once or twice. Celia was trying to ask about the original layout of Gerald's house. She planned to reunite the two homes, bring them back to their twin status."

I rubbed my temples. I was developing a headache.

"So, Gerald Buchanan didn't think the ghost in the house was Walter, his great-grandfather who committed suicide? He thought it was someone else?"

"Oh, yes. I told him it wasn't the suicide at all. It was the murder that was the problem."

"What murder?"

"If I knew that, we could put the matter to rest, couldn't we?" Meredith said, as though I'd asked her to predict the upcoming lottery numbers. "Something happened years ago, something that haunted Walter Buchanan and every one of his descendants in that house. I've tried everything I can think of, but the spirits won't talk to me."

Maybe that was where I came in.

Chapter Eighteen

"Rotten piece of undead *scum*," I said.

Kenneth flickered for a moment before coming back to stride alongside me with a rolling, almost perfectly smooth gait as I hurried toward my car.

"What did *I* do?" he whined.

"Were you trying to sell the house out from under Matt? And the investors?"

"I swear I don't remember," he said, hands—one hand, actually—up in front of him as though to ward off attack.

I let out an exasperated snort.

"*That's* probably what got you killed," I mumbled. "It probably had nothing at all to do with an ancient treasure map."

"I've been thinking a lot," Kenneth said, keeping up with me easily. "I hate to admit it, but that sounds like something I would have done. I seem to have been rather materialistic, if I do say so myself."

"You think?"

"I'm ... I'm feeling really crappy about the way things went. I think I wasted my life. And now it's too late."

There was genuine regret in his voice. I let out a weary sigh. It was hard to stay angry with a remorseful ghost.

"I don't suppose you could make up for any of that wasted life by finding some way to help with the current situation?" I asked as I climbed into the car.

Kenneth appeared in the passenger seat, looking askance at my broken window.

"If I were you, I'd go talk to that photographer," he said.

It was the logical next step: Take a look at the photos from the party. But I felt wary. I wasn't sure about this photographer guy, and Graham's warning rang in my ears.

Someone had gone after the crate at the storage yard, and then the piano at my house, and then must have followed me and searched my car. How did I know Zach wasn't involved? He didn't *seem* involved, but could I trust my assessment of men's character these days?

"You think I can trust this guy?" I asked the ghost.

"Oh, I'm sure of it. Tell you what, I'll be there, just in case."

"In case of what?"

"You know, if you need me."

"I thought you couldn't do anything ... material."

"I'm learning. I scared you yesterday, didn't I? I think I could step in. Besides, really, I don't think it's a problem."

I checked my watch. It was after four and I was supposed to meet Luz and our friend Stephen for dinner.

And before that, I needed to drop by the St. Francis Wood job site and check on the progress with the landscapers and the faux finishers.

I rummaged in the bottom of my satchel, but couldn't find the card Zach had given me yesterday. But I write a semiannual feature for the *San Francisco Chronicle* about my favorite local remodel, so I know a few folks at the Home and Leisure section, including one very indiscreet woman in personnel: Nancy Jorgenson.

Armed with only the name "Zachary something," it took me all of two minutes to find the photographer's phone number and to get a quick character reference from Nancy, who told me Zach was "a real doll, I've known him since he was a boy." That was no hedge against subsequent criminality, I guessed, but I was going to take it for what it was worth.

I called. Zach told me he would love to get together, but that he was on a shoot at the moment. We agreed to meet tomorrow at one at his place.

"I'll see him tomorrow," I said to Kenneth as I put away the phone.

Disappointment rolled off him in waves.

"Don't do that," I said.

"What?"

"That . . . sadness thing. It's creepy."

"What sadness thing?"

"Whatever it is you do to make me feel your misery."

"I'm thinking you're projecting here," Kenneth said. "I don't know what you're talking about."

And just like that, he disappeared.

Was this the secret? All I had to do was insult the man—the *ghost*—and he'd leave me alone?

Well, I thought, *that should be easy enough.*

But somehow I knew it wasn't going to be quite that simple.

Absinthe is a trendy, fabulous restaurant in the Hayes Valley neighborhood of San Francisco, with a French art nouveau style and a totally rocking chef, a woman with a butch blond haircut and tattoos on her arms who had recently enhanced her celebrity status by taking part in a televised chef contest. Or so my friends who watched TV told me.

Luz, Stephen, and I sat in our favorite horseshoe-shaped booth, near the bar, right up front in the thick of things.

"That darling waiter is totally flirting with you," Luz leaned over to Stephen and whispered.

He whirled around, looking back at us in disappointment when he realized Luz was talking about a man.

"Why does everyone think I'm gay?" Stephen asked with a theatrical sigh.

"Maybe it's because all your best friends are women," I said.

"And you're a clothing designer," Luz added.

"And your name's Stephen," I said.

"A lot of straight men are named Stephen," he protested.

"That's true, but then they go by Steve," Luz said.

He laughed. "I suppose you're right."

Stephen was tall and thin, pale, with dark, dramatic features. He could easily have played the part of some eighteenth-century romantic poet dying of consumption. Like Luz, Stephen was an old friend from my academic days. He had been a student of political science until he realized that his doctoral dissertation bored not only his family, friends, and academic mentors but even himself. In an act of bravery that some people called foolish, he chucked the scholarships and grants he had cobbled together and set off to pursue his real love: designing clothes and costumes. He had recently been rejected for an internship with the San Francisco Opera and was trying to figure out his next move, career-wise. For the moment he was working as a barista at Starbucks.

Luz and I were taking him out to dinner to cheer him up. Luz probably had some sort of ulterior motive that involved getting me out of my own head, as well. It didn't much matter to me at the moment—I was on my second hot and dirty martini and felt quite content.

"Mel's had quite the active love life of late," Luz announced.

Stephen turned to me in anticipation.

"That's a bit of a stretch. I said that I'd been asked out lately."

"By whom?"

"Vincent Hutchins. He lives next door to Matt Addax's house on Vallejo."

"Must be loaded, in that neighborhood. Is he a hottie?" asked Stephen, helping himself to a plate of multicolored olives.

"He is, actually," I said. "You two would make a cute couple."

"Very funny."

I laughed. "But there's something a little odd about him."

"You mean the part where he still lives with his mommy?" asked Luz.

"Yes, though I live with my daddy, so I can't really throw stones," I said. "But he's lied to me a couple of times, and I can't figure out why. And something's been nagging at me: Why would Celia Hutchins want someone like me to go out with her son?"

"Because you're a catch," Stephen jumped in with the unquestioning loyalty of a true friend.

"You're smart, and wicked funny, and gorgeous," added Luz without missing a beat.

"And pretty darned interesting," said Stephen.

"Thanks, guys, I appreciate the ego boost. Seriously, though—no false modesty here, but if Celia wanted grandchildren, wouldn't she go after a younger woman, or a more conciliatory woman?"

"You *are* awfully stubborn," Luz said, motioning to the waiter to bring her another lemon drop.

"Look who's talking," I said with a smile. "Do you think Celia might want Vincent to spend time with me for other reasons? Something to do with getting her hands on Matt's house? Or something hidden *in* the house, maybe?"

"Like what?" Stephen asked. I realized I hadn't told my friends about my dubious discovery in the walls. Best not to involve them.

"Never mind," I said, sipping my martini. "She was probably just bowled over by my kick-ass wardrobe."

Stephen beamed.

"The police officer worries me," said Luz. "You said there was something weird about him, too, right? A rogue cop could be seriously bad news."

"I never said he was a bad cop. He just seems a bit . . . uninterested in the crime. I don't suppose your sister knows anything . . . ?" Luz's sister Carmen was a beat cop. I doubted they ran in the same circles as homicide inspectors.

"I actually mentioned it to her already, but she doesn't really know him," Luz said. "She said she heard he was a drinker, but that could apply to half the police force."

"As it is, Lehner hasn't done anything to me. He doesn't seem to have done anything to anybody, other than bring Matt up on charges. But even then . . . frankly, he hasn't been talking to the obvious witnesses, anything like that. And Graham said that the cops seemed to want him to declare it an accident. Now that I think about it, maybe in his own strange way, Lehner's trying to help Matt. I just don't know."

"What are you even *talking* about?" Stephen said with a puzzled smile. "You're sounding a little crazy, Mel, I gotta tell ya. Luz, you were right to call me. She definitely needs to be spending more time with sane people like us."

"Yeah, I know." I smiled. "You guys might need to step in soon and lock me away."

"Let's talk about something else," Luz said. "Mel, I was thinking, maybe we all should flip a house together. You, me, and Stephen."

"Because you're suddenly independently wealthy?" I asked.

"You know I've been doing research for my new place. And I've been watching a lot of those shows—it doesn't look that hard, especially with your talents."

My friends and family are quick to point out that I harbor Luddite tendencies. One of them is that I refuse to watch cable. As a result, I am unfamiliar with the plethora of home improvement shows, but I am all too aware of them. Rarely does a day go by that a client doesn't seek to enlighten me by sharing something they saw on a TV show, or trying to lower my price by doing it themselves. Like most things, though, it's always a whole lot harder than it looks.

"Don't even *think* about it, Luz. I'm serious." I shook my head. It was going to take plenty more martinis before I got into the house-flipping business. I was barely keeping my head above water as it was. "Not in this market."

"Okay, what I want to hear about—what I really *came here* for," said Stephen, changing the subject, "was to hear about the gorgeous man from your past."

"Graham?"

"Come on, girlfriend, you can tell me. After all, I'm your gay best friend, remember?"

I laughed.

"Luz tells me he's pretty hot."

"Last night he tried to tell me not to work on Matt's site."

"How'd that go over?"

"About as well as you'd expect. I started on the job this morning."

"You're such a romantic," Stephen said.

"How about the young guy?" Luz asked. "The photographer? He had a little thing for you, I'm pretty sure."

"I'm going to see him tomorrow to look through pictures from the party. But I told you, I think he was only looking at me that way because I was holding a gun on him."

"Now you're telling me I missed *gunplay* while I was busy foaming lattes?" Stephen took a big gulp of his Chardonnay and gaped at us, one after the other. "Next time I am *so* going to lunch with you guys."

The next morning I awoke at my usual five o'clock, but I felt great despite the late night. I hadn't dreamt about

Kenneth, or any other ghosts for that matter. In fact, I seemed to be seeing Kenneth less and less lately, which was really working for me.

I dressed and went downstairs to the office, returning e-mails and attending to paperwork until I smelled coffee.

As I passed the living room I noticed that Dad, Stan, and the boys were getting ready for their camping trip: The floor was filled with little piles of things like personal first-aid kits, canteens, flashlights, duffel bags, and Dad's ever-present camping checklist. Last night, upon coming home in the dark, I was startled by the sleeping bags hanging on the clothesline to air out. All of it gave me a twinge of sweet nostalgia: We spent a lot of time in the woods as a family when my sisters and I were kids. My dad was happiest in the mountains, and Mom was game, if not ecstatic about trying to keep three girls happy and healthy in the wilderness.

We learned a lot on those trips. Hiking, swimming, basic survival skills. On my eighth birthday I graduated from a BB gun to my first .22 rifle. We used to shoot aluminum cans off of tree stumps; whoever hit the most cans got extra ice cream. That's one reason I was such a good shot. Probably also explains why I was a chubby kid.

"Hey, babe," Dad said as I walked into the kitchen. He had already put bread in the toaster and was frying bacon in an iron skillet. "Hungry?"

"No, thanks," I said through clenched teeth. I couldn't keep the words from bubbling up. "Dad, have you *ever* known me to eat breakfast?"

"Seems to me you used to like Cream of Wheat like your mama used to make. Or was it oatmeal?"

"It was both, but that was Charlotte," I said. "And Daphne always liked ham and eggs. I never liked anything. I'm the cranky one, remember?"

"Oh, I think I've got that part down pretty well," he said with a smile.

We both chuckled. I sipped my coffee. One thing Dad and I always agreed on: really good French roast. Our current favorite was locally roasted Blue Bottle Coffee.

"Dad, do you know that Stanislaus River area at all?"

"Well, I've done a little exploring around there, but not much. We usually went up to Ralston Lake, which is a little north of there. But you know that."

I nodded. "If a person had a gold-country map from, say, the 1870s, how likely would it be to find the same place-names, that sort of thing?"

"Most of that stuff was temporary—those mining towns rose and fell within a matter of months sometimes."

"Have you ever heard of gem fields in California?"

"What kinds of gems?"

"Diamonds? Rubies, emeralds . . ."

"Nah." He shook his head and extracted strips of crunchy bacon from the grease, laying them carefully on a paper towel–lined plate. "Gold. Copper, silver, minerals of all types. But no diamonds."

"That's what I thought."

"Your mom and I used to take you kids around to explore those old ghost towns from time to time."

"I remember."

"I used to enjoy the tar out of that. The really good places aren't usually marked on maps; you have to ask around to find them. And you're free to explore the old mines and get a feel for the place. They're too far off

the beaten path for the bleeding-heart government bu-
reaucrats to step in and close 'em down to save us from
ourselves."

I just smiled and sipped my coffee. I was getting
craftier with age. He wasn't dragging me into a political
debate that easily.

"Hey, Dad, would you be willing to ask around, look
a place up while you're in that area? As far as I can tell,
it's probably not too far from Stan's cabin."

"What kind of place?"

"A gem field."

"*Gem* field?"

"An old one, played out years ago."

"What do you want me to do if I find it?"

Good question.

"Take some photos, I guess, chat with the locals. In
case anyone knows about it being a gem field, knows the
story behind it."

"Sure, I never mind a reason to check out the local
bars."

"I said locate an old gem field claim, not get a beer."

"Where do you think the old-timers hang out?
They're the ones who know whatever there is to know.
I'd place my bets with them over a library any day." He
started buttering thick slices of toasted sourdough. "So,
I'm almost afraid to ask, but how's it going at Matt's
place?"

"I've got Nico's guys started on demo, salvaging as
much as possible. They're keeping an eye out in case
they find anything pertinent to Matt's case."

"And what's happening with that?"

I shrugged. "I can't seem to get a call back from Matt's
high-powered lawyer. Probably doesn't know why I'm

asking questions. But at least Matt's out on bail. From what I hear, I guess the cops, or the prosecutors, are still working up their case against him."

"Yup, he told me that last night when he dropped the boys off. Nice enough guy for a hippie."

I smiled. "Matt Addax hardly qualifies as a hippie."

"Needs a haircut in the worst way."

"So do I."

"You're a girl. Girls are supposed to have long hair."

I suddenly caught a whiff of something besides coffee. Dread washed over me.

"Do you smell that?" I asked. "Is that . . . cigar smoke?"

"Oh, yeah," Dad said. "Friend of Stan's came by last night, brought him a cigar from the Dominican Republic. We opened the windows, but . . . you can still smell it, huh?"

"Oh, good." I relaxed back against the counter.

"Good? I thought you'd be all over his case. Thought you hated smoking."

"I do; it's just that . . . Well, it's the weirdest thing. Every time I'm in Matt's Vallejo Street house I could swear I smell fresh pipe smoke. Nobody else seems to notice. It's getting to the point where I feel like those people who smell eggs or oranges right before they have a stroke."

Dad looked up at me. "You . . . hear anything odd?"

"As a matter of fact—"

"*Son of a bitch*," muttered Dad. "Is this the first time? You haven't mentioned anything like this before."

"Anything like what?"

"You feel something cold, see little lights floating around, anything like that?"

"Dad? What are we talking about here?"

He resumed buttering toast, remaining silent for so long I thought he wasn't going to answer.

"Your mother had it," he said finally.

"Had what?"

"That . . . whatever you call it." He gestured with the butter knife. "Third eye, whatever."

"You're saying Mom was *psychic*?"

"Sort of. Not reading people's minds or anything like that. Just when it came to . . . ghosts. Spirits. Whatever you want to call it."

"How come I've never heard this before?"

"It isn't the sort of thing normal people want to broadcast."

"I'm not talking about broadcasting, I'm talking about informing your family." I paused for a moment, sipping my coffee and trying to absorb this news. "How often did she see these supposed ghosts?"

"She wasn't scared of it, anything like that. It was just a sense she had, visions sometimes. For instance, she was the one who always chose the houses we bought and flipped—she'd check them out for good vibes before she'd let me buy anything."

"I can't believe this."

"I was always afraid you got it from her. Remember that place in the Sunset?"

I nodded. We lived there when I was in third grade. I loved that house and had cried when we finished the re-model project, sold it for a neat profit, and had to move out.

"You had an imaginary friend."

"Anthony." I nodded. I remembered thinking I was far too old, at age eight, to have a made-up playmate. I tried to keep it a secret, but Mom found me talking to him more than once.

"He wasn't so imaginary."

I stared at him.

"Your mom saw him. Poor little kid died way back when the house was being built, some kind of carriage accident."

Which would explain his old-fashioned clothes: button-up shoes, brown knickers that came just under his little knees, white shirt with a lacy frill at the collar. I remembered him vividly: the tinkling sound of his voice, the cold weight of his funny little lead soldiers.

"So what does all this mean? I have to go through life talking to ghosts now?"

He shrugged. "After that boy, you never mentioned anything else. I thought maybe you were okay."

"But you say Mom had this?"

"Sort of. Tell the truth, I didn't really want to hear about it. But she had something—I tell you that much."

I was born and raised in California's Bay Area, a region spectacularly open-minded about just about everything—with the possible exception of social conservatism. So I didn't feel like a freak, exactly; and frankly it was a relief to know, deep down, that I wasn't insane.

But for the last several years I'd wanted nothing more than to be left alone. Yet here I was living with two men, two boys, a dog, a ghost, and now how many other undead who would be free to visit and chat whenever they darned well felt like it?

Apparently, they didn't even need to sleep. *Super*.

Chapter Nineteen

The revelation about Mom was . . . not shocking exactly, because in a way, deep down, I think I already knew. But it was akin to realizing your parents have a sex life: It's one thing to recognize it somewhere in the dusty recesses of your mind, quite another to confront it late one night with the lights on.

And as for what this "power," or "third eye," might mean for me . . . I was particularly unclear on that part.

Speaking of haunted houses, before going into the city today, I wanted to stop by and see a man about a ghost. Or two.

The assisted-living facility, Felicity Gardens, was nothing like the nursing homes I remembered visiting as a kid. There were no funky smells, no endless linoleum corridors with people sitting alone in wheelchairs. In fact, this place reminded me of a European-style inn: a restaurant to one side, a living room with a fireplace on the other, and a sweeping circular stair leading to the second floor.

When I asked after Gerald Buchanan, the fiftyish,

well-coiffed woman at the front desk mimicked Meredith's words: "It's good for him to have visitors."

"Doesn't anyone come to see him?"

"Not many," she said as she led the way to his room on the second floor and gestured toward his door. She dropped her voice and leaned in as though in confidence. "Only one, actually. And he was a *police* officer."

She left me at Gerald Buchanan's door.

My second knock was answered by a tiny man, seemingly shrunken with age. Bent over a walker, with only a tuft of white hair atop his pink, age-spotted head, he looked ancient. And angry.

"I don't want to go to the *goddamned* symphony. I don't want to go to pottery class, or exercise class, or go see a goddamned movie. I don't give a good goddamn about the current Frida Kahlo exhibit at the MOMA. I want you to cook my food, and then *leave ... me ... alone*. How hard is that for you people?"

"Mr. Buchanan, I don't work here. My name's Mel Turner, and I wanted to ask you about your house. Your former house."

Gerald tried to slam the door. It bounced off one leg of his walker. He started to swear again.

"Just a couple of questions." I put my hand out to hold the door open and moved toward him, compelling him to back up. "I promise I'll make it quick."

Grumbling, he turned around and made his laborious way back into his one-bedroom accommodations. The sitting room was nicely furnished, with a huge television, a comfy-looking La-Z-Boy, and a little kitchenette with a minifridge and a microwave.

He collapsed into the recliner. I closed the door and brought a chair over from the small café table.

"I don't mean to bother you, sir, but I don't know whether you heard that something terrible happened a few days ago in your old house."

Rheumy eyes looked over toward me. "What?"

"The police officer didn't tell you?"

"That cop? I told that goddamned cop to leave me alone."

"What was he asking you about? The murder?"

"Murder? Nah." His chuckle turned into a cough. "He thought there was money in that house. A whole fortune, just sitting in that place somewhere. Idiot."

"What kind of fortune?"

"The man came in here and sat down just as neat as you please, goes on to tell me his whole sob story. Like I care. How he started drinking, and wound up screwing up his marriage, and how his wife left him and took the kids. How he went into rehab and now he needs money to get his family back. Then he asked me about the gems."

He laughed and coughed again.

"What gems?"

"From the goddamned gem field, years ago. Don't tell me you've never heard of 'em. That's why you're here, too, right? You been snooping around at the—whaddayacallit?—the historic society downtown. There's those papers that say my family had a gem field back in the day. But I got news for you: There *are* no gems. It was all a scam."

"What kind of scam?"

"Those gems, they weren't worth a thing. They were rejects, worthless."

"But I read that your great-grandfather had them assessed by respected jewelers. Even Charles Tiffany."

"Everybody had get-rich-quick on their brain back then. Maybe they wanted to be in on the next gem rush. I don't know and I don't care. All I know is those rocks were worthless. The two prospectors salted the mine field with cheap gems, stones they bought as seconds. It was all a scam, and when the prospectors got bought off, they went and disappeared with their ill-gotten gains."

"And you're very sure there was nothing hidden in the house, somehow? Could Walter have hidden valuable gems somewhere?"

"Nah," he scoffed. "That's what that cop kept asking, too. If there was something there, don't you think I would have found it over all those years? I did all my own repair work there, you know. I'm pretty handy."

I thought of some of the former owner's "repairs" we had found in the house: He had made one electrical connection with parts taken from a miniature train set. It was a wonder the whole place hadn't burned down years ago.

"And why would Walter kill himself if there was something real?" Gerald wheezed. "He couldn't stand the disgrace of being duped. Or maybe . . . maybe it was something else. But he killed himself; that much is sure."

"Your old neighbor, Meredith Montgomery, mentioned that you might have sensed another presence in the house."

He gazed at me, his lips drawn tight and disapproving. "Yeah. Maybe."

"And you don't think it was Walter Buchanan?"

He shook his head. "It haunted Walter. Still does. It . . . it haunted me, too. Finally I just gave in and sold, and came to this goddamned place where people won't leave me alone."

"Meredith mentioned that you sat in on a séance or two."

"My neighbors," he scoffed. "Not one of 'em has come by to visit—not that I'd want them to. Meredith called once or twice. And Celia was all right, but that kid of hers was rotten."

"Vincent?"

"He was a bad kid from the start. And then, when I was gonna sell the house, he started up the rumors, talking about how it was haunted."

"But I thought you agreed that it was haunted."

"Back in my day you kept that kind of information to yourself. Don't have to go hanging your dirty laundry out for everyone to hear."

"How did Vincent spread the rumors? Who did he tell?"

"Went on the goddamned whaddayacallit? The Internets. Told the world, I guess. When I went to sell the house, the buyer showed me all these things he printed from the computer. The Realtor said I had to admit it, and then the guy offered less because of it. God damn it."

"This was Kenneth Kostow?"

"Yeah. Guy cheated me out of plenty, I tell you what."

My mind raced as I drove across the bridge into San Francisco. Did this mean Vincent and Kenneth had been working together to lower the price of Gerald's house . . . or had Vincent had been doing it for his own reasons? Maybe he was trying to help his mother in her acquisition of the property, and Kenneth stepped in and took advantage of the situation. In which case Vincent might have reason to be angry with Kenneth.

And Gerald said the gem field was all a scam ... but what if not everyone believed that? What if Kenneth and/or the other investors thought the gems were still hidden in the house? That would explain why they came after the items we took from the house to put in storage.

Once again, I felt relieved to pull up to the St. Francis Wood job site and turn my thoughts to the work at hand.

The landscapers, as usual, had accomplished a great deal in very little time. It was always amazing to see a team of ten people swarming over a yard, transforming it almost overnight from a weed-pocked junkyard into a bucolic haven. This was especially true when clients had the money to invest in mature plants. Even the trees looked as though they'd been there for years. The Zabens now had a beautiful sandstone pathway leading up to and around either side of a central fountain, three pools of descending size topped by a figure of Pan. Water tinkled merrily; it would attract birds once all the workers were gone.

Sod had been laid on either side of the pathway, which was rimmed with flowering shrubs and vines. Lately many Californians were opting for naturalized gardens, which were low maintenance and drought-resistant. Not the Zabens: They had worked with a landscape designer I recommended to create a traditional manicured French-inspired garden.

Inside, the faux finishers had transformed the living room walls with a parchment finish and completed painting the mural in the playroom and clouds on the girls' ceilings. A border of monochromatic seashells, painted in various sepia tones, marched just below the dental molding on the sage green walls of the girls' bathroom. The master bath was bordered in a wispy painted garland of ivy and cupids, sanded back and glazed over so it looked as though it had been there for years. The tumbled stone of the separate bath and shower surrounds set it off perfectly. The sink was hammered copper, and sat above the counter like a bowl. Alongside the Tuscan-inspired architecture, the huge bathroom also included modern conveniences like radiant heat under the stone floor, non-fogging mirrors, and a huge flat-screened TV.

Raul was installing the handmade blown glass I had bought from Bendheim architectural glass in Oakland, near Alameda. The sheets of glass were precious; expensive and gorgeous, marked by the tiny bubbles and uneven surface common to glass made the old-fashioned way. It wasn't practical to use in every window, but I loved placing bits and pieces here and there. We were using amber, red, and blue glass in the transoms above the bedrooms, so when the lights shone through, there was a lovely glow on the other side.

The last time I was at Ohmega Salvage, a beautiful "junkyard"—more like an antiques store—in Berkeley, I had stumbled across a pair of arched, paneled, Gothic-style wooden doors. I convinced the Zabens to let us use these rather than the new master bedroom doors that were on back order. After all, the new doors would have to be faux-distressed, whereas these were already old, and beautiful, intact but wearing their history proudly. Unfortunately, most reclaimed doors don't come with their own frame, which made fitting them into new construction tricky at best. The doors' distinctive arched tops did not match the current frame, so we had one of our best carpenters working on the solution. He almost had it.

I still needed a perfect rectangular leaded-glass piece

to use in the door between the kitchen and the dining room. As usual, I could have a new one made, but I'd rather find an old one. Clearly I needed to make some time to scout the salvage yards.

Finally, I got a worker to help me pack two heavy porcelain-covered iron sinks into the back of my car. They were chipped and stained, in need of help from the Sink Factory in Berkeley. The sink doctor would cure what ailed them.

Secure that all was proceeding well at the Zabens' house, I headed back toward Vallejo Street. The careful demolition was moving along nicely. The men still hadn't found anything special in the walls, but they'd put together quite a collection of salvaged items: woodwork, hardware, doors.

The only place I hadn't inspected thoroughly was the basement. I had been down there months ago, when I did the initial house inspection, but not since.

I still couldn't find a key, so I took out my tools and removed the door from its hinges.

As in most basements, steep stairs led down into what seemed to be a dark pit. It was no wonder that so many horror novels featured cellars—they tend to bring out the inner claustrophobe in us all. But when I flipped on the overhead light—a simple incandescent bulb hanging from a cord—it revealed nothing more sinister than a musty smell, an uneven brick floor, and a massive octopus-type heater with elephantine ductwork reaching up through different parts of the house. Despite its impressive physique, the heater hadn't functioned in years.

I studied the newly built brick wall that blocked the

old pass-through to Celia's twin house. Laying my hands on it, I tried to sense something. I had no idea what. I was one sorry psychic.

I knocked around at the base of the wall, pulling some of the loose floor bricks away. There was no foundation laid; it looked as though the opening from the floor to the low ceiling had simply been bricked up. The floor had been laid in bricks also, but not well. The mortar was thin and insufficient for the task of lying on damp dirt for years. Cement, and even bricks, wick moisture up into themselves. Mortar will eventually crumble if it doesn't have a chance to dry out.

Meredith said Celia had bricked over bones. My stomach turned. What was she referring to?

Just as the thought popped into my head, Kenneth appeared, crouching down near the pile of bricks. I could feel mournfulness coming from him—this was more than his typical depression.

"What is it?" I whispered, hoping no one overheard.

He didn't answer.

It didn't take Brittany Humm to point out that when a ghost seems particularly mournful in a dirt basement that has been strangely bricked over, there might be something to check out.

I looked at my watch. Twelve thirty. I was supposed to meet Zach-the-photographer in half an hour. I needed to get washed up and on the road.

"Kenneth?" I asked again. "Can you tell me what you're feeling?"

He just shook his head and shrugged.

I hesitated, torn between investigating further and making my next appointment. Finally I decided talking to the living would tell me more than hanging out with the dead. Plus . . . I wasn't entirely sure I was ready for what I might find.

The basement—and its secrets—would have to wait.

Zachary Malinski lived in a 1940s-era apartment building near the corner of Divisadero and Golden Gate. He buzzed me in through the huge mahogany front door and told me he was on the first floor, to the left. The long, old-fashioned hallway was completely lined—floor, walls, and ceiling—in original wood paneling. Glass windows in the apartment doors, all of which had been painted over, made the place seem almost like a converted office building, but it was really just a holdover from a time when people weren't afraid everyone at the door meant to hurt them.

A door opened and Zachary Malinski stepped halfway into the hall.

His dark hair was artfully tousled. He wore faded jeans, black socks, and a very white T-shirt that strained slightly across his broad chest. Talk about your Diet Pepsi commercials.

"I was so glad you called," he said with a warm smile as his sherry brown eyes looked me up and down. His voice sounded amused.

"I wanted to ask you a few more questions," I answered. Strictly business.

"Come on in."

He stepped back and gestured me through the small foyer into a single fifteen-by-fifteen room barely large enough for a neatly made double bed, a trunk serving as a bedside table, a small desk with a laptop computer on it, and an old-fashioned wooden desk chair. One huge sidewalk-level window cast light on the newspapers, photographs, and correspondence that covered just about every horizontal surface. To the right was a cramped galley kitchen, off the foyer was a bathroom, and there was a single closet off the main room. Apartment life in the big city.

"Have a seat; make yourself comfortable," said my host, gathering newspapers off the bed and stashing them in a recycling bin under the desk.

Zachary sank into the desk chair.

I perched on the edge of the bed, feeling awkward at the implied intimacy. As in the exterior hallway, the walls of the apartment were paneled in a beautiful cherry wainscoting that reached at least five feet. The wall surface above was chock-full of tacked-up black-and-white photographs: faces mostly, a lot of children. I don't know much about photography, but these shots were beautiful, soulful. The plate-rail ledge displayed brightly beaded handicrafts, carved figurines, and woven baskets. Mementoes of a rich life.

The decorations reminded me of the apartments of my friends back in the anthropology program, or my own room for that matter—where every item had a story attached, rather than being picked out by a designer, as was the case in most of the wealthy homes I worked on.

"So what can I help you with?" asked my host.

"I wanted to ask you some more questions about the party the other night."

"I thought you were a contractor."

"I am."

"So how come you're acting like a cop?"

"Have they spoken to you yet?"

He nodded. "Yesterday. Why are *you* looking into it?"

"I'm just trying to find out what happened," I evaded. "Matt's a friend."

"A 'friend'? You had a crush on him when you were young, right?" Zach teased with a crooked smile. "Tell the truth."

"I was there when—when we found Kenneth. It's a hard image to shake."

"Ah. I see."

"Matt Addax is incapable of killing his friend with a nail gun and a saw. Think about it. You know him."

"I do, a bit." Zach nodded. His hands were clasped around one knee, and he observed me with a sort of relaxed but astute mien. This went on for a long moment. Just as I was starting to get nervous, he continued. "So you think you can tell, just like that? What evil lurks in the hearts of men?"

"Not just like that, but I trust my gut." Did I? Trusting my gut had led me to marry the wrong man. But that was romance; this was friendship. I had always had good taste in friends.

"You want some orange juice? Vitamin water?" Zach asked.

"No, thanks."

"So, I used to trust my gut," Zach continued with our previous conversation as he rose and stepped into the galley kitchen. "Then I spent some time in Darfur—all over Sudan, actually. After what I saw there, I decided I don't know much about how far people will go, given the right motivation."

He poured himself a tall glass of orange juice and put the carton back in the fridge. His words had been casual, as though recounting his trip to the mall. But as he turned back toward me, his eyes held mine. Eyes far too old for his face. Eyes that did not quite reflect his boyish smile.

I couldn't think what to say.

"Anyhoo, you want to look at the pictures—is that it?"

"Do you have them already?"

"At an event like that, I shoot digital. Instant gratification." He swung his chair around to face his computer and started clicking.

"Did you notice anything odd going on?" I asked as I came to stand behind him. "Anyone with a gun?"

He laughed and shook his head. "If someone had whipped out a gun, I would have bounced. It was a group of liquored-up socialites—women in full makeup, a lot of them in high heels—none of whom knew what they were doing. The whole thing was pretty surreal, to tell you the truth."

Zachary put the pictures on a slide show setting, stood, and insisted that I take the desk chair. He then hovered over me, one hand on the back of the chair, the other leaning on the desk. His forearm was sinewy but strong-looking. I caught a whiff of Ivory soap.

"I even took a few with my tiny camera, to get candid shots. People don't even realize I'm shooting them when I use it."

I turned my attention to the pictures, not knowing what I was looking for. I noticed the wallboard hanging oddly in one photo, the lacy red bra in the foreground. Could the wallboard have been hung to hide the box Graham and I had found? I clicked through several pictures of Matt and Kenneth clowning around.

Kenneth held an electric drill in one hand, while Matt held the nail gun. My heart caught in my throat.

"Which of these are you going to print?"

"None of them. Kenneth hired me, after all, and I'm not really a paparazzi type. I was just there for the human interest story—no need to rat out the celebs' wild parties. Especially after what happened."

"A journalist with a conscience?"

"I'm not a journalist. I'm a photographer. There's a difference."

"Ah," I said, not sure what to make of the young Zachary Malinski. "How is it that you didn't hear about what happened there? It looks like you keep up with the news," I said, gesturing to the stacks of newspapers all over the apartment.

"I read international stuff, the *Guardian*, *Le Monde*. I never pay attention to local. My bad."

I flipped through the rest of the photos. I recognized Jason, and Vincent from next door. And the restaurateur who had made a splash last year with his trendy new spot in North Beach—Rory Abrams.

Most disturbing, though, was a picture of Brice Lehner. Homicide Inspector Brice Lehner. What was he doing at Matt and Kenneth's Do-It-Yourself Demo party, and why hadn't this come up at any point in the investigation?

Or maybe it had. I didn't exactly have sources in the police department. Maybe it was an entirely innocent association, he had informed his superiors, and they decided he should stay on the case. Or maybe there really was something fishy going on. How could I find out?

"Do you know this guy?" I asked.

"Met him at the party, briefly. But I was working, not socializing."

As the photos continued to appear, I saw that several

were marred by what looked like tiny white starbursts or light smudges.

"Did you notice that several of these photos seem to have little light streaks, like this?" I asked, pointing one out.

"It's not that unusual. You get that many people together in an area, lots of activity, light glints off of all sorts of things."

I nodded.

"Either that or the place is full of ghosts, and those are their orbs, or energy traces."

Startled, I looked up at him.

He was grinning. "I'm *kidding*. Speaking of ghosts, you look like you've just seen one."

Embarrassed, I turned back to the photos, but there wasn't much else to see. No obvious murderers lurking in the background, no blood trails or sinister faces in the shadows.

"Thank you for showing these to me," I said, getting up. Zachary didn't back up, so as I stood I essentially thrust myself right into the circle of his arms.

He looked down at me, smiled, and stepped back ... slowly.

"You want to, you know, get a cup of coffee sometime?" he asked. "Or better yet, I could help you with your case."

"It's not a case," I said, flustered. Did he just ask me *out*? "I mean, I'm not a private detective or anything. I was just asking a few questions."

"Where were you going to ask questions next?"

Only when he asked me did I realize that, indeed, I had planned my next move.

"I wanted to talk to the bouncer at the party. Do you know him?"

"Sure do. Robbie. I recommended him to Kenneth. He works over at the Vixen's Lair."

"Where?"

"Tell you what, I'll take you," Zach said, grabbing the leather jacket that had been hanging on a nearby coat-rack. His manner was utterly relaxed, and yet when he moved he did so with unexpected speed.

"I don't really need company. . . ."

"Have you ever been to the Vixen's Lair?"

"No . . . I mean, I've heard of it. But I've never exactly gone in. I don't think I'm their target audience."

Malinski grinned. "Are you kidding me? Strip joints love it when women come in."

"In any case, I don't need an escort."

"I wouldn't let you go there alone."

"I don't—"

"Look, I know these guys—they're a lot more likely to talk to me than to you. Besides, you'd be doing me a favor. I'm going nuts in here. I don't have nearly enough work to keep me busy lately, and I've read all my news-papers. I might have to resort to the local news soon, and you *know* that's scraping the bottom of the old barrel."

Chapter Twenty

"How do you know this place so well?" I asked as I pulled into a spot at the curb not two blocks from our destination, near the corner of Columbus and Broadway. I was pretty excited about the miraculous spot—North Beach was famous for impossible parking. Maybe Malinski brought me good parking karma.

"I do their glamour shots."

"Ah."

"Whatever it takes to pay the rent."

"I'll bet."

"It beats working in fast food."

"On so many levels."

He grinned. "It's a tough job, but somebody's gotta do it."

Outside of the Vixen's Lair, blocking the doorway, stood a tall man with a belly so big he looked pregnant. His black embroidered shirt was worn loose, his head was shaved, and a dark goatee defined the broad planes of his face. As he smoked, gold chains glinted on his chunky wrist. He reminded me of one of Nico's many jumbo-sized nephews. I imagined any one of them could play for the NFL.

He was speaking to a pretty Asian woman, half his size, wearing a red corset over a frilly white dress reminiscent of Victorian undergarments.

"Zach, sweetie, where you been?" The woman gave my companion a hug before standing back and looking me up and down. I had the sense she was sizing me up. . . . I just wasn't sure what for.

"Heya, Tam, Robbie, what's up?" Zachary nodded to them both.

"Who's this?" Tam asked, a slight frown marring her smooth forehead. "I like the dress, but she's too old to dance."

"She's not here to dance," Zach said with a laugh. "This is a friend of mine, Melanie Turner."

"Call me Mel," I said.

"We need to ask Robbie a couple of questions," Zach said.

"Don't take too long," she said, displeased, turning toward the door. "Bad enough we got cops coming by lately. It's like a doughnut shop, but with naked girls."

"So, Robbie," Zach began, "did you see anything strange the other night at the party, anything at all?"

Robbie shook his head, his gaze skittering nervously up and down the street. He started literally wringing his large, mittlike hands.

"I heard about this on the news. But Kenneth was fine when I left—I can't believe this happened."

"Have the police talked to you?" I asked.

He finally looked up at me, a flicker of alarm in his flat hazel eyes. He shook his head.

"Do I gotta talk to the police?" he asked, a note of petulance in his voice. "That sort of thing don't work out so well for me."

"You might be able to give the police some information they could use, even if it doesn't seem useful to you."

On the other hand, Matt had already told the police who was at the party. If they weren't knocking on doors and talking to people, was it up to potential witnesses to track down the investigating officers?

Besides, the more I thought about it, the more it seemed like Kenneth must have been hurt the morning *after* the party. He couldn't have survived otherwise. So maybe none of these questions were relevant.

"I did see one thing," Robbie said. "Some of them, like that Rory Abrams guy—you know him? He's a real foodie—and the next-door neighbor, they were ripping down walls, going at the lath and plaster pretty good, like, opening up the holes and crawling back in there."

"Like they were looking for something?" I asked.

"Maybe." He shrugged his meaty shoulders. "Probably just having fun."

Tam poked her head out of the black curtains that shielded the door. "You guys done yet? Bad for business, folks just hanging around. Either come in or go away."

"We're going," said Zach. "Thanks, Robbie. See you later, Tam."

It was late afternoon, but already North Beach's famous nightlife was starting to ratchet up. Tourists and locals alike filled the sidewalks, in search of great Italian food, fun bars, good music, and girlie shows.

"How about I take you to dinner?" Zach suggested as we walked away from the Vixen's Lair.

I hadn't been asked out in ages. And now, within a few days, Vincent Hutchins and Zachary Malinski were both asking me out? Meanwhile a man had been killed, Nico had been attacked, my storage unit had been broken into, Graham had a black eye, a ghost was following me around. . . . Coincidence, or could this all be connected?

My stomach clenched. I hated the thought of interpreting any attraction a man might feel toward me as part of some kind of malignant behavior . . . but since everything that had happened with my ex-husband, I was more than a little cynical about hidden motivations and their seemingly close association with Y chromosomes. Since I wasn't going to make it to Paris in the foreseeable future, at the very least I should shy away from male-induced craziness here at home.

And it hadn't escaped my notice that there were now any number of suspects in Kenneth's death. No wonder the police weren't asking more questions. They probably figured they'd just stick with the first suspicious character and call it a day.

"Earth to Mel . . ." Zach said with a smile. "It was meant to be a simple 'yes' or 'no' question."

"I'm sorry; you took me aback. If you don't mind my asking, how old are you?"

"How old do I look?"

"You look young."

Zach fell in step beside me as I started walking up the hill.

"I'm not that young."

"You're a lot younger than I am. You're barely older than my stepson."

"How old is he?"

"Fifteen."

"I'm nearly *twice* your stepson's age."

"It's not that big a gap."

"How old are *you*?" he asked.

"Thirty-eight."

"Aha! I got you. You're only nine years older than I am."

"They're a long nine years. Important. Formative, even."

"I'm sensing the age thing is a problem for you. Tell you what, we won't call it a date. At least let me help you with this case."

"As I said before, it's not a 'case.' I'm just a contractor who seems to have a hard time keeping her nose out of things."

"Awesome. I'll help. Where're we headed?" Zach asked with the upbeat tone of a kid going to an arcade parlor.

"I want to talk to that restaurant owner Robbie mentioned. It's right up the street."

"Rory Abrams? Perfect. Great food."

And just that easily I gave in. The last thing I really wanted to do was to show up at a chic restaurant solo, dressed in my usual inappropriate attire, to try to talk with a "real foodie" about whether he might have killed Kenneth Kostow because he found out Kenneth had sold the house with the intent to abscond with all the money. Or whether, perhaps, he thought there was something valuable in the walls at Matt's house, and he had been willing to maim and kill to get to it.

"On the way," said Zach, "let's play a game I call Who the heck *are* these people? And what are they doing on Columbus Avenue in broad daylight? Don't they have *jobs*?"

I couldn't help but smile at Zach's enthusiasm. Besides, this was a question that often occurred to me as I drove around on my daily tasks.

"This guy, for example," Zach said in a low, confidential tone as we passed a tall, preppy-looking young man. "Trust fund, Dartmouth education, sang in an a cappella group and is just beginning to admit to himself that he misses his fellow frat boys more than his perfect size-two blond girlfriend. Give him two weeks here, and he'll find his way to the Castro and realize that, deep down, he's cut out to be a leather daddy."

I chuckled.

"And this one." He nodded subtly toward a thin, long-haired young woman in a tie-dyed T-shirt. "Born Stacy Roop in Bitterwater, Wisconsin, is looking for either Haight Street or Berkeley, and will soon change her name to Willow."

"No." I shook my head. "Nature names are *so* last century. The young ones are all named after Celtic goddesses."

Zach favored me with his crooked grin. "Now you're getting it. Epona, then."

"Morrigan."

"Arianrhod."

"And this one"—I leaned in to Zach and whispered as we passed a thin, goateed young man with a composition book stuck under his arm—"is under the mistaken impression that Jack Kerouac still lives."

"Next alley over," Zach said aloud to the presumed

poet. He pointed toward the tiny mural-decorated alley named after the famous beatnik writer. "Right between Vesuvio's and City Lights bookstore."

He and I shared a smile.

"We're here," Zach said.

All I saw was an old-fashioned, weather-beaten sign in the shape of a boot. It advertised a shoe repair shop.

"Where?" Just as the word was leaving my lips, I peered in the darkened windows and realized it was a restaurant.

"Nobody hangs restaurant signs out anymore," Zach explained. "This used to be a shoe repair, so they just kept the funky old sign."

"What's the name of the restaurant?"

"Shoe Repair."

"Seriously?"

"They figured since they kept the sign, they'd keep the name."

"Then how do people know it's a restaurant?"

"That's the point—only the people on the 'in' know."

"I'm never on the 'in,'" I said. "Anyway, it doesn't look like they're open yet."

"Stick with me, soul sister," Zach said with a wink, rapping smartly on the window and gesturing at an aproned man behind the bar. Sure enough, the man came over, unlocked the door, greeted Zach, and went in the back to get Rory Abrams.

"You know him?"

"Not really. Sort of. I sort of know everybody. I'm a photographer—I get around. I did a spread on the restaurant when it was new. That's how I met Kenneth as well."

Abrams was a large man with a well-trimmed beard,

looking a lot like one would expect of a chef who enjoyed his own cooking a mite too much. A fine sheen of sweat covered his broad brow.

When I introduced myself as a friend of Matt's, and as the general contractor working on the house, he was eager to talk. We took a seat at a small table in a corner near the bar, while two women in white aprons laid out place settings on the tables in preparation for the evening crowd.

"Try this," he said, setting out some fresh, crusty bread, olive oil with herbs, and olives, both bright green and khaki. Also, there was a tiny plate of some sort of paste.

"What is that? It's delicious."

"It's a kind of truffle pesto. Can't tell you my secrets, though."

What he could tell us, apparently, was that he was a dedicated foodie, on the new wave of Italian/French-inspired restaurants. He dropped any number of names, which I'm sure I would have recognized had I been one of those on the "in." There were days when I forgot the names of dearest friends; I couldn't imagine a day when I would manage to keep up with local celebrities. He regaled us with tales of his dedication to organically grown local veggies, just like Alice Waters at Chez Panisse. Now, that name even I recognized.

I used to eat at Berkeley's Chez Panisse from time to time when I was married. Daniel and I would meet after class, and though I would have been happy with any number of inexpensive ethnic restaurants, Daniel preferred to go to the latest wildly expensive—some might even say overrated and overpriced—place that had been written up in all the local rags. But Chez

Panisse deserved its reputation as an incredible place to eat, and Alice Waters had revolutionized much of the business by stressing the importance of using local organic produce. On top of everything else, she now worked with local schools to teach kids about growing their own food—amazing how many city kids had never seen a vegetable grow from the ground. Waters was an admirable addition to the Bay Area scene.

But by and large my patience with foodies was limited.

"I wondered if you could tell me anything about the arrangement you had with Matt Addax and Kenneth Kostow with regard to the house in Pacific Heights."

Abrams insisted on pouring us each a glass of a Sonoma Cabernet.

"That was such a tragedy with Kostow. Will there be a memorial service, do you know?"

"Actually, I don't know. But I'll check into it." With everything else going on, I'd never thought to ask. I wondered whether Matt had been able to arrange anything, whether it had even crossed his mind. I guessed we'd all been pretty busy, but I still felt guilty. Kenneth hadn't mentioned anything, but it seemed like a pretty egregious oversight, considering.

"Were you good friends with Kenneth?" I asked.

"I doubt Kenneth had what you'd call close friends. An associate, certainly, and we had a few nice evenings together. That last party was a hoot, I'll tell you that much." He took a drink of wine. "Hey, even with what happened . . . Matt called me and told me I didn't have anything to worry about with the investment. He told me you were fixing the place up, and that it would be ready soon."

"'Soon' is a relative term. As soon as possible would be a better way to put it."

"I'm going to need to see a return on my money, the faster, the better. I'm tired of always serving other people's wines. I want to try my hand at it, get into the vineyard business."

"Do you know anything about the history of Matt's building?" I asked.

"I understood it had been in one family since it was built, the same family as the man who built it way back when."

"That's true, but I was—"

"How would that affect this? This was a simple, straightforward business arrangement."

"Have the police questioned you about the party?"

"Someone called. I told them I hadn't seen anything, and that was the last I heard of it."

"Do you happen to know the homicide investigator on the case, Brice Lehner?"

I thought I saw a flare of recognition in his eyes, but he got up to grab another open bottle of wine.

"You have to try this one, too," he said. "I know it's sacrilege to carry European wine in a California restaurant, but you have to hand it to the French. They know their Côtes du Rhônes."

The wine was hitting hard on my empty stomach. I hadn't eaten anything but a quick samosa at an Indian café earlier today. I snacked on bread to soak things up.

"So you do know Inspector Lehner?" I pushed. "He was at the party, wasn't he?"

"I may have met a guy named Brice, but there were a lot of people there."

"Brice is a pretty unusual name."

"Okay, but how was I supposed to know he was a cop?" He looked around the restaurant. "He wasn't exactly flashing a badge. Anyway, last I heard it wasn't a crime for a cop to go to a party."

"But why—"

"Hey, Rory," Zach broke in. "You know how to make a small fortune in the wine business?"

"How?"

"Start out with a huge fortune."

Abrams laughed and excused himself, just for a moment, to attend to something in the kitchen.

"Why didn't you let him answer?" I asked.

"He did answer."

"When?"

"He answered by not answering. Why is this such a crusade for you? Do you honestly think that Rory Abrams sliced off Kenneth's hand?"

It was hard to imagine. But then, who could have?

"Besides," Zach added, looking slyly over at Rory, "if we play our cards right, he'll comp us dinner. I've seen him like this before."

I looked out the window to see the lights of Columbus flickering on, crowds forming, the whole place starting to feel festive. I felt a surge of—what? Something unusual. The desire to relax and have fun. How long had it been since I'd been out with a man—other than sweet Stephen, of course? I had been feeling sorry for myself and defensive for so long I had forgotten that I used to enjoy this sort of thing.

What would it hurt? Besides, except for the work boots, I was even sort of dressed for it, in my own way.

I made a phone call. My father was excited I was on a date and said he'd take care of the boys, not to worry.

"Say hi to Graham for me," Dad said.

But the fellow at my elbow wasn't Graham; it was a man nine years my junior. I was suddenly very worried about sagging. But after another glass of excellent, full-bodied wine, it slipped my mind altogether.

Chapter Twenty-one

"**W**hy don't you just stay here for the night, or what's left of it?" Zach said hours later after he'd driven us back to his apartment. I was in no shape to drive. "No funny business; you can stay in my guest bed."

"What guest bed?"

"Well, I generally take the right side near the window, so the other side's for guests," he said with a crooked grin. "Seriously, we can put pillows or something in between us if it will make you feel better, but we're grown-ups. I'm sure we could survive a night in the same bed. I won't try anything. Scout's honor."

It was so late I called Caleb, figuring he would still be awake at this hour. Keeping things vague, I told him I was spending the night in the city.

"With Graham?"

"No, of course not."

"With who, then?" the usually uninquisitive boy wanted to know.

"Just a friend."

"What kind of friend?"

Maybe I should have called my father instead.

"I'll talk to you tomorrow, Caleb."

"We're going camping, remember?"

"Oh, I forgot. You'll be back on Tuesday?"

"That's what your dad said. I think."

"All right, I'll call in the morning."

I hung up and closed my eyes. Just for a second. The bed felt very soft.

"Come on," Zach said, putting his hand out for me. He pulled me up and around the side of the bed. He flipped back the covers with his other hand, then yanked open a drawer and pulled out a T-shirt. "Why don't you change out of those clothes, put this on, and then crawl into bed. I'll fix us some cocoa, give you a little privacy."

I took the T-shirt and cradled it, smelling the scent of laundry detergent.

"Thanks, Zach. I feel like an idiot."

"Hey, none of that. You should hear some of my stories."

He took me by the shoulders, turned me around, and gave me a gentle shove in the direction of the bathroom.

When I woke up the next morning I felt as though I had been unconscious, rather than just asleep. There was a little wet spot of drool on the pillow. I had the sinking feeling that I might have been snoring.

Was it any wonder that Zach was able to keep his gentlemanly distance?

Perched upon the wall of pillows in the middle of the bed was a note, and upon the paper sat a bottle of Excedrin. Bold, all caps handwriting told me that Zach had to leave for a photo shoot but I should feel free to use his shower, his computer, even his razor.

I lay back and squeezed my eyes shut for a moment. I go out on my first date in . . . well, since before I was married. And this is how the evening ends up.

Clearly I shouldn't be allowed out of my cage yet, unsupervised.

I checked my phone, which I had assiduously avoided all night. Seven calls. Three from Graham Donovan.

Ugh! I had completely forgotten I was supposed to meet him for dinner last night to show him the gem field map. What a loser.

My head pounded. I downed three Excedrin and two big glasses of water.

It was already nearly eleven, but I turned on Zach's computer and took another look at the photos from the party, just in case. Rory and Jason were both investors in the house, and they were present at the party. If Inspector Brice Lehner was there as well . . . could he be the final investor, the one Matt hadn't known about? According to Gerald Buchanan, Lehner had a drinking problem. Could he have ended up at the same New Leaf rehab clinic, where he could have met Matt and Kenneth? And was there anything illegal about a police investigator investing in a property, assuming the entire proposal was on the up-and-up?

Glancing at the clock again, I remembered I was supposed to meet Matt at the Vallejo Street house today. Now. I splashed some water on my face, did what I could with lip gloss and an eye pencil, stopped for quick caffeinated inspiration at Martha & Bros. Coffee Company, and zoomed on over.

"Wasn't that the same dress you were wearing yesterday?" Kenneth asked on the way.

"None of your business."

"You wouldn't go out with me—when I was alive, I mean—but you'll spend the night with that photographer? That makes no sense at all."

His outraged sensibilities made me smile.

"None of this is any of your damned business. You were the one so hot on me talking to him. And anyway, why shouldn't I spend the night with him if I want? I'm no longer married, and he's a smart, good-looking man."

"He's a boy."

I changed the subject. "Hey, what did you see yesterday in the basement at Matt's house?"

"I didn't see anything. But there's something really . . . *sad* in that basement. Can't you feel it?"

"I felt *your* sadness."

"You did?"

I nodded.

"It's sad . . . and frightening. I don't go down there alone."

"A ghost is afraid of the other ghosts? What's it going to do, kill you?"

"Very funny."

Matt was as good as his word; I spotted his shiny black BMW as I pulled up to the house. I found him inside, chatting with Spike. Spike gave me a quick rundown of the demo progress, then went back to join his crew.

"Matt, was Brice Lehner at the rehab clinic with you?"

Pause. "Yes."

"Homicide Inspector Brice Lehner was at the New Leaf clinic with you and Kenneth," I repeated.

Matt nodded.

"Why didn't you *say* anything?" I asked. "How can he

be acting as the investigating officer on this case if you and he have a prior personal relationship?"

"He's still a professional," Matt said. "Just because we knew each other doesn't mean he's neglecting his duties. In fact, he's been trying to help me out."

"And he's also an investor in this house project, isn't he?"

Matt sighed, his blue eyes weary as he looked around the still-messy living room. "He's a good guy, Mel, really. So he had a problem with alcohol. It happens to the best of us. It's a disease, you know. You wouldn't blame a person for having cancer, would you?"

"I'm not talking about his alcoholism, Matt. But if he's an investor in this house, he might have had a particular interest in making sure Kenneth didn't sell it and take off with the money."

"What?"

I realized I hadn't filled Matt in on all the details yet.

"It looks as though Kenneth was trying to sell the house, to reap the profit."

"And what about all of us?" Matt looked at me, aghast.

I shrugged. Matt was smart; he didn't need me to spell it out for him.

"Wow," he said. "I don't know what to say."

"Matt, do you think Lehner could have done this? Maybe he found out about Kenneth's scheme to sell the house, filed the lien papers to slow him down, then confronted Kenneth sometime after the party and . . . lost it."

"No. He would never do that."

"You wouldn't have believed Kenneth would double-cross you, either, would you?"

Matt just shook his head, looking blankly out the window.

"Have you ever found anything here in the house, in the walls? Maybe Kenneth mentioned something, or you heard stories about it?"

"No. But I wasn't really here in the house that much, to tell you the truth. Not like Kenneth. I mostly just worked on design."

The men wanted to knock off early for the holiday weekend, so I paid them and watched them tramp out.

Matt, too depressed by our little talk to get to work, left along with them.

The instant I was alone, the place felt lousy with ghosts. The smell of a pipe in the parlor. The rattle of a newspaper.

As I entered the front room, I had a clear vision of what the parlor had looked like, set up for a séance. I've always had the ability to visualize the original sense of a house: floor plan, wall treatment, woodwork details. When I remodeled the Victorian that Daniel and I lived in on Clay Street, I could practically see it unfold in front of me. I had always assumed it was just a knack. But now I realized it was much more.

I remembered again the boy, Anthony, whom I thought of as my imaginary friend, so many years ago. When I closed my eyes I could still see his child's toys, could feel his small hand tugging at my skirt, hear his high-pitched laugh.

"You see them, don't you?"

I jumped nearly out of my skin, letting out a little yelp.

"You scared the *hell* out of me!" I snapped.

"Sorry about that," Kenneth said, not looking particularly sorry. He did, however, look rather tragic and wan—and he was wearing nineteenth-century garb. Like a proper ghost.

"What are you wearing?"

"I found these. Yesterday. When we were in the basement. Don't you like them?"

"You look like you're an escapee from your local community theater."

"You're a fine one to talk," he said. "Look in the mirror lately?"

"Touché," I said.

"But I can tell," he continued. "You can see the others."

"Not really. Not as clearly as I see you, that's for sure."

"But you sense something?"

I nodded. "Who's here in this house besides you, Kenneth?"

"An old guy with a white beard."

"Is he a pipe smoker?"

"Yes. How'd you know?"

"I can smell it."

"And there's another one. An angry guy. Don't really know what his story is. Nobody uses names."

"Can't any of them tell you why you're still hanging around? Or why they are?"

"I'm telling you, they treat me like I'm barely visible. Like you." He collapsed onto the second-to-last stair and put his head in his hands. "I'm such a disaster. I can't even make a proper ghost."

I slumped onto the step next to him. He had been a real schmuck in real life. But now I felt bad for the guy.

"Maybe . . . maybe this is your chance to do something really good. To help Matt . . ."

"With what? I can't remember anything useful."

"Can you tell me anything about what was going on

with the finances? You tried to sell the house and just keep all the money for yourself?"

"I guess. I don't remember."

"So you can't recall if that's why you were killed? Could it have to do with the gem field map?"

"Gem field Matt?"

"What?"

"I thought you said 'gem field Matt.'"

"I said 'map,' not 'Matt.' Wait—was that what you were referring to at the hospital? The 'damned *map*,' not 'Matt'?"

"I don't get it."

"Maybe you were trying to tell the nurse you were killed over the *map*, Kenneth."

"I guess you could be right."

Okay, so what would this mean? I could give the box to the authorities, say I just dug it up and found the map, and tell them my theory about the nurse getting the words wrong. And then what? Would they go along with it and exonerate Matt . . . or was this another crazy, irrelevant idea?

"Okay, so the bearded guy here," said Kenneth suddenly. "He claims there's something to do with jewels."

"As in the map?"

"I have no idea. He's not exactly clear. But you might want to look into it."

"Next time I am *so* getting a more knowledgeable ghost," I muttered.

"Hey, I'm doing the best I can here. I don't know what the hell's going on. For instance, I told this guy to speak to you directly, but he says, and I quote, that you're 'getting there but not ready yet.' Unquote."

My stomach fell.

"That makes it sound like I'm going to be visited by other ghosts. Kenneth, I swear, I am *not* becoming the conduit for spirits. You hear me? This is *so* not how I envisioned things. When I go to Paris to hide from people, that includes dead people. *Especially* dead people. You get me?"

"Like I'm in charge around here. I reiterate: I don't know what the hell's going on."

He disappeared.

"Kenneth, come back here!" I yelled.

No answer. No more pipe smoke, no rattling newspaper, no forlornness, nothing.

Apparently I had a lot to learn with regard to proper ghost etiquette.

I called Dad on his cell phone.

"Have fun last night?" Dad asked.

"Yes, thanks," I replied, my head still pounding from way too much fun. "Where are you guys?"

"Still driving east. Thought we'd check out Murphys before we set up camp. Nice little town. Couple good bars. The boys'll enjoy it, I think."

Murphys . . . That rang a bell. "If you're in Murphys, will you ask them about a rock-hound convention in town last fall?"

"What about it?"

"Ask . . . if the rock hounds were looking anywhere in particular. Ask if they were looking at that Jumping Falls claim, the one on the map."

"Will do. Hey, don't forget to check on Dog."

"He's not with you?"

"Carsickness, remember? He's with Tom next door—Tom's a dog lover. But you should pick him up later."

After hanging up, I pulled on my coveralls and screwed up my courage to go down to the basement. For one thing, the ghosts seemed to have gone elsewhere. Even if they were still around, I was finding them much more annoying than frightening lately, thanks to my frustrating—and rather banal—interactions with Kenneth. In fact, at this point I was almost looking forward to having a conversation with whatever phantoms might be attached to the house. They were invisible witnesses to everything that had happened here over the years, after all.

Plus I had the handgun from my dad's house in my satchel. It wasn't loaded, but still. . . . I know it went against my father's credo, but even an empty gun would give a person pause. Just in case.

The door was still off its hinges, making the doorway to the basement a forbidding black rectangle. I switched on the overhead light and made my way down.

I stepped off the stairs onto the damp bricks.

Whispers.

I whirled around, but saw nothing more threatening than thick cobwebs and a couple of rusty old paint cans.

The whispers continued. Urgent. Unintelligible.

Swallowing hard, I tried to regain some of my recent bravado. *Annoying*, I told myself. *Annoying and confused. They can't actually do anything to hurt you.*

I had to hand it to this ghost, though—the vague, barely audible whispers were far creepier than anything Kenneth had ever managed to pull off. If it hadn't been for my recent experiences, I'm sure I would have run screaming out of the house by now. Instead I thought of my mother. She didn't let the spirits she found in houses frighten her; on the contrary, they helped her to choose great old homes that she and my father then flipped, allowing them to build up a successful business and to provide for their family.

If I had inherited even a fraction of her abilities, I wouldn't let the whispers frighten me. *Remember what Brittany Humm said*, I told myself. *It's a privilege.*

I made my way to the bricks between the houses and started removing some of them from the floor. They came up so easily it seemed as though they had recently been disturbed.

Under one, I saw something that appeared white. Bonelike.

I let out a breath. If there were actually bones here, I would have to call in a forensic anthropologist. Probably shut down the job site for a number of days.

Still, surely any bones would, indeed, belong to some poor animal, as Meredith had suggested. No one would simply brick over a human skeleton in their basement, would they?

As I was about to gingerly replace the bricks I had moved, I saw something else. Something metal. A chain. With a small medallion attached.

Wiping away the mud, I saw it was a St. Christopher medal. Words on the back were written in Italian.

The whispers increased in volume, still unintelligible but more strident.

Okay . . . Walter Buchanan had supposedly been haunted by a ghost. But the buildings were new when he built them. What ghosts would have been lingering? Could it be an Italian Catholic ghost? Perhaps someone Walter had buried in his basement? Like a prospector who had duped him? The man to whom Buchanan had signed over Norton notes, one of the men in the photograph with him, holding up their hands in celebration?

If that was true ... he wouldn't have any reason to be angry at me, would he? I could help him, maybe. Just like I was—sort of—helping Kenneth.

I let out a deep breath, closed my eyes, and concentrated, trying to invoke the spirit, somehow. If I tried hard enough, could I talk to it with my mind?

It didn't escape me that I started seeing Kenneth very much against my will, and even now he seemed to show up only when he wanted to, rather than when I wanted to speak with him.

Nonetheless, I figured I might as well try. Doing yoga was the closest I came to achieving any sort of altered state. I took a deep breath, sat down on the damp bricks, yanked my work-boot-shod feet into as close to a lotus position as I could manage—which wasn't very close—and laid my hands, palms up, on my knees.

"Mel?"

Letting out a screech, I wheeled on my haunches and wound up falling backward on my butt in the mud, whirling around with the gun in my hands. Aiming.

Graham jumped off the basement stairs to crouch behind them, hands in the air.

"*Don't shoot!* What is *wrong* with you?" he yelled at me from his hiding place. "And you were accusing your *father* of being gun crazy. *Damn*, woman."

I closed my eyes and blew out a breath. "You shouldn't sneak up on a person like that. In a basement, no less."

His eyes went past me to the upended bricks

Eyebrows raised in question. "What's up?"

"I really don't know," I said, feeling unaccountably guilty.

"Uh-huh. You've got something buried in your basement now?"

"Don't look at me like that. It's not like I put it there."

"What is it?"

"Could be nothing," I said with a shrug.

"Or it could be . . . ?"

"A skeleton? Maybe?"

"A skeleton. Oh, goody."

"I think I'd better call in a forensic anthropologist."

"I thought *you* were an anthropologist."

"I was a cultural anthropologist, not an archaeologist. I followed Daniel around on a lot of his digs, but I'm not qualified for something like this." I tore my eyes away from the bricks and looked back at Graham. "What are you doing here, anyway?"

"Exactly what I swore I wasn't going to do: worrying about you. You and I were supposed to meet for dinner last night, remember? You weren't answering your phone. I called your dad and he said you were out with me." He shrugged. "So I worried."

"I'm sorry, Graham. That was terrible of me." My already sour stomach took a turn for the worse.

"You okay?" he asked. "You don't look so great."

"I might have had a little bit too much to drink last night. And coffee on top of that."

"How about we get out of here, I make a couple of calls—though I guarantee you we won't get a forensic specialist out here on the holiday weekend—and we go get some lunch?"

"That's the best idea I've heard all day."

Chapter Twenty-two

"Graham, could I ask you something?" I said over our meals at Rose's on Union Street.

"Shoot."

"Do you believe in ghosts?"

"Is this a trick question?"

"No."

He shook his head, taking a bite of his overstuffed sandwich.

"Never?"

Graham sat back in his chair and studied me. "I take it you think you've seen a ghost?"

I could feel myself blush. I ducked my head and took a sip of my iced tea.

"Then again, I guess there are ghosts, and then there are ghosts. Your mama, for instance ... she sure knew how to pick a house." My eyes flew up to meet his gaze. "Look, Mel, I don't believe in ghosts per se, but anyone in the trades will tell you there are some projects that are blessed, or cursed, from the start. Some houses just have worse feelings than others. Like your Vallejo Street project, for instance."

Cursed. It sure seemed that way. A body—two if you counted a possible skeleton in the basement. But it called to me, this house. The elegance of its arches, the melancholy chambers leading one to another. If my mother's gift was finding enchanted homes, maybe mine was redeeming the ones that seemed condemned to misery. Or maybe I was just more at home when surrounded by melancholy and despair. They had been my loyal companions these past few years, anyway.

Time to change the subject. Sort of. I brought the copy of the gem field map out of my satchel and handed it to Graham. He spread it out on the table, studied it.

"I keep thinking Kenneth's death has to do with this map. I know it sounds crazy, and I'm sure the police would agree. It's probably just as simple as Kenneth's getting mixed up with the wrong people, trying to sell the house and dupe everybody."

"Probably," Graham said with a nod. "Of course, that wouldn't explain why they went after the crate, and then the piano."

"I thought you thought this was a wild-goose chase."

"I don't know what to think. I feel like someone was looking for something in that house, and the box and journal were the only apparent 'treasure' to be found. But now ... ?" He trailed off with a shrug.

"My dad's going to look up the gem field, if he can find it, while they're in the area."

"Even if they can locate it, they won't find anything more than dirt and rocks."

"I'm sure you're right, but you never know."

"You know what raw diamonds look like?"

"Lumpy diamonds?"

"Rocks. Plain old rocks. Rubies are even worse."

"Really?"

"Really."

"So you're saying I should have them sifting through all the gravel in the field?"

"I imagine others have done so, through the years. If they find the right place, and it used to be a gem field claim, it would have been scoured clean by hundreds, maybe thousands, of tourists and rock hounds through the years."

"But if gems look like regular rocks, how do they know none of the rocks are diamonds?"

"Seriously? Besides the fact that others would have looked already?"

I nodded.

"Because diamonds don't just occur randomly in fields, Mel. They're associated with volcanic pipes in very particular locales. And they sure as hell don't turn up next to rubies."

"They don't?"

He looked at me a beat too long before talking. "Didn't you ever take basic geology? Weren't you studying anthropology?"

"Once again, cultural anthropologists study *live* people. It's not archaeology."

"Still, a course or two might have been relevant."

"Thanks for the impromptu college counseling. You're just a few years too late."

He smiled. "Whatever happened with your degree? Did you finish up the PhD?"

I shook my head. "I'm an A.B.D."

"What's that?"

"All But Dissertation. Also known as an L-O-S-E-R."

Graham smiled and took a long pull on his beer. "I wouldn't say that."

"Mmm. I say it plenty all by myself."

"So why didn't you finish?"

"I don't know, exactly. It seemed like one thing after another at first. I went with Daniel to South Africa, where he was teaching for a semester, and then we wound up in Venezuela for nearly a year. All of which would have been fine if it had had anything to do with my dissertation topic, but it really didn't."

"Which was?"

"Mexican and Central American immigrants in the United States. Their strategies for economic success, cultural adaptation, attitudes toward education, that sort of thing. With an emphasis on women's roles within the family, what I called maternal authority."

"Sounds like worthwhile research."

"Sure. But hard to do from South Africa and Venezuela. I tried to keep writing, but I kept getting caught up in other things. Local stuff. I worked on a maternal and infant health project in rural South Africa, and then with a micro-lending group in Venezuela. Fascinating but not exactly on track, if you know what I mean. And then things changed between Daniel and me—"

I cut myself off as I realized who I was talking to. I had never shared this with anyone. . . . Why was I spilling my guts to Graham Donovan, of all people?

"Sounds like you did some valuable work, even if it wasn't pertinent to your research question."

I shrugged. "I found it hard to write when everything was falling apart. And then when Mom . . ." I trailed off, and took another drink. "Some people find their refuge in their work. Apparently I'm not one of those people."

"I don't know about that. Seems to me you've allowed the construction business to take over your life pretty thoroughly. Some might even say you were avoiding certain other aspects of life."

"Other aspects of life? I have no other aspects of life."

"That was my point."

"How about you, Graham? You've remained remarkably mute about the rest of *your* life, outside of your work as an inspector for a government bureaucracy."

"You say 'bureaucracy' like it's a bad thing. You know better than most where we'd all be without OSHA to enforce workplace safety laws."

"That's true. But I always thought . . . I thought you wanted to start your own business. Weren't you going to be part of the green revolution?"

He shrugged and looked around the restaurant.

"Things don't always work out the way we'd hope."

Ain't that the truth.

"I needed to find a job with benefits," Graham said after a long silence. "Several years ago I married a woman who was . . . more like a friend than a lover. We still are friends. She had a pretty serious bout with cancer; afterward she decided friendship wasn't enough from a relationship, and she moved on."

"You're saying you got a job at OSHA to provide for her, and then when she got healthy she dumped you? That seems . . . rotten."

"It wasn't quite that cut-and-dried. Jessica had a new lease on life when the cancer went into remission, and she made a number of changes. One of those included me. She decided she was only going around once, and she wanted different things from life. We didn't have any children, so there was no real family to keep together. Frankly, I would much rather she be honest with me, as she was, than to stay with me, miserable and unfulfilled, out of some misplaced sense of obligation."

"You sound very evolved," I said. "I'm still in the 'I hope my ex-husband dies in some violent and bloody way' stage."

Graham chuckled. "Well, there's always a bit of that in any divorce, I suppose. You'll probably feel different about him over time. On the other hand, though I cared for her, I was never in love with Jessica the way you were with Daniel."

"I don't know whether it was ever real love," I said, looking into my iced tea.

"Don't put it down. It was something strong, and it made sense to you at the time."

"Have you been in therapy or something?"

He smiled. "I've just had a lot of time to think. Anyway, my marriage was the last time I pull the knight-in-shining-armor act. I'm hanging up my lance."

"And yet you came looking for me in the basement."

"Yeah, well . . . I was doing it for an old friend."

"You and I are old friends now?"

"I meant your father. He asked me to look after you while he was away."

"Oh, great. That's not patronizing at all."

Graham grinned. "He's old school. And you attract trouble."

"Lest you forget, Graham Donovan, I've got a Glock in my purse."

*   *   *

After lunch I remembered Brittany Humm had mentioned that her soon-to-be father-in-law had a jewelry store on Union Street. I called and asked her whether she thought he would be willing to talk to me about gemstones. She told me that while her father-in-law would not be in the shop today, I was in luck: Ralph would be there, and he knew everything there was to know about diamonds. She gave me the address.

"I need to make a quick stop at a jewelry store," I said to Graham as we walked down the busy street full of shops and restaurants. "I want to talk to a man about a diamond. Now that we're spending so much time together, my father will be expecting some sort of public declaration."

Graham looked over at me, startled.

"I'm joking," I said, laughing. "Good Lord, man, you look pale."

The man behind the jewelry counter was in his sixties, slight, bent at the shoulders as though he spent a lot of time hunched over his jeweler's glass.

Brittany was right: It didn't take much prompting to get Ralph wound up talking about diamonds.

"Ya gotta know your four C's: cut, color, clarity, and carat weight. Of all of these, the only one influenced by man is the cut. The others are pure chance, determined by fate or God or whatever you believe in."

"But not all diamonds would be cut, would they?" Graham asked. "Not if they were considered of lesser quality?"

"No, they wouldn't. Since the wrong cut can take away tens of thousands of dollars of worth, expert cutters are in high demand. They use the flawed ones for practice, or sell them for industrial use. Only about

twenty percent of mined diamonds are considered jewelry quality."

He brought out a black-velvet-covered tray filled
with glittery gems and looked up at me with sly eagle
eyes.

"Real pretty, aren't they?" he asked, shoving the tray
toward me.

"Lovely. Do you have any rough, uncut diamonds I
could look at?"

He frowned slightly, whether at the loss of a potential
sale or the unnaturalness of a single woman standing beside a handsome man and not lusting after a diamond
ring I couldn't be sure.

"Just a minute," he said, as he disappeared into the
back of the shop, past the EMPLOYEES ONLY sign.

"You're ruining all the man's romantic illusions,"
Graham murmured, leaning back with his elbow on the
counter and looking down at me with a half smile.

"We're here for business, not romance. Unless you
really did want to ask me to marry you?"

"Seems to me I tried that once."

"Really. Was that a proposal? I don't remember the
'marry me' part, just the 'don't get married' part."

"As you know, I'm a man of few words."

"Uh-huh," I answered.

Luckily our new best friend, Ralph-the-jeweler, returned before we went too far down that perilous con-
versational path.

He brought out another swath of black velvet and
then emptied a little bag of its contents. Several small
stones, about the size of a pencil eraser, tumbled out.
They looked like lumpy, murky brownish gray rocks.

"Watch this," Ralph said as he brought a small work

lamp over and held one of the stones in front of it. When backlit, the stone was translucent, making it look like a dirty glass pebble.

"I guess you really would have to know what you were looking for," I commented.

"That's for sure. The brilliance that we associate with diamonds comes from the faceted cut, as I was saying before. But even before you cut these open, you would be able to tell they aren't high quality because of the crystalline inclusions, clouds, feathers, internal graining— it all affects the clarity. Diamonds below the grade of I-3 aren't considered gems at all."

"But they're still useful for industry, right? I'm in construction, and we have diamond tips on some of our drill bits and saws."

The man looked me up and down. Then he met Graham's eyes.

"You let a pretty little thing like her work in *construction*?" He shook his head in a what's-this-world-coming-to gesture. First we disillusioned him with our lack of engagement, and now with a woman not only working but working in the trades, no less.

Graham just smiled. "I'm trying to keep her too busy to get into trouble."

Ralph chuckled.

"Back to the diamonds . . ." I urged. "Industrial uses?"

"Right. They're coming up with new uses all the time. Since they're the hardest mineral, they're used to polish or degrade other material. Grinding and cutting purposes. Boring machines. They used a diamond window on a probe they sent to Venus. As technologies develop, so do the uses. And they only need a tiny part of a diamond. So sometimes they sell for much more than a gem would per carat. The 'bort,' as they're called, will only be about one-sixtieth of a carat."

"Oh, I see," I said. "Can't they manufacture diamonds now?"

"You better believe it. But to do it right takes a lot of time and expense—those of really high quality can cost more than natural diamonds, at least industrial-grade ones. Hey, you wanna hear something weird?"

"You bet I do," I said.

"There's a group out of Illinois that makes diamonds out of the ashes of loved ones. They made one out of Beethoven's hair, and I heard they got Michael Jackson's hair from that Pepsi commercial where it caught on fire? So they're gonna make diamonds out of that, too. I imagine they'll be more expensive than real diamonds, for instance."

I felt just a tad queasy. Ghosts were plenty for me. Wearing jewelry made out of a dead person's ashes ... it was too much.

I glanced down at the tray of diamond rings sparkling in the afternoon sun streaming in through the front window. What with their weight of tradition and expectation, they made me nervous. I had given Daniel back his beautiful, expensive ring when I left him. It had weighed me down in more ways than one. I remembered thinking at the time that I would never wear another, and now that they were becoming so associated in my mind with death ... I doubted I ever would.

Chapter Twenty-three

While we were on Union Street I had a key to Matt's house made for Graham. He promised to see whether he could expedite proper treatment of the bones in the basement so that the project wouldn't be put on hold for too long.

Meanwhile, I decided to spend the rest of the afternoon salvage-yard hunting. I still needed a few items for the Zaben job—including that leaded window—and it wasn't too early to start looking for Matt's project.

Before heading over the Bay Bridge to go "thrifting," I called my dad.

"We're in Jumpin' Falls now, but there aren't any falls. Just an old mine shaft and a big empty field. The hotel manager remembered the rock hounds coming into town, said they were digging around out here. Apparently it's a pretty well-known site."

"Did they ever find any real gems, do you know?"

"Nah," said Dad. "There never were any, according to the locals. Apparently the whole thing was just a con.

But every once in a while folks come across some of the poor-quality stones that the prospectors used to pepper the field. Guess some of these rock hounds get a kick out of that, maybe more than finding real gems, even. They're a quirky bunch, those guys."

"Okay, thanks, Dad. How are the boys?"

"Having a great time. We're about to go check out the mine."

"Be careful." I had a sudden vivid memory of crawling through old abandoned gold mines with my dad when I was a kid. I loved the scary chill that hung in the musty air, the thrill of inching through the pitch-black shafts, never sure what lay around the next corner. My mother refused to go in, and used to wait in the car with my less adventurous sisters, telling my father and me that she'd call for rescue if we weren't out by nightfall. I always thought she was a spoilsport; now I wondered whether she was avoiding the unhappy spirits of miners who'd lost their lives in search of precious minerals. Mining has always been a dangerous occupation.

I headed to the East Bay and dropped the sinks stowed in my car at the Sink Factory. There were some great architectural salvage yards in Berkeley, but they had been discovered long ago—which meant that they now knew how much their stuff was worth. I wanted a junk store, the kind of place where serendipity trumped supply and it was still possible to find treasures stuck underneath stacks of moldy magazines.

So I headed north on 580 to Richmond.

On the way I passed the Rosie the Riveter monument, which paid homage to the diverse workforce—including historic numbers of women and African Americans— who labored here in the Kaiser Shipyards during World

War II. These days, Richmond was the kind of town that many Oaklanders were wary of, which was saying a lot. Their murder rate rivaled ours.

Even *I* had to admit that Uncle Joe's Salvage, on Macdonald Avenue, was in a questionable part of town, not the kind of place I'd want to wander around in after dark. On the upside, there was a little place, Cj's, right across the street that offered delectable barbecue. Even though I had eaten lunch not long ago, I had a Pavlovian response as I neared the salvage yard. I salivated as I smelled the meat grilling.

I bet Dog would love to gnaw on some rib bones, I thought, already making plans for dinner.

My tires popped and crunched on loose gravel as I pulled in through the gate. It was almost closing time; only two other cars and one beat-up truck sat in the potholed parking lot. The entire yard was surrounded by a barbwire-topped chain-link fence, and the massive, hangarlike metal structure was secured with bars over high, grimy windows and roll-down metal security gates that blocked the huge doorways at night.

Outside, a good acre of land was strewn with bathtubs, sinks, toilets, slabs of limestone and marble, garden materials like statuary and birdbaths and stepping-stones. Inside was a maze of wooden building materials, furniture, tools, electronics, old LPs and cassette players, "vintage" clothing, doorknobs and hinges and mannequins and vintage roller skates complete with key. A giant plastic swan loomed over the register; below it, a rubber hand held a sign: SHOPLIFTERS WILL BE DISMEMBERED.

I felt my spirits lift. Other people went for spa treatments, or out to a nice dinner when they wanted to treat themselves. I poked around mildewy, funky places like this.

The young acne-scarred man at the register near the main entrance flipped through a glossy magazine of bling-covered rap stars, not even looking up as I passed by. "Uncle" Joe liked to take off fishing for days at a time, and in his stead he employed a succession of sullen, uninterested, barely awake young men and paid them minimum wage. As a result, it was pretty much a help-yourself situation, which I enjoyed. I liked being left alone to peruse the potential treasures.

I made a quick loop, circling the perimeter to make sure there weren't any new acquisitions I just had to possess. Usually the good stuff had to be dug up, but every once in a while there would be something sitting out in plain view, an item that had just arrived, hadn't yet been shoved back in a corner to be covered with flower pots and chrome kitchen organizers and a collection of *Tiger Beat* magazines, circa 1987. Last summer I had stumbled upon an old steamer trunk, complete with faded sage green velvet lining, the original hangers, and shelves. It now served as a de facto bookshelf in my bedroom.

Finally I ended up in the far corner of the building, looking through a wild assortment of doorknobs. The originals in Matt's house had been glass, not faceted but big and round, like miniature crystal balls. I knew I could find reproductions online, but they weren't the same. I wanted knobs that reflected the times.

People would buy an old Victorian somewhere like Richmond and West Oakland and immediately strip it of all the doorknobs, hinges, lighting fixtures, even built-in cabinets, in order to sell them for easy cash. Antique doorknobs could fetch twenty, maybe up to forty dollars each. By the time one stripped a whole house, it added up. The items were replaced by cheap reproductions from an inexpensive home improvement center, thereby leaving the house soulless and strangely off-kilter, like a great old carriage without wheels. Naked. Undone. Unloved. And more likely than ever to be torn down with the next sale.

As I scavenged through the dusty knobs, I found lots of cut crystal, including some that had turned a pale lavender with time and exposure to the sun. I used to collect these naturally colored glass bottles and knobs when I was a kid, convinced that they were "amethysts" and I would be able to sell them for a fortune. My dad burst my bubble when he informed me that the lead in the crystal reacted to sunlight, whereas true amethyst was a type of quartz often found in geodes.

The lavender doorknobs might not be fit for jewels, but they were lovely nonetheless. I had seen the glass used in decorative mobiles and lamps, where the light shining through showed off the subtle light purple hues.

After some time I realized that the light streaming in through grimy windowpanes was turning orange with the early evening. Vaguely I wondered whether I was the last person here, whether the man at the register was waiting impatiently for me to depart. I assumed he would let me know, eager as he must be to get home.

I turned. A man stood in my path.

"Zach?"

"Mel, what are you doing here?"

"Shopping. What are *you* doing here?"

"Taking some shots," he said, gesturing to the heavy camera hanging around his neck, as though I could miss it. "Well, isn't this a coincidence."

Quite.

I didn't believe a whole lot in coincidences. Especially lately. I tried to peer around Zach to check whether the young man was still at the register, but I couldn't see past the endless row of doors. I cast a quick glance around the back of the building—no one. Just me and Zach.

"Well, I was just leaving anyway," I said. "Thought I'd pick up some barbecue from Cj's. Have you tried it?"

"Not yet. Smells great."

There was a great clatter as the metal safety door at the front fell toward the ground. It reminded me of being nearly trapped in the storage facility with Graham. I made a move toward the exit. Zach stepped in front of me.

"We need to talk."

"Sure—let's talk over barbecue. My treat." My heart was starting to pound, and it had nothing to do with Zach's big sherry-colored eyes and sweet expression. I moved toward the front door again, and again he shifted to block my path.

"Let's talk here, Mel. Have a seat." He gestured toward a 1960s asymmetrical upholstered divan.

My eyes flew to the front doors. *"Oh my God!"*

Zach whirled around to see what I was looking at.

I ran, knocking over a large ceramic pot holding dozens of wooden poles, hoping they would hinder his chase.

"Mel, stop!" Zach said, sounding close on my heels.

"*Help!*" I started yelling and pushing everything in my path I could lay my hands on—signs, corbels, small chairs. Finally, I started throwing doorknobs. I used to play softball in high school; I still had pretty good aim.

"I'm not going to hurt you!" Zach ducked behind a bunch of doors, swearing under his breath. "Just calm down and stop yelling. I gave the clerk twenty bucks to ignore us. It's just you and me."

The lights went out, plunging us into darkness. We both fell silent for a long moment.

Zach switched on a flashlight and cast the beam around. "Listen to me, Mel. They think you have something."

I crawled along the floor, hoping my eyes would adjust quickly to the lack of light. Besides Zach's flashlight, the only illumination was from the streetlights outside.

Luckily I was in the tool section. I desperately tried to think of anything I could fabricate into some sort of rudimentary weapon. When would I start listening to my dad? Gun control be damned—my hands itched for a pistol. I remembered then that I did have a Glock with me, but it was in the satchel I had dropped while running from Zach. And in any case, I had no bullets, severely limiting the effectiveness of the weapon.

As silently as I could, I squeezed into a small tunnel behind a row of stained-glass windows.

"Did you take something from Matt's house?" Zach continued, sounding closer. "A package of some sort?"

I flashed on the map and the journal, safe at the historical society.

"I told them you were clean, but they're pretty sure you've got something. And I get the distinct impression they won't stop until they get it."

I watched as he walked down the corridor, beaming his light this way and that.

"What I'm worried about at this point is that they're violent," he said.

Gee, ya think?

"You've got to believe me on this: I had nothing to do with Kenneth's death. I didn't even know about it until you told me the next day. They asked me to look around the house that day you found me there, that's all. But at this point . . . I'm involved whether I want to be or not. And you might find this hard to believe, but I'm the one standing between you and them getting really nasty."

Everything was gray and black shadow figures. Part of me really didn't think Zach was out to hurt me, but a whole other part of my brain shouted at me: *You can't trust men, no matter what you're feeling. You're no good at character assessment when it comes to the males of the species.* With an exception for Stephen. And Nico. My dad, of course. And Stan. And Caleb. And Matt. And . . . Graham?

Aha! My hands landed on a can of aerosol something. I had no idea what. But it would serve as a weapon. If I was sure Zach meant me harm, I wouldn't hesitate to risk blinding him in self-defense. But as it was . . .

Feeling a bit calmer now that I had a weapon in hand, I inched my way behind cabinets holding artists' frames and tried to think. What I really needed was some way of incapacitating Zach temporarily, just enough to get him tied up so I could escape and call the cops to come pick him up. Maybe he would be able to explain everything, tell us who killed Kenneth.

I felt around in the dark, and miracle of miracles, my hands alighted upon a piece of heavy twine used to bind several paintings together. I worked the knot out of it and carefully pulled it out from under the canvases.

I set about tying loops in the twine, doubling them for strength.

Crawling over to the steep aluminum stairs that led to the loft, I scrambled up them.

Zach ran toward me.

I stood just out of reach, my feet at the level of his head. I kicked out, and managed to land a good blow on the side of his head. He dropped, but he wasn't knocked out. They never went down that easily in real life. Still, before he could catch his breath I jumped on top of him and slipped a loop of twine around one raised wrist, while threatening him with the aerosol.

"Mel, calm down!" Zach yelled.

"I feel very calm," I said as I reached out to loop more twine around his other wrist. Before I knew what hit me, he grabbed me and flipped me. We rolled around, but Zach had the obvious advantage. He loomed above me, holding me by my wrists over my head. Our harsh breathing rang out loudly in the empty building.

"Chill *out* for a second," he said, banging my wrists slightly against the floor for emphasis. "*Listen to me.* I'm trying to help you, believe it or not. Rory was sure there were gems somewhere in that house, and he thought maybe you had a bead on them. It's not like he was going to keep them for himself or anything. He was going to split them with everybody, all the investors."

"Uh-huh." I squirmed, but Zach held on tight.

"He was just worried that you'd abscond with them in the meantime."

"*Me?* Why would he think that?"

"Jason told him contractors are known for taking off with the loot they find in the walls. And after the other night at dinner, with you asking all those questions about Brice Lehner, he got especially nervous."

"Tell Rory that there *are* no gems to be found. It was all a scam."

"It *wasn't* all a scam," Zach said. "That's the whole point. The two prospectors had to show Buchanan proof in order to get his backing."

"But they were just inferior gems to convince Buchanan there was a fortune to be had in raw diamonds and rubies."

"They must be worth something anyway; otherwise why would everyone be trying to track them down? Maybe Buchanan tried to save face by mixing in a bunch of his wife's jewelry with the duds."

"That's what they're after, then? This is what Kenneth was killed over?"

"I told you, I don't know anything about that." Zach shook his head. "I was just looking for a package in the house somewhere, some hiding place, that's all."

"And that day we met you in the house? Were you looking for them then?" I asked.

"Rory said there would be a couple of men over at the house that day, they would let me in, and I should help them to look for something in the walls. They were cleaning up the study, but I didn't know what went down, I swear. I didn't even know about it until the day after."

"Zach, I've crawled under and around and through every part of that house by now. There *is* no treasure to be had." But I was lying. I had figured out where the gems might be hidden.

"I guess that's why Rory wanted me to follow you around. Just in case you knew something."

He rose off me a little, just enough to flip me over and tie my hands behind my back with the very twine I had used on him. I kicked and squirmed as much as I could, but I was no match for Zach's strength. Then he marched me over to the door corral, which was a huge wooden structure filled with hundreds of doors standing on end.

Doors had been stacked to block both exits. And now Zach was doing the same, stacking them, standing them on end, at the sole remaining opening. He was trapping me here. I felt helpless, idiotic. And more than a little panicked.

"Zach, this is crazy! Why are you working with these guys? I know someone who knows your mother."

"My mother?" He seemed genuinely taken aback.

"Nancy, in personnel at the *Chronicle*. She knows your mom."

"Huh. Anyway, I reiterate: I'm a good guy in all of this."

"Which would explain why I'm tied up?"

"Trust me on this: You're safer here. They have no idea where you are. In the meantime, if you just sit tight, I'm going to get all the investors together and figure out what the hell's going on."

"The house is all locked up," I said, rather inanely. As though a couple of simple locks would keep them out if they really wanted in. They got in to clean up the scene of the murder easily enough.

"The last place any of the investors want to be right now is Matt's house, believe me. They're trying to distance themselves from all of this."

"But—" I began, but he cut me off.

"Don't try to move these doors by yourself," he warned. "They'll fall in on you. And don't call the police. As I think you know by now, they have a contact in the police department. Just try to relax until morning. The guy working here will dig you out as soon as he gets here in the a.m."

"Zach! Don't leave me here!"

But he was gone with a clatter of a security door.

Blind rage gave me energy and a clarity of purpose.

First things first. It took me most of the night, but I finally got loose, managing to cut through the twine by rubbing against the rough edge of a loose hinge on a door. Then I stacked doors one on top of another, putting together a makeshift set of stairs. I hoisted myself up onto the wooden partition, over the top, crash-landing amidst mannequins and a rack of faux fur coats.

What now? If I called the police and reported Zach, I would be in for hours of questions and filling out forms. Plus, if Inspector Lehner had been an investor in the house, had placed a fraudulent lien against it, and then was hunting for the gems himself . . . who was to say he wasn't the murderer? Or at least a conspirator? And if he was that ruthless, why would he stop at hurting *me*?

The security door was chained shut. I rifled through the papers and effluvia behind the cash register, just in case an extra key was lying around or hanging on a hook somewhere. Nothing. I had to get *out* of here.

If Nico hadn't been in the hospital recently—by virtue of working for me, no less—I would have called him. I didn't know Spike or any of Nico's nephews well enough to ask them to rescue me in the early hours of the morning. I was by far the handiest of any of my friends; Luz and Stephen could both be referred to, at best, as "athletically challenged." And Graham . . . well, that would just be too embarrassing on all fronts.

Finally I decided to take care of it myself. I found a heavy pair of bolt cutters in the tool area, and though it took another hour, I managed to cut through the chains on the metal security door, and then those on the parking lot gate.

By the time I was on the freeway, the first light of dawn had arrived, and my rage had morphed into angry determination. I went home and got myself a gun and bullets—Zach had taken the Glock, along with my cell phone. I stopped by our neighbor Tom's house; he was up early for his shift at Pacific Gas and Electric. Dog went wild when he saw me, forgoing his usual laid-back demeanor for the joy of reunion.

"Are you all right?" Tom asked, clearly worried at my appearance. Though I'd used the bathroom at home, I hadn't taken the time to clean up.

I knew where the diamonds might be. Looking at the amethyst doorknobs had given me an idea. And just in case I was right, I wanted to retrieve them before the goons figured it out. Zach had told me no one would be poking around Matt's house this morning. This was my opportunity.

"Oh, I'm just peachy. Thanks for the dogsitting."

"Anytime. My daughter thought she'd died and gone to heaven. Loves dogs. I might just have to make a trip to the pound, pick up one of our own."

I was just about to offer him Dog, but bit my tongue. Big brown eyes looked up at me in mute adoration. We had fed him, and named him, sort of. Dog was here to stay.

Chapter Twenty-four

Looking back on it later, I probably shouldn't have been so eager to lay my hands on the gems that I went to the house alone, without arranging for backup. But I had my loyal canine by my side, a loaded Smith & Wesson in my satchel, and a near blind rage egging me on.

I entered the house. Awaited the ghosts. Nothing.

I went upstairs to the den. This was where I always smelled Walter Buchanan's pipe, heard the rattle of his newspaper.

One of the carpenters had set up a circular saw in this room, just like the one that had taken Kenneth's hand, and then his life. They hadn't known about the other one here, clearly, and since I had told them to leave this room alone they figured they wouldn't have to work around it. Still, talk about your déjà vu ...

I sat for a moment, just taking in the room. The prospectors Nelson and Giametti had conned Walter Buchanan into a scam that led him to disgrace, as well as to a great loss of fortune. Walter had been left in this house, alone, to face his ruin.

Had Giametti come back for some reason? Was he lured by the promise of more money, or angered by the Norton notes he was given instead of real money? Had Buchanan killed the man, kept the jewels and the money he had paid him, and then, in a fit of shame and remorse, killed himself?

And now the two remained here, locked together forever, in this home?

Pipe smoke enveloped me suddenly. I still couldn't see him, but I felt Walter Buchanan's presence. Sad. Rueful. Penitent.

I approached the ugly fireplace surround that Gerald, Walter's great-grandson, had made all by himself. The river rock reminded me of the smooth stones at Ralston Lake, where we had scattered Mom's ashes. Shells and smaller pieces of gravel and strange translucent stones were stuck in the cement as well, willy-nilly.

I knelt before it, passed my hands over the rock.

Picking up a hammer and a screwdriver, I started to chip away at the mortar, just a little.

But what if I accidentally chipped the next Hope diamond? Could a person chip a diamond that easily?

The light fixture in the entry hall.

Murky, crystalline stones . . .

I had to use the twelve-foot ladder to reach. Usually, according to my own stringent workplace safety standards, I would never allow one of my people to climb a tall ladder without assistance nearby. But I wasn't afraid of heights. And I couldn't wait.

I reached the third rung from the top, the last one

you're supposed to stand on before risking losing your balance. I reached up to the fixture . . .

Dog barked.

The ladder rocked. I grabbed it in reflex.

I looked down to see Jason Wehr. And Robbie, a red motorcycle helmet still tucked under his beefy arm. Apparently the murderous investors club wasn't meeting this morning, after all.

Dog barked some more.

"Brilliant, Mel. Just brilliant." Jason smiled up at me. "I was hoping you'd figure it out. I racked my brain, swear to God. Didn't want to think it was all some sort of wild-goose chase."

Where was my *gun*? My mind flashed on my satchel, which I'd left in the den. Brilliant, indeed.

"What are you talking about?" I asked, all innocence. "You want this ugly light fixture?"

Uncertainty clouded his expression briefly, but then he smiled again. "Those are the gems, though, right? It finally dawned on me—I was so set on a bunch of glittery jewels that I didn't realize how ugly raw gems could be."

"You were working with Kenneth on this?" I asked, taking a deep breath and trying desperately to think. "Trying to find the gems?"

Wehr shook his head. "I wouldn't say Kenneth was working with *anyone*. He was planning on absconding with the money for the house. You need a hand with that?"

"I think I need tools," I said, my voice shaky.

"Shut up, stupid mutt," Robbie growled at Dog.

"Don't worry about it, Mel. Robbie here will get it. He's good at that sort of thing."

Robbie rattled the ladder again, and I grabbed it with one hand, the other holding on to the light's ceiling mount. It hadn't been properly installed. Even if it had been, the screws wouldn't hold my weight; as it was, I could already see it pulling away from the ceiling.

"Oops." Robbie laughed as I clutched tight.

"Don't be mean, Robbie," Jason chastised.

"You don't need to do anything stupid," I said.

"Oh, I won't," Jason said. "I'll leave that up to my friend here."

"Robbie," I said, "think about this. Tam will be so disappointed."

He shrugged his big ham shoulders. "Whatever."

"I guess it's time for another construction accident," said Jason. "Sorry, Mel. This will ruin Turner Construction's safety record, I'm sure. But I don't see any way around it at this point. I do feel bad for your father, though. Maybe he'll finally pull himself together, step back in."

I looked down at the inlaid stone of the entryway floor. If I landed right, it wouldn't kill me. But somehow I thought Robbie or Jason would take care of that part soon enough.

"Wait. *Wait*," I said. "I can give you the map."

"What map?"

"The gem field map."

"I never wanted the stupid gem field map!" said Jason. "Kenneth kept mumbling about the damned map, but what I wanted was the diamonds. I never meant for him to die, you know. I even tried to stop the bleeding, but then you pulled up, and I guess we panicked."

"How did you even know about the gems in the first place?"

"I read about them when I was researching the house, and then met up with a bunch of rock hounds, who told me the whole story."

"The diamonds aren't good quality, anyway," I protested. "They're all seconds, no good for jewelry making."

"That was back then," Jason said. "In today's market they'd be worth a small fortune for use in high-tech industries. That, on top of the money from the house, was enough. But with Kenneth selling us out and then trying to take off with the money for the house, I would have been left with less than nothing."

"What do you need so much money for, anyway, Jason? You're an award-winning, sought-after architect, aren't you?"

"I have to complete my project. My Eden. Do you have any idea how much it costs to get something like that off the ground? Kenneth told me he'd help me put investors together. He convinced me I'd make a tidy profit off flipping this monstrosity of a house. Then he tried to sell the house out from under us. Now I'll at least get my money back, and those diamonds are a sure thing. Hey, yank one off for me, while you're up there," he said. "I want to see one up close."

"One of these?" I said, toying with one of the blobby crystalline shapes. I was still playing for time.

He nodded.

I grabbed hold of the mounting plate, and yanked as hard as I could. The whole fixture came out of the ceiling, raining plaster upon the men below. Balancing as best I could, I held the lamp in my arms and pulled diamonds off, one after another, hurling them at my attackers.

Diamonds are just about the hardest rocks around. And I've got good aim.

Dog started going wild, barking and running around in circles.

Robbie was going for his gun, ducking the whole time. He kicked at Dog.

I threw the entire light fixture at Jason, and jumped from the ladder on top of Robbie.

This was one of those moments I was glad I was a solid, substantial woman. Even a man of Robbie's size went down under my weight and the force of gravity. The gun fell away from us, skittering along the stone floor.

We struggled. Robbie flipped me over and fell on top of me. He was huge. Heavy. The breath was knocked out of me. Before I could move, he wrapped his mitt-sized hands around my neck.

He squeezed.

I choked.

Dog barked incessantly.

Panic surged through me. My muscles ached with the effort of keeping my neck taut, fighting off the agonizing pressure of his hands.

Jason scrambled around us, picking up the raw diamonds.

Black spots danced in front of my eyes.

Dog lunged, biting Robbie on the upper arm. Robbie yelled, released one hand from my neck, and stretched it out, reaching for his gun.

Kenneth!

He popped up in my peripheral vision, just to the side of us. Holding his arms overhead, his hand curled like a claw, the other a bloody stump, he snarled. Dog yelped and ran, tail between his legs.

Then Robbie screamed and leapt off of me.

Kenneth had managed to materialize enough for others to see him.

Jason squealed as well. Both men ran up the stairs, away from the apparition.

Kenneth chased after them, laughing maniacally, the very stereotype of a bloodthirsty, vengeful spirit.

I heard the whine of the circular saw upstairs, and the men screamed again.

Massaging my neck, I collapsed on the ground and tried to catch my breath.

Brice Lehner burst in through the front door, his gun drawn. He ran to me and knelt beside me.

"Are you all right?"

I nodded. "They're upstairs." My voice was raspy; it sounded unlike me.

He ran up the stairs.

With a sudden burst of strength, I followed.

Jason and Robbie were in the den. Jason kept wiping his hands, à la Lady Macbeth, as though to clean them of blood. Robbie just held his arms over his head, whimpering. The saw was running, ready to cut. But the cord wasn't plugged in.

"Get them away!" Robbie yelled.

"All right, everyone just relax," Inspector Lehner said, looking frightened himself. "It's okay. You're both going to come with me, and nobody gets hurt. Understand?"

Two other uniformed officers stormed up the stairs and joined us in the den. Lehner instructed them to take Robbie and Jason into custody; they cuffed them, read them their rights, and led them out.

In the reflection of the French doors, I caught a quick flash of two men: one in simple miner's attire, the other in a fine smoking jacket. Buchanan and Giametti, I assumed. They disappeared as soon as the inspector spoke.

"What the hell just went down here?" Lehner asked me.

"I think it's called justice. Who called you? How did you know to come?"

"This whole thing ... it spun out of control. I guess you know by now that I was involved? It was supposed to be just a regular investment opportunity." He shook his head. "And then it turned out Kenneth was trying to cash in on the house, and Rory and Jason started talking about the possibility of finding jewels in the walls. ... But Jason took things too damned far. Still, I didn't have any evidence to connect him to Kenneth's murder. I've been tailing him for a few days, figuring he might try something stupid."

"Thank you for coming." I tried to swallow. My throat felt bruised, along with my knee and arm.

"I'll need to get a full statement from you." Lehner hesitated. "We could probably leave out some of the details about saws working without electricity, that sort of thing. Best to move on, I think. I've seen a lot of things over the years, and some don't bear investigating."

"That works for me."

I heard Dog barking hysterically, and ineffectually, from downstairs.

"Could I go get my dog first?" I asked. The inspector agreed, and I was able to give him my full statement with my new canine companion sitting at my side. Dog leaned into me, and I returned the hug as I talked. He was my hero.

"One more thing I wanted to ask you," Lehner said

to me half an hour later as we finished up. "About Kostow's body . . ."

"What about it?"

"You want it? Morgue held on to it for a while, but they couldn't find any relations. It's sad, people go through life without family, friends."

But Kenneth wasn't without friends. Not really. Matt was his friend.

And I guessed I was, too.

Chapter Twenty-five

" D'ya suppose he wanted to be cremated?" asked Matt the next day, as we met with the funeral directors.

"Yes," Kenneth said. "Definitely."

"Cremated. Definitely," I said.

Matt looked at me, eyebrows raised in question.

"We talked about it once," I improvised.

"Let me guess—was this when you were threatening to kill him?"

I laughed. "It may have been then, yes."

"Meet me in the bathroom," Kenneth said to me in a dramatic whisper, as though Matt could hear him.

"I'll be right back," I told Matt.

In the women's room I could look Kenneth in the eye by meeting his gaze in the mirror.

"Stick a fork in me—I think I'm done," Kenneth said.

"Done?"

He nodded. "I feel ready to move on. . . . It's hard to

explain, but I think I needed to get back to my body, somehow. Finish things up."

"So that's it?" I asked.

"I think so. I actually did a good deed, managed to scare the crap out of those guys so they didn't kill you. Of course, you wouldn't have been in that position in the first place, if not for me, I know . . ."

"I don't blame you, Kenneth."

"You know, now that it's too late, I remember that morning. I woke up, hungover, of course, with a gun in my face. I guess Jason had been looking all night for the diamonds, with no luck, and he really thought I had taken them, hidden them somewhere. He also found out about my plan to sell the house. Philip Singh went to eat at Rory's restaurant, drank too much, started bragging about the new house he was getting from me for a steal."

Kenneth shook his head, his eyes looking off into space. "Robbie was Jason's muscle. They kept asking me where the gems were, over and over. Jason made Robbie put his gun down—I don't think they ever meant to actually kill me—but they used the nail gun on me, and then the saw. It was terrible."

That seemed like an understatement.

"They panicked when they heard your car pull up," Kenneth continued. "Jason tossed Robbie's gun and they took off."

"The police weren't able to recover any prints from the gun," I said.

"Yeah, they were both wearing latex gloves. Matt provided them for safety at the party—he said you made him promise to supply safety equipment. Ironic, huh? Anyway, they just went out the fire escape and left me there. . . . After that, I couldn't even think."

"I'm so sorry, Kenneth."

He smiled. "You and Matt are giving me a real memorial service, and I feel good. Grounded."

I had wanted this moment, yearned for it. But now that it was here I felt sort of choked up.

"Well, then . . . so it's time to move on?"

"I think so."

"To what, do you know?"

He shook his head. "No, but I feel uncharacteristically optimistic about it. Talk about a chance to turn over a new leaf. And I don't mean that in the sense of the rehab clinic."

We smiled, our gazes meeting and holding in the mirror.

"Good luck, Kenneth. It was . . . nice to know you. Strange. Surreal even, but nice."

"Good-bye."

And just like that, he was gone.

"It's not going to bite you," I said, stifling a smile.

Matt crouched over a peeling paneled door lying atop two sawhorses, in the front room of the Vallejo Street house. His blue eyes were barely visible through dust-covered safety goggles. The lower part of his face was obscured by a cartridge respirator rated for lead— the kind that made everyone look like World War I insect-people. His long, graceful fingers clutched the random orbital sander, holding it away from him as though it were a dangerous animal.

"Really, Matt," I continued. "You have to hold power tools like you mean it, show 'em who's boss."

Matt said something in response, but his words were muffled by the mask and drowned out by a loud compressor that switched on right at that moment.

Dog looked over his shoulder laconically, disturbed by the loud noise but not motivated to actually budge from his makeshift cardboard bed in the corner. Now that I gave him his motion sickness pills, he was becoming a real construction pup, accompanying me everywhere. His mellow demeanor was a good antidote to my frenetic daily schedule.

He wagged his tail and gave a low *woof* of welcome, looking toward the front door.

"Heya, Dog," Graham said as he walked into the room. He wore his work uniform: Cal-OSHA shirt, jeans, boots, and a clipboard under his arm. "What's Matt saying?"

"Not sure," I chuckled. "Probably had something to do with going back to guitar playing. Either that or he was suggesting where I might shove my random orbital sander."

Graham returned my smile. "What are you up to?"

"Are you asking that in an official capacity?"

"Not really. Actually, I thought you should know that I've given Cal-OSHA two weeks' notice. I'm turning in my clipboard."

"Are you serious?"

"I hear the Green Revolution is upon us. Wouldn't want to let it pass me by."

"That's so exciting, Graham! I'm really happy for you. You'll be great."

"I stopped by to let you know that the forensics came back on the skeleton in the basement," Graham said. The anthropologists had taken a couple of days to dig everything up and document the burial area. Then they took the remains back to their lab, releasing the house

for further construction. "It's a male in his twenties or
early thirties; they can't date it to a specific year, but it
fits into the timeline you suggested. The medallion you
found was from the era as well. It looks like you're probably right: It's Giametti."

"What will happen with the bones? Will he be given
a decent burial?"

"As soon as they finish up all the tests he can be laid
to rest. You suppose Matt would volunteer to pay for
it?"

"Now might not be the best time to ask," I said with
a smile, watching as the sander once again rotated right
out of Matt's grasp.

I was glad for Giametti—I hadn't felt his presence in
the house since his bones had been removed, and now
that his story was known I hoped he would be able to
rest. It must have been horrific to remain here in this
house, all these years, with his own murderer.

Walter Buchanan, on the other hand . . . I still caught
whiffs of his pipe, sensed his guilt and shame from time
to time as I walked through the halls. I hoped he might
move on, too, now that his secret was out, but until he
spoke to me directly, it was hard to know how to help.
Maybe I should ask Meredith to come check it out, or
I could always consult with Brittany Humm. Or even
Celia. We could set up a séance. I smiled again, this time
at myself. It was hard to believe that I now knew a handful of people with whom I could theorize about lingering ghosts and haunted houses.

"*Bollocks!*" exclaimed Matt as he whipped off the
glasses and mask. His face was red and sweaty underneath. "I give up. Maybe I could try, ya know, some other

aspect of the job. For instance, I'd be happy to run for doughnuts. Or how about *your* job? I'd even be willing to wear your fancy dress costumes."

"That's the whole point," I said. "You can't have my job until you understand construction."

Graham raised his eyebrows in question.

"I insisted that Matt get a hands-on feel for the job," I explained. "If he's going to be flipping houses, he needs to know how it's done."

"Or I could just hire a professional," said Matt. "Which is what I thought I had done."

"Even if you have a contractor do the actual work, wouldn't you feel better if you understood what the builders were talking about?"

"Not really, no," said Matt, crouching by Dog and caressing his silky but dusty brown coat.

"I take it the charges were dropped?" Graham asked Matt.

"Thank heavens," Matt said. "With the others in custody, I'm off the hook. Even the inspector admitted misconduct and intervened on my behalf."

"Glad to hear it," said Graham. "So, what's next for you, then?"

"Basic carpentry," I said.

Matt rolled his eyes. "Guess I'm here for the duration. I don't seem to have much choice. She's the boss."

"Yes," said Graham, casting me a significant look. "Yes, she is."

Handprints. On the ceiling.

Dammit. My mind cast about for a way to explain
them to my clients. The marks weren't flat, the kind that
could be explained away by someone using their hand to
steady themselves while teetering atop scaffolding or a
tall ladder. Rather the prints looked as though someone
had dragged five fingers along the surface of the ceiling's wet plaster or paint, resulting in a subtle chicken-
scratch pattern fanning out in concentric circles around
the hole for the light fixture.

Not to mention the marks hadn't been there yesterday.

As with so much of what happened on this job site, it
was disturbing.

My clients Carlotta and Jim Daley stood amidst the
construction debris and dust. The workers had finished
for the day, so the house was quiet aside from the coo-
ing of eight-month-old Quinn, who squirmed in a pad-
ded pouch slung across his father's stomach like a baby
kangaroo.

Together we gazed up at the twelve-foot-tall coffered
ceiling of what would be an elegant dining room—once
the walls and ceiling were painted, the old light fixtures
rewired and remounted, and the inlaid wood floors

sanded, stained, and polyurethaned. The Daley's new home, an 1890s Queen Anne Victorian in San Francisco's Cow Hollow neighborhood, was structurally sound—a pleasant surprise, and rare for structures from that era—but decades of operating as a boarding house for drifters, down-at-the-heels bachelors, and homeless cats had left its mark. The home's bones were exquisite, but the rest of it required plenty of renovation, repair, and ornamentation. Queen Anne Victorians were celebrated for their elaborate decorative designs and lavish "gingerbread" details.

Which is where I come in. Mel Turner, general contractor, Jill of all trades. I pride myself on tackling the historic renovations my competitors find too difficult or not worth their time.

I had been trying—and failing—to ignore or explain away the string of strange events that had plagued this particular project from its inception: lumber and drywall going missing and then showing up in the yard; work gloves and safety goggles *right there* one moment and gone the next; rusty old dead bolts locking and unlocking although the keys had long been lost; footsteps resonating overhead when no one was upstairs. Already a handful of my workers had walked off the job, unwilling to deal with the disturbances.

This wasn't my first run-in with the unexplainable. Much to my shock, I had encountered the ghost of a former colleague some months ago. But since then, other than vague sensations of welcome—or of being decidedly unwelcome—in historic homes, I hadn't had any other ghostly experiences. Perhaps I had lulled myself into a false sense of security. I wanted to believe it had been a one-time deal, like the measles. Once you had it, you were inoculated.

Looked as if I was getting a booster shot whether I wanted it or not.

"What's on the ceiling? Are those . . . handprints?"

the petite Carlotta asked in her heavy Russian accent, a frown marring her otherwise smooth brow. Dark, wavy hair hung halfway down her back; her big brown eyes were limpid, her posture languid. She had just celebrated her thirtieth birthday, but she appeared much younger. In part this was due to her penchant for wearing gauzy baby-doll dresses, a wardrobe choice completely unsuited to a foggy San Francisco December.

Since I was known for my own inappropriate outfits, I wasn't about to cast any stones. Still, whenever I was in the same room as Carlotta, I had to stifle the entirely uncharacteristic urge to bundle her up in a big fluffy sweater.

If Carlotta inspired such protectiveness in someone as cynical as *me*, I could only imagine what havoc she wreaked within the average heterosexual man. Which might explain why Jim Daley, an affable guy, organized their lives so she never had to lift so much as a toilet brush.

"Yep, they look like handprints to me," I said.

"Maybe from the painters?" Jim offered.

"Sure, that must be it," I lied, hoping he didn't notice there wasn't a paint brush in sight. This project was nowhere near ready for the final decorative stages; we hadn't even started with plaster repair and mud. "We'll take care of it—don't worry. You won't even notice them once we're done."

"Great." Jim was a typical thirtysomething Bay Area high-tech professional: He wore stylish eyewear, his hair was artfully tousled, and he spent what few leisure hours he had training for triathlons or bicycling up Mount Tamalpais. At least he had until his son was born. Lately he had thrown himself into parenthood. Which was a very good thing—Jim was better cut out for the role than Carlotta, who seemed bemused, if not outright discomfited, by her wriggling, demanding infant.

At the moment, Quinn was enthusiastically gumming

Jim's thumb, a long thread of drool marring the front of Jim's shirt as if a giant snail had left a trail.

"He's cutting a tooth," Jim said with an indulgent chuckle.

I returned his smile. Jim was a sweet guy. A tad on the obsessive side, but nice enough. Plus, as a principal in a successful Internet start-up, his pockets were deep enough to return this Queen Anne to its former glory. As much as I hated to admit it, that was an important trait in a client.

"Is very dusty. Dust everywhere," Carlotta commented, her nostrils flaring as she glanced around the dining room.

"Yes. That sort of thing's hard to avoid on a construction site, I'm afraid."

"Oh, by the way," Jim said, "I've taken the liberty of calling in a green construction consultant."

"An outside consultant?" I clamped down my annoyance and tried to keep a neutral expression on my face. I felt territorial about my construction site. When a general contractor was on The Job, they owned The Job. There was a reason my workers called me the General for short.

Besides, I was pretty knowledgeable about the green-building movement myself. I implemented a number of such building techniques whenever I could, salvaging as much as possible of the original moldings, hardware, and building materials not only for their historic value, but also to keep from filling our landfills with perfectly usable items.

Apparently my attempt to cover up my feelings was not entirely successful. No surprise there. I'm not great at diplomacy.

"No worries," said Jim. "I'm sure you two will get along great. It just makes me feel better to have an expert on the job. And as a matter of fact, he mentioned that you know each other: Graham Donovan?"

"Oh, yes, I do know Graham," I said, my emotions reeling even more. The sexy green contractor was an old friend of my father's and used to be an official inspector for the state of California—in fact, he had helped shut down a job site of mine not too long ago. And ten years before that, Graham had made a romantic play for me, trying to dissuade me from marrying my now ex-husband, Daniel. Unfortunately, Graham had been right in his assessment of Daniel, which mortified me for a number of reasons.

Quinn's adorable coos escalated into a fretful whimper. His chubby legs danced and his tiny arms flapped.

"I'd better go feed the baby," Jim said. "Coming, honey?"

"You go. I come in a minute." Carlotta's mouth tightened and one side pulled down in a little grimace. I'd noticed that look before. It was usually directed at unpleasant tasks, or just about anything to do with her son. Still, in her big eyes was a mixture of eager concern and trepidation. I found Carlotta difficult to warm to, but a small part of my heart went out to this young woman, so far from her home and with a baby that she was finding hard to love. My maternal experience was limited to the ready-made stepson I'd acquired when I married his father. Caring for an infant would be tough for anyone.

"Take your time," Jim said, kissing the top of her head. "Let's order Thai tonight—what do you think?"

She shrugged.

"Indian?" The baby's distress was spiraling, his whimpering ceding to crying.

"Is greasy."

"Pizza?" Quinn started to wail for real.

"We decide *later*," she said.

"Okay, sure. Just let me know when you're getting hungry." Jim headed down what was formerly a servant's hall to a back staircase that descended to the garden-level apartment the family was inhabiting during construction.

It was tough to work around clients who insisted on remaining onsite during the renovation. Aside from the obvious comfort problems of the dust, the noise, and the early-to-rise hours of the construction crew, there were aspects of the job that clients really didn't need to see. There were also the occasional, but inevitable, minidisasters: broken windows or fried wiring, and any number of "oopsie" moments that we would fix in time, but which I'd rather not have the clients witness.

My dad, the original Turner of Turner Construction, taught me never to allow clients in the home while it was being worked on. Maybe because I was a woman—not a gruff ex-Marine like Dad—or because I lacked sufficient backbone, I had a hard time enforcing this policy. Carlotta and Jim had insisted on remaining in the house in the one-bedroom "in-law" unit downstairs. As I got to know them a little, I learned the driving force behind their intransigence: Apparently Carlotta was terribly homesick for dear old Mother Russia. Personally, I didn't see how an ornate Queen Anne Victorian in San Francisco's crowded Cow Hollow neighborhood could possibly remind her of home—a country I knew mainly from repeated viewings of *Doctor Zhivago*—but what did I know?

They wanted to stay, and they were paying the bills. In the high-end construction business, the one with the checkbook rules. And until I could convince my father to take over the business again, I did the best I could.

I adored working on the historic structures. And my laborers, after some initial resistance to taking construction direction from a woman, had come to respect my knowledge and abilities, and their consistent paychecks. But the clients . . . the clients pushed my interpersonal skills to the brink. To be fair, I'd been in a bad mood since my marriage had gone down the drain, and all I really wanted to do was run away to Paris and lick my wounds in some fourth-floor Left Bank garret for a year or ten. But when my mom passed away unexpectedly, my dad needed my help. So I stepped in to run Turner Construction, fully intending to resume running away in a few months, as soon as Dad was back on his feet.

That was more than two years ago. I wasn't a single step closer to sipping a café au lait while watching the sun rise over the Seine.

"Crazy," Carlotta said, rolling her eyes. "He drive me crazy."

"The baby or Jim?"

"Both. Mel, I must ask you some advice."

"I'm not much good at advice, Carlotta. . . ." For reasons I have never been able to understand, a lot of clients sought my counsel. Maybe I sent out an unconscious "Ask me!" vibe. Maybe they thought a general contractor could fix anything, from a cracked foundation to a broken marriage. Maybe I had "Big Ol' Softie" written across my forehead. Whatever it was, I was in fact the last person anyone should turn to for advice about their personal life. Got a leaky faucet? I'm your gal. Trying to expedite a construction permit down at city hall? I know who to talk to. Problems with your love life? You'd be better off soliciting marital advice from Elizabeth Taylor.

"I think we have uninvited guests here in this house." Her fingers played with the filigreed crucifix that hung on a chain of fine silver around her swanlike neck.

"I'm sorry?"

"Spirits. Ghosts. The souls of the dead who are still with us."

Offering marital advice was sounding easier all the time. "I . . . uh, why would you think that?"

"At night, I hear knocking. And footsteps."

"There could be any number of expla—"

Carlotta gazed at me intently. "Please, Mel. I did research. It is said the spirits of the departed do not like to have their surroundings disturbed. And the renovation work, it disturbs surroundings, no?"

"Well, sure, that's sort of the point. . . ." I couldn't dismiss Carlotta's fears out of hand, especially with everything that had been going wrong on the job site. Still, I didn't want my clients getting caught up in the vortex of fear and confusion that the crossover of spirits could cause. What I really should concentrate on, I thought with sudden resolve, was getting them to move out while I brought in some ghost busters. Or whatever it was they called themselves. I was *not* in the mood to go through this again.

"And when I go . . . when I go into Quinn's room, sometimes there is a black cloud."

"A black cloud? In the baby's room?"

"No, following me. I can feel it over my shoulder. As though it is trying to get in the room."

I swallowed, hard. The one ghost I'd gotten to know well was annoying, but at least he never lurked over my shoulder in the form of a black cloud. That was just plain scary.

"I put up amulets," said Carlotta. Her voice started to shake, and tears welled in her huge eyes. "And sprinkle the holy water. I try to tell the ghosts to leave. I was very forceful, but it makes things worse. Now they are worse."

This would explain the smudge bundle I had noticed earlier lying amidst bits of wood and wallboard. The scent of burnt sage reminded me of walking down the street in nearby Berkeley, but I never did understand what it had to do with cleansing homes of bad vibrations.

"You know, it's always unsettling to live in a home while we're doing construction," I said. "The knocking could be a twig against a windowpane or the sound of old pipes. And the creaking in the walls—"

My attempt to explain the unexplainable was interrupted by the high-pitched whine of an electric drill. The power tool started to spin atop a temporary plywood worktable. No one was near it.

Carlotta and I stared at the spinning contraption.

"Must be an electrical short," I lied again as I hit the "off" switch and unplugged it. "Happens all the time in these old houses—"

"Is no short," Carlotta said, her tone fatalistic. "Is ghost. Maybe more than one. Have you found history of the house?"

I shook my head. Restoring a historic structure properly meant thorough research on its past. But a trip to the California Historical Society hadn't turned up anything on the Daleys' Queen Anne Victorian or on the family that originally built it. Nothing at all. And that was odd. As cities go, San Francisco isn't that old, or that large. It's usually easy to find paper trails left behind by its well-to-do citizens, whether through articles in the newspaper's society section, or tax records, or architectural blueprints. But not this time. It wasn't that the history of the place was sketchy. It was nonexistent.

"You know the lady who used to live here?" Carlotta asked.

"The Cat Lady? I've heard of her."

"Yes. The Cat Lady. I saw her yesterday. She ran away but I made her to talk to me. She admit to me she leave this house because of the ghosts. She say they try to kill her."

Our eyes met.

"That's a bad thing, no?" Carlotta demanded.

Why, yes, I thought. In general, death threats were a bad thing. Death threats from ghosts? Even worse.

Carlotta's gaze shifted to a spot behind me, and her eyes widened. Her face went pale, her body rigid. I swung around to see what she was looking at.

But I saw nothing except the kitchen door, standing open.

Wait—hadn't it been closed?

And then I saw it: a footprint in the dust on the floor.

I turned back to Carlotta just as she wobbled, then crumpled. I grabbed her before she could fall to the floor.

Another print appeared, then another. They were coming toward us.